Baby, It's Cold Outside

WHEN I FALL
IN LOVE

Baby, It's Cold Outside

A Novel

SUSAN MAY WARREN

summerside
PRESS™

Summerside Press™
Minneapolis 55337
www.summersidepress.com

Baby, It's Cold Outside
© 2011 by Susan May Warren

ISBN 978-1-609362-15-7

Scripture references are from The Holy Bible, King James Version (KJV).

All characters are fictional. Any resemblances to actual people are
purely coincidental.

Cover design by David Carlson | www.studiogearbox.com
Cover image: Getty Images
Interior design by Müllerhaus Publishing Group | www.mullerhaus.net

Summerside Press™ is an inspirational publisher offering fresh,
irresistible books to uplift the heart and engage the mind.

Printed in USA.

For Your glory, Lord

CHAPTER ONE

Thursday, December 22, 1949

If she could, Dottie would simply erase the next three days off her calendar.

More than any other holiday, Christmas had the power to rip her asunder. A thousand tiny shards of excruciating memory bombarded her as she ventured through Berman's Grocery store on the annual requisite journey to pad her pantry for the holiday.

Christmas was for those with something to celebrate, with family, and the hope of a better tomorrow. Even Berman's Grocery store believed that. As if emboldened by the optimism of the new decade, and casting away the specter of rationing over the past five years, they advertised a holiday special on Rock Cornish game hens at thirty-nine cents a pound.

Dottie Morgan picked up the packaged hen. It fit well into her gloved hand, weighing two pounds, maybe a bit more. In all her forty-four years, she'd never had a Rock Cornish game hen.

Behind her, a mother in the bakery section corralled two giggling schoolchildren. Dottie peeked at them—Minnie Dorr, with her little tykes, Guy and Hazel. She recognized the grade schoolers, dressed in their blue-checkered wool jackets, belts hitched around their bulky waists and sweltering in their knitted caps, from the library's young readers program. Six-year-old Guy could wheedle right under Dottie's skin like a burr.

Or, a curl of warmth, if she let him.

Dottie turned away from them, dropping the hen back into the cooler. She didn't need a cart but hung her wire basket on her arm, passing by the turkeys. She hadn't purchased a bird in...well, she knew she shouldn't have stopped by the store on the way home from work. Today, the place bustled with women stocking up for the holiday, celebration in the air, and it only stirred up the old aches.

Near the canned cranberry sauce hung an advertisement of a jolly Saint Nicholas slaking his thirst with a Coca-Cola, smiling upon two pajama-clad children surrounded by gifts.

At the end of the bakery section a giant velvet stocking bulged with candy canes, Pfeffernusse cookies, and popcorn balls.

A display of iceskates and holiday lights reminded patrons to visit Berman's Hardware, next door.

On the radio, Bing Crosby crooned out "Silent Night."

Memories simply couldn't be dodged at Christmastime.

Dottie stilled, her hand on a bag of flour, as she watched widow Cora Sundeen march past, her blond hair pulled back from her pretty face and tucked into a black boiled wool hat. Her son hung onto the hem of her matching coat. His ruddy cheeks and blue eyes could devour Dottie whole.

Cora caught sight of Dottie and slowed, her face betraying a second of hesitation before she produced a smile. "Mrs. Morgan! I was just telling Cliffy how, when I was young, we'd celebrate Christmas Eve at the library, with cookies and a story."

SUSAN MAY WARREN

Dottie calculated when she'd last seen Cora, seated at her knee at the library's Christmas Eve reading, and put the woman at twenty-seven, or older, which meant little Cliffy must be nearly six. Cora probably had only a handful of memories of her fallen soldier husband.

"Oh, Cora…" Dottie looked away, perspiring under her wool coat, wishing, yes, she'd driven straight home. Who needed Cornish hens and eggnog, and plum pudding and fruitcake? After all, who exactly would Dottie cook for? "You know I haven't had the Christmas story hour…well, it's been a few years."

"I know." Cora's voice lowered. "But perhaps it's time to start the old traditions again." Her arm curled over the shoulder of her son. "For the next generation."

Dottie had no next generation, but she refused to show that on her face. "Have a lovely holiday, Cora," she said. She added a smile to soften her librarian tone and turned away from Cora's fading smile.

The radio announced, "I'll Be Home for Christmas," and Dottie headed for the door.

Tomorrow. She could return tomorrow when the place might be nearly abandoned, every woman in Frost, Minnesota, at home preparing for the holiday weekend.

She just about plowed over Lew Parsons ringing the Salvation Army bell just outside the door. His red velvet Santa-arm hung folded and pinned to his shoulder and he greeted her with a smile.

"Merry Christmas, Mrs. Morgan." He used his schoolboy tone, despite the fact that he had last year married Henrietta Fitzpatrick and now had a child on the way.

Dottie tacked on the appropriate smile. "And to you, Lew."

She probably should dig into her handbag and find a dime, but she couldn't slow. She just might be suffocating, choking on the sweet aroma of too many families who had somehow survived this wretched decade.

As if to add gloom to her mood, the pewter Minnesotan sky had begun to drizzle icy droplets of despair, eating away the meager dusting of snow.

Dottie wrenched open the rusty door to her father's faded yellow International Harvester truck and climbed onto the bouncy bench seat, the springs whining with the December cold. She'd long ago thrown a blanket over the seat, opting to cover the worn holes rather than replace the car. She wrestled the gearshift into place and eased the truck out of the dirt lot. The rain pinged on the windshield like bullets, as if it had already begun to turn to sleet. She turned on the wiper blades, but they cleaned only a pitiful swath in the middle. She leaned over the wheel to navigate as she turned onto St. Olaf Avenue and headed out of town.

Frost never suffered for holiday decorations. The entire town turned out in early November to embellish the lamps along the road with white pine boughs, hang lights from Miller's Café and Soda Fountain, and add sparkling lights to Benson's Creamery and the gilded window of the *Frost Weekly News* and the First Bank. The Snowflake Theater listed tomorrow night's opening of *Holiday Affair*, featuring Janet Leigh and Robert Mitchum. Across the street, J.C. Penney boasted a window-sized red-berried wreath over their second-floor window, and at the end of the street, in the circular garden in front of the Frost Community Center—formerly the Germanic Center—the towering blue spruce glowed with twinkly lights against the rain.

Only the star remained absent from the top of the tree. *Perhaps it's time to find the old traditions again...*

No. Not yet.

She watched Father O'Donnell throwing plastic over the wooden crèche in front of St Peter's Catholic Church, then turned left onto Third Street, driving past the community center. Movement inside suggested the local women's auxiliary bedecking it for tonight's dance.

The five o'clock whistle at the mill echoed over the soggy town.

The rain had begun to turn to ice, crystallizing on the windshield. The wiper blades bumped over the glass as they sloughed off the moisture. She passed Central Park, the cottonwoods and oaks shiny with an icy glaze, then crossed the creek at North Street. The river flowed, angry with icy chunks, its spittle grimy below the bridge.

When her father—land owner, banker, mayor of Frost—built their turreted Victorian on the outskirts of town, he'd expected the town to grow and overtake his vast acreage and add to the family coffers.

Unfortunately, the town had grown toward the flour mill side of town and toward the train depot and beyond, so that the ornate green Victorian with the gingerbread trim and two balconies sat lonely under the knotted embrace of a grove of ancient cottonwoods, resembling something out of a Grimm storybook.

The house overlooked Silver Lake on the south side—more a slough now than a respectable lake. In November, wild turkeys and pheasants took refuge between the stiff cattails and dry milkweeds dissecting the parchment ice. How many times had she wakened to old Barnabus's wild spaniel barking, or the bone-jarring crack of Gordy's 16-gauge shotgun shattering the pre-dawn air?

Worse, of course, was when she bolted from the bed, her face to the icy window, as if she might catch her son Nelson out there beside Gordy in the misty dawn, wearing his grandfather's rabbit shopka, dressed in his brown canvas coveralls, leaning into Gordy's every word.

Dottie fully blamed the loneliness of this holiday on Gordon Lindholm.

She made out the white pine in her front yard, blowing in the onslaught of the storm. Twenty-plus years it had centered the yard, protected the house from vagabonds who might like a peek into her front windows. Too many branches had turned rusty over the past few years—she would need to prune it to keep it alive.

Hard head stone from the hillside and fields made up a wall that partitioned the main driveway from the Third Street extension. She eased the old International up the hill toward the barn, which served more as a garage for her father's eccentric collection of cars and electronics. Like the 1929 roadster. Her father had also owned a Packard Clipper, a sedan he'd purchased right before his death. Dottie had shipped it right back to Minneapolis when it arrived, months later.

Her father always did live too extravagantly. Too many big dreams.

She'd inherited that bit from him, she supposed. But she

couldn't blame her father's peculiarities for the tragedy of her brief marriage.

No, the state of her life, the lonely creak of the barren house, could only be attributed to her own desperate mistakes.

Dottie slid out of the truck, the rain soaking through her wool coat, the mud slopping over her black dress boots as she tramped to the door of the barn and opened it. She drove the truck inside and parked. In the breathy expanse of the barn, the rain stirred the musty smell of forgotten hay, the remnant odors of the horses that once dwelled within, only bony Ollie left to lounge in the corner stall. Her grandfather's winter carriage sat dusty and abandoned in another stall, age rusting its steel runners, cracking the two leather bench seats.

Dottie checked on the feed for the horse. Someday she should sell the animal. He hadn't been ridden in years, ornery as an old mule. In fact, only her son had ever been able to cajole the horse into service.

She closed the barn door and hiked up to the house, her stomach already relishing the beef soup she'd left in the ice box. Tomorrow, perhaps, she'd purchase one of those game hens, stuff it, and roast it for Christmas day.

Maybe even set the grand table in the dining room for one.

For Nelson, she might try to acknowledge the day of God's grace for the world, even if His grace hadn't been extended anymore to her.

Or, perhaps, and more likely, she'd stay home, under her mother's wedding ring quilt, and listen to the silences collect her memories.

If she could summon the courage.

The rain turned her skin to ice, dribbling down her back by the time she reached the mudroom door. Stamping her frozen feet on the mat, she hung her coat on the peg, noticed the woodpile needed stocking, then opened the kitchen door and entered the heat of the house.

Or, rather, no heat. An icy breath clasped the grand house with its too many rooms—fifteen total—in a crisp silence. No clanging of the old coal stoker, no heat blasting from the giant grate heater in the middle of the family room floor. The chilly floorboards protested, however, as she walked across the kitchen, plunking her purse onto the oak table.

She listened to her heartbeat, closed her eyes. If she wanted—she didn't even have to try hard—she could hear Nelson's voice, feel his presence entering the kitchen after her. *I'll check on the stoker. The auger might be clogged. I'll go break it free.*

The rain battered the window and she saw Nelson in her memory, his shoulders broad now, hardened by playing football, or chopping wood, or even loading flour at the mill. He grabbed paper and matches to restart the stoker, tugged on her father's work jacket—now his—tucked on a derby, and headed outside, around the house to the cellar door.

He had a song on his lips, something from *Jack Armstrong, the All American Boy.*

> *Wave the flag for Hudson High, boys, Show them where we stand.*
> *Ever shall our team be champions.*

Known throughout the land. Rah, Rah. Boola boola, boola boola, boola boola, boola boo...

She sighed as the song faded into the deathly still of the house. How she longed to hear him breaking apart the coal, the hammering pinging through the catacombs of their house until finally the auger began to turn again. The fire would rest in the coal furnace, heat whisking out of the giant floor grate and into the house.

If she looked up, she might catch him carrying the heavy clinker out to the debris pile behind the barn.

No. See, too easily Nelson crept into her hollow places, entering without permission. She ran the palm of her hand against her wet cheeks then retreated to the back room. Stepping into her father's high-topped galoshes, she grabbed paper and pulled on the work jacket. Nelson's scent clung to it, woodchips and teenager sweat, the smell of coal and oil and grease, and way too much charm.

That charm got Nelson out of trouble too many times. Probably what cajoled Dottie into agreeing in that brief, wretched moment to allow him to march off to war.

She stepped outside into the rain, hunching her shoulders against the pellets of ice now sleeting from the sky as she splashed through the slick yard to the cellar. The hasp lay unlocked, and she wrenched open the door, hesitating before she closed it behind her to keep out the rain. Once, when Nelson was about fourteen, the latch had flipped over, locking him inside for two hours. She'd found him sitting in the cold, pounding on the floorboards, after she returned from work.

Dottie tugged on the overhead electric light and checked the coal stoker. Unlit, indeed.

The coal man had dumped her allotment into the bin in early November. It remained half full of dark chunks, too many of them the size of anvils. Putting on her gloves, she climbed into the bin. Sure enough, a chunk wedged between the auger and the stoker hole. Grabbing the sledgehammer, she picked it up—not without a groan, and dropped it onto the coal. It broke in half. She dropped it again, and the piece tumbled free.

She climbed out of the bin, listening to the wind whine outside. It shook the cellar door.

Taking the paper from her pocket, she shoved it into the middle of the clinker inside the stove, added a piece of coal, and lit it.

The furnace flickered to life, flames gnawing at the paper. The auger began to churn coal into the stoker. Until the house heated, she'd curl up in a quilt and build a fire in the family room.

She removed her gloves, laid them on the steps, and pushed on the cellar door.

It didn't move.

Again.

She heard the hasp rattle against its mount, but it didn't give. She closed her eyes. Then, with a cry, she banged her hand against the door, hard, sharp. The action was probably too violent, for pain spiked through her, up her arm, into her shoulder.

The door only shuddered.

She turned on the steps, sat down, and lowered her head to her hands, listening to the memory of Nelson's song fade into the howling wind.

They'd probably find her frozen, emaciated body sometime in May.

* * * * *

"Come down from that ladder, Violet Hart, before you get killed."

Violet ignored Otis and finished screwing in the lightbulb before climbing down. She turned to the janitor, dusting off her hands before tucking them into her cardigan pockets. "It's dark in this hallway, and I thought you'd gone home for the day. Sorry."

"I know you had some sort of man's job in the army, Violet, but you're back in civilization now. Let a man do his job." He folded up the tall ladder, hiking it onto its side. "I'll take care of the maintenance of the city buildings, thank you."

He had a waddle that went with his belly and sixty years on the job. Violet shook her head. She couldn't even change a lightbulb without offending mankind?

She caught her reflection in the display case—the one filled with the Oglala Sioux artifacts found around the area—arrowheads, pottery, a donated blanket from one of the locals.

Violet had turned into Donna Reed's dour librarian before her very eyes. No, wait, Donna Reed had been much too beautiful to end up as a librarian, even if George Bailey hadn't asked to marry her. Some handsome suitor would have certainly come knocking at her door. But four years after the war, Violet had begun to admit there would be no *It's a Wonderful Life* happy ending for her.

No, instead of shopping for groceries or planning a holiday meal for a husband and family three days before Christmas, Violet found herself returning to the children's reading corner and picking up the scattering of children's books—*Make Way for Ducklings* and *Curious George,* the Beatrix Potter series.

The rain knocked on the leaded glass windows of the Frost Library, the late afternoon shadows draping over the shelves and long study tables like dust coverings. The building imprisoned a chill, the behemoth coal furnace in the basement still not enough to heat both the library and the city hall.

The chill contributed even more to Violet's appearance as a spinster librarian, with her long, knitted brown cardigan buttoned over the white blouse. And, to keep her legs warm, she wore pants, something Mrs. Morgan raised a thin eyebrow to two years ago when she showed up for her new position. But she'd remembered the younger, unconventional Dottie Morgan of her childhood and taken a chance.

Violet shelved the books back in their places in the graded reader nook, nearly sitting down with *The Little Engine that Could* as she heard in her head Mrs. Morgan's storytelling voice, the one she'd grown up on.

That Mrs. Morgan inspired a world beyond the prairie hamlet of Frost, bordered on all sides by boring farmland, a dirty creek, a pond turned marshland. In Mrs. Morgan's voice, the children of the town waged battle with evil Mr. MacGregor and wandered the Hundred Acre Wood with Piglet and Christopher Robin. They uncovered mysteries with the Hardy Boys and Nancy Drew, the Five Little Peppers, and sometimes, Mrs. Morgan even displayed a fresh copy of a Big Little Book—Dick Tracy or Tarzan, Buck Rogers, Flash Gordon, or even Jack Armstrong, wonder athlete.

Nelson usually commandeered the Jack Armstrong books.

Violet could still see him climbing on the wooden chairs or hiding behind the shelves as he waited for his mother to close up the library. Or, in his later years, stopping by to drive her home, his shoulders wide in his Frost High letterman's sweater.

Violet might have even harbored a crush on Nelson, despite his being a couple years younger than her, with his unruly tawny brown hair, shorn short on the sides and curly on top, those deep prairie sky-blue eyes, filled with a charming mischief. He had a way of turning a girl's insides to soft caramel, inspiring the men with athletic memories of their childhood as he sank baskets and ran for touchdowns. In fact, who, really, in Frost hadn't loved Nelson T. Morgan?

The town's love for Nelson didn't help Violet's cause any either. Because if it weren't for Violet's service in the WAACs, she wouldn't have been among those women who "stole a man's job and freed Nelson to be shipped off to war."

So many of their young men might have been spared if Violet hadn't usurped their behind-the-frontlines jobs.

She had a feeling that Nelson wouldn't have been one of those filing clerks left behind on American soil or changing the tires on the army colonel's jeeps or even running one of the chow lines. Still, the town hardly embraced her when she arrived home at the depot two years ago, and with their stares she'd felt the specter of his death on the back of her neck.

No wonder Dottie abandoned storytelling hour, spending long hours locked in her office, turning over most of her duties to Violet. And yet, no one wanted to take her place in the story nook. Even Violet, thank you very much. Taking Dottie's place felt like a prophecy. Or an epitaph.

Even, surrender.

Violet would not end up like widowed, lonely, dowdy, and pinched librarian Dottie Morgan.

Violet arranged the children's chairs into the traditional circle, turned off a study light at one of the long pine tables, then gathered up her handbag and camel wool coat. This morning, ice crusted the puddles in the dirt driveway, and with the grim pallor of the sky, she'd also grabbed an umbrella, along with a plastic accordion rain hat and her boots.

In fact, Violet might be even more of a librarian than Dottie, who'd worn a pair of stylish black dress boots today, as if she hadn't quite forgotten the woman she'd wanted to be.

As she locked up, balancing the umbrella above her, Violet heard the train whistle moan over the blanket of dark weather suffocating the town. She calculated roughly ten minutes before the post office closed at 6 p.m.

Maybe today she'd find a letter waiting. She could almost imagine Alex's Christmas greeting in her box, in that tight, precise handwriting. If she could, she'd will it there, along with his agreement to visit her this holiday season.

Five years ago he'd made the promise. It seemed time to fulfill it, and she'd gently—without sounding desperate or angry or even melancholy—suggested it. Minneapolis wasn't far, on the train at least. A half-day's ride at most.

The rain pelted the sidewalk, and when the wind splattered it into her face, Violet realized it had turned to sleet. She hunkered down against it as she strode past Berman's Hardware, the grocery lot, now full of cars, then the bank and the florist. Her stomach growled as she passed Miller's Cafe. She'd managed a cold mincemeat sandwich today, and dinner seemed nowhere in sight, what with her mother pressing her into duty for tonight's Christmas social.

Violet shook out her umbrella, holding the door open for Ardis Weiss at the post office. Inside, the gates had already closed at the desk, but the area to the post office boxes remained accessible. She found her wooden box, unlocked it, and held her breath.

Yes. A small white envelope lay crossways in the box, the size of a Christmas card. She pulled it out, her breath catching.

No, wait—she recognized her *own* handwriting scrawled on the front of the envelope. A stamp across the top—RETURN TO SENDER—in blood red screamed out to her.

Return to Sender?

She ran her thumb over the directive. How—but only three months ago he'd sent her a postcard from Chicago, and before that, St. Louis. And...well, yes, their correspondence seemed rudely one-sided, but *Return to Sender?*

Movement beside her made her glance over—she spied Esther Jamison in her periphery and tucked the envelope into her pocket, swallowing hard to find a smile, in case the organist from the Lutheran church greeted her.

Mercifully, Esther shuffled past without acknowledgment, sorting through her mail. Violet made it out into the street without choking on the ball of heat in her throat.

Return to Sender.

It took a moment before she realized rain wetted her face as it plinked upon her rain hat, sifting into the collar of her coat, warming, then dribbling down the nape of her neck. She opened the umbrella and ran a gloved hand over her cheek. So that was that. She probably should have expected it, really. After all, with all the other younger, beautiful women available—women who hadn't sacrificed their marrying years to the service of their country—she didn't truly expect him to take the train all the way from Minneapolis on an icy winter night, Christmas weekend, no less, and find a woman he'd only met once, during the early years of war at Fort Meade, Maryland.

The lights from the community center at the end of Saint Olaf Street glowed, but Violet stood in the rush of the wind for a moment, a cold hollowness pressing through her.

It should be easier to be alone. She had so much to be grateful for. She and all of her brothers survived the war, she had nieces and nephews, a job, and a family.

So Alex had moved on, let go of their friendship. Violet would take it as a sign that she should too.

Enough of these shiny dreams of a home, a family, a life that might be waiting for her after the war.

Perhaps she should take over story hour at the library and resign herself to weaving stories with happy endings rather than living one.

The community center bustled with activity as she pressed inside, shaking off her umbrella. Members of the Ladies Auxiliary, her mother somewhere leading the charge, worked to transform the old dance hall into the annual Frost Christmas celebration. Miriam Wilkes wrapped the middle cement pole with greenery, a battalion of women that included two of her sisters-in-law dressed the long punch table with a crimson tablecloth, crystal punch glasses, and trays of brownies and cookies. Soon, the members of the Hungry Five Band would arrive to set up on the stage at the far end of the room. The place smelled of the new decade—balsam and pine, sugar cookies, nutmeg, and cinnamon-spiced cider. A promising decade of celebration, free of war and sacrifice.

Violet shucked off her jacket and hung it in the coatroom. She found her newest sister-in-law, Hattie Grace, kneeling on the floor by the kitchen entrance, plugging in a stringer of colored bulbs that ran along the ceiling. "I can't believe this entire string of lights won't work. I just wasted an hour."

She sat back, ran her hand behind her head to tuck up a wayward loop of blond hair. "I just want to go home and take a nap."

Violet gave her a grin, holding out her hand to lift her off the floor. "A nap? You're not supposed to be tired. You're only nineteen. Talk to me when you hit twenty-nine." Or thirty. She could barely think it. Two weeks and, well, she'd be an official spinster, wouldn't she?

Return to Sender.

Right.

"Oh, it's just the baby. I've been so tired since…" Hattie pressed her hand over her mouth. "Violet, I'm sorry. I forgot you don't know yet."

Violet had stopped moving, although somehow she managed to keep breathing. Baby? Hattie Grace, her kid brother's wife, was already expecting? But they only married three months ago. But perhaps, like everyone else, they felt the urgency to start their family, join in on the celebration of life.

"No, of course, that's wonderful." And Violet even made it

sound that way. She reached out, embraced Hattie. The girl would have to gain some weight if she wanted to keep her baby healthy.

Hattie hung onto her arms. "Johnny was going to tell you tonight when we were together. Really. At the dance, with the whole family. Only your mother knows." Hattie pressed her hand to her mouth again, this time to hide a smile, a little giggle.

Truly, Violet could be happy for Hattie, for Johnny. He'd barely seen war, had enlisted a day after his eighteenth birthday, dropping out of school and entering basic two weeks before D-Day. He hadn't made it to Omaha Beach but managed to tromp about Europe for the cleanup fourteen months later. As far as she knew, he hadn't even fired his weapon.

Not that she'd even been issued a weapon, but she'd seen more action changing tires for officers in London, France, and Berlin than Johnny ever had acting as an MP for starved Germans. She hadn't even had a furlough, not once, in four years. That should count for at least an acknowledgment on the Fourth of July.

Hattie reached down, unplugged the lights. "I guess I'll have to find a new strand."

"Wait one moment." Violet walked over to a table by the door and removed a lamp from it. Then she plugged it into the outlet near Hattie and turned it on.

Nothing. "I think this outlet isn't working."

"I tried the strand in the outlet by the stage. It didn't work there either."

"Could be the breaker is blown for these outlets. Let me see what I can do."

Violet plugged the colored lights back in, returned the lamp, then headed for the utility closet near the kitchen. Snapping on the overhead light, she moved back beyond the mops, the buckets, and the brooms, and found the utility box. Yes, one of the fuses had blown. She unscrewed it, found a new fuse from the cardboard box on the shelf nearby, and screwed it in.

"It's on!" Hattie yelled from the dance hall.

"Violet? When did you get here? What are you doing?"

She didn't have to turn to know the owner of the voice. She could nearly see her mother standing in the hallway, probably carrying a tray of cookies, wearing one of her old homemade checkered aprons over her black party dress, her graying hair rolled back from her face, her red lipstick perfectly applied.

No dour widowhood mourning for Frances Hart.

Violet closed the box and turned to answer her mother as she pried herself from the closet. "The fuse was blown for the Christmas bulbs."

"And of course you had to fix it. Why didn't you ask Roger, or even Johnny?"

"Because Roger and Johnny aren't here, and I'm perfectly capable of fixing a fuse, Mother."

Violet accepted the tray of brownies her mother settled in her arms.

"Well, that's the problem, isn't it? You're always perfectly capable. You don't need a man."

Violet ignored her and headed to the serving table. Probably she wouldn't make it home to change before the dance tonight. Not that it mattered, anyway. She could count on one hand the remaining eligible bachelors in Frost. Clyde, from the feed store, and Tony, the janitor at the school. And don't forget Father O'Donnell, in his midforties. But he was a priest, so that really didn't count.

She set the tray on the table, did some rearranging.

The band members began to arrive—Lew and Bobby, toting their trumpets, Howard lugging in an upright bass. Another man she didn't recognize tromped in behind them, stomping his feet. He carried what looked like a suitcase, although maybe it fit a saxophone.

Perhaps the Hungry Five had added a hungry sixth. Oh, see, life wasn't so despairing when she could laugh at herself. She would survive Alex's *Return to Sender.*

"I can't believe it's raining, three days before Christmas." June, her oldest sister-in-law, the one married to Thomas, corralled her seven-year-old with a grab at the back of his shirt. She and Thomas married right after high school, a year before he shipped out. "So much for the Christmas spirit."

"We don't need snow to have Christmas, or Christmas spirit."

"It would help. Poor kids, it's not the same as when we grew up. With sleighs and horses mushing up and down Main Street and kids skating on Silver Lake and story hour at the library."

"And the star. I miss the star." This from Sara, the tall, elegant daughter of the town doctor, married to Roger. Violet felt short and dour next to her lanky blond sister-in-law. Sara had served as a navy nurse, stationed in London. When Violet returned, she'd thought they'd share that kinship.

Apparently, serving Uncle Sam as a nurse held a different prestige. And Sara's return to town heralded a parade of men to her door. Roger had fought them all off to win her heart.

Sara ran her hands over her extended belly. "When I was young, I could see the star from my bedroom window, like it had been plucked from the night sky and set right in the middle of Frost."

"Dottie and Nelson made that star when Nelson was about five, I think." Frances added a batch of Krumkake to the table.

"The tree seems so dark without it," Sara said.

"Where is it now?"

"Well, I suppose Mrs. Morgan has it, somewhere in that creepy house of hers," June said. "She stopped putting it up the year after Nelson—"

"Shh. Not today, Junie," Frances said. "Today is a day of hope."

"All the more reason to put the star up." Sara arranged the punch cups on the table. "Maybe we could get another one."

"Oh no, Sara. That's just not right," Frances said, moving the napkins for the addition of the punch bowl.

Sarah turned to Violet. "You know Mrs. Morgan—can you go ask her for it?"

Ask Dottie for her son's star? "I don't think—"

"It's a great idea," June said. "Don't you think so, Tripp?"

Perfect. Violet's nephew had to nod, to grin at her with that gap-toothed smile.

"Listen, Dottie just wants to be left alone. Trust me on this. I know you all remember her as the woman who made books come to life, but frankly, she's not that woman anymore. She's...well, she's..." Violet didn't want to use the word *dead*, not today, but—

"She used to be a real firecracker." Frances had moved around the table, begun arranging the napkins. "Highfalutin—her daddy owned most of the town back then. She had suitors lining up on her doorstep. And then TJ Morgan motored into town the summer after she graduated from teachers college in his bumblebee-yellow Studebaker roadster. She took one look at that gangster, with his dark wavy hair, hypnotizing blue eyes, and dangerous swagger, and turned into a flapper right before our eyes. Cut off her hair and ran away with him."

"Mother!" June said, putting her hands over Tripp's ears. He wriggled away.

Frances shrugged. "It's true. I guess we all should have expected it. Dottie was always so independent, so feisty. She even played women's basketball at Mankato State Teachers college. But six months later, when TJ landed in prison and she returned home pregnant, I can assure you we thanked the good Lord we'd missed that bullet. Of course, she asked for it, behaving the way she did, but no one can deny she had a blessing out of that Nelson." She smiled at Violet. "I had hoped Nelson might fancy you."

"Oh please, Mother." If she could, Violet would run from the building at top speed.

"It's true. You remind me, in a way, of Dottie. She and you are both such free spirits." Frances patted her cheek. "It's difficult to catch a man when you're flitting about, I suppose."

"I was hardly *flitting about*, Mother. I was serving my country."

"You were changing tires. Let's not over-glamorize your role in the war effort." Frances sighed. "Sweetheart, no man is going to marry a gal who can change her own tires. Men need to feel needed." She looked at June and winked. "Even if we know the truth."

Right now. The earth could open right now, gobble her whole, and Violet would go to glory with joy.

But Frances hadn't quite finished. "And it wouldn't hurt you to wear a clean dress, a little lipstick, perhaps. You could put some effort into your appearance. We Hart women have to work at it a little harder than the rest."

Hardly. Her mother had a natural, shapely beauty at age fifty that turned the heads of the widowers in town. But yes, Violet, a true Hart, had inherited her father's wide lips, dull mud-brown hair, strong hands, and less than womanly silhouette. She had to work at femininity doubly hard.

Return to Sender. Perhaps Alex had simply remembered her in her greasy uniform, her hair pulled back with a scarf, her unpainted face, and realized that, back then, the air of desperation could cloud a man's mind. With so many women single after the war, he could certainly do better than plain and even mannish Violet Hart.

"I'll try to change before the dance, Mother," Violet said quietly.

"That would be wonderful. Now, can you grab a broom, sweep up some of the drying mud? We need a clean dance floor."

But Violet slowed on her way back to the utility closet, her gaze falling on the naked treetop outside in the square. She saw Dottie, sitting night after night in the puddle of her office light, alone. Eating a piece of cold chicken for lunch, muscling that old truck into gear as she pulled away from city hall.

She used to be a real firecracker.

Even when Violet was a child, Dottie intrigued her, the murmurs surrounding her circumstances always just a little unintelligible, a woman of mystery and adventure.

Night fell upon Frost like coal dust, the sleet swirling now, lighter. They could use the lighted star as a beacon to draw townspeople to the dance.

If she headed out to Dottie's, Violet might escape, at least for an hour, to gather her fortifications for tonight's predicted loneliness.

And...what if she could talk Dottie into joining them at the dance?

Violet caught a glimpse of herself in the pane of glass, her dark hair wet and bedraggled with the storm. Yes, she might need some spiffing up before the dance, but who was she kidding? Every man in town, eligible or not, knew she was the girl who spent more time under the hood of her father's tractor than learning to waltz. She didn't even know how to dance.

Still, she reached back, pulled the bobby pins from her bun, shook out her hair. Then she grabbed her coat, her plastic rain hat, her umbrella.

"Mother, I'm taking Father's car out to Dottie's place." She was the only one, besides Johnny, who knew how to drive it anyway. She opened the door and noticed that the ice had turned to thick, fluffy flakes, hurtling down from the heavens, accumulating in a light layer.

"I'm going to get the star."

* * * * *

Jacob Ramsey III always had an answer for disaster, a way to untangle life, a word of hope to solve any problem.

But today, he had to arrive before the daily mail if he hoped to save the day.

He set down his suitcase—still packed for Davenport—and stepped aside to avoid being skewered by the umbrella the pretty dark brunette wielded. He swept off his hat, held open the door, but she barely seemed to notice him as she called out to someone behind her.

Jake did register it as odd that she might be driving, but then again, his mother had taken the Stearns Runabout for a tour around Lake Michigan a few times. Nearly killed an apple man, but still, she'd managed the wheel, the brake. He'd heard of women driving during the war also.

In fact, most likely Violet knew how to drive, what with her ability to fix army trucks, jeeps, and other vehicles in the army motor pool.

He'd like to see that—a woman with a wrench in her hand.

But first he had to find her.

Jake drew in a breath and picked up his suitcase, approaching a group of women at the punch table arranging pastries. The older one wore her years on her face, in her stern features, her dark hair dappled with just the barest threads of gray. Red lips and a black party dress suggested she refused to surrender to the onslaught of age. He glanced at the others then said, "Hello, I'm looking for someone and I'm wondering if you could help me."

The older woman looked up at him, wiping her hands on her apron. "I hope so—I know everyone in Frost. Are you visiting for the holidays?"

Visiting? He didn't exactly know how to describe it. "I'm just...delivering a message, really. I'm looking for a woman named Violet Hart."

A younger woman—blond—and a pregnant woman frowned at him. "What do you want with her?"

Behind her, the band had begun to unload, the trumpets warming up their horns. He'd happened upon a party of sorts. When he'd disembarked at the train station, under the torrent of sleet, Jake had simply ducked his head and fought his way to Main Street, hoping to find a hotel. The lighted dance hall beckoned like a safe harbor.

"She was a friend…of a friend. In a way. Or…well, I just need to talk to her. Do you know where I might find her?"

"She's not here." This from a woman who hiked a small boy onto her hip. "She just left to get a star for the tree outside." The child—cute, with dark blond curly hair—squirmed off her hip. "The dance will start in less than an hour. She'll be back before then. Please stay. Have some cake."

He didn't want cake. He'd lose cake, right on the wooden dance floor. No, Jake had no hope of holding anything down until he talked to Violet. Until he explained why his mother had sent back her letter.

Until he told her the truth.

"How long ago did she leave?"

"You passed her when you came in," said the blond.

Oh, he felt like a cad. The brunette, with the long, chocolate-brown hair, the lethal umbrella. Perhaps he should have guessed it, but she'd never sent a picture, so… "Where did she go?" He didn't look at the older woman, who had crossed her arms across her chest, looking very much like Svetlana when he invaded her kitchen, but smiled at the young, pregnant one. She looked like someone who might offer a poor guy a hand in his time of need.

Indeed. "Out of town, to the south. Go until you see a big green house—it looks like a fairy tale house. And has a stone fence around it. It's not that far, about a half mile out of town."

He tucked up his collar, a shiver starting at his tailbone. Perfect. He hiked up his suitcase.

A half mile should give him plenty of time to figure out how to tell Violet that for the past four and a half years she'd been writing to a dead man.

CHAPTER TWO

Realistically, by New Year's someone might come looking for her. But with Christmas upon them…and Gordy wouldn't dare venture over from his side of the pond.

Dottie had done a thorough search of the cellar and found nothing useful—no peach preserves, no droplets of water trickling down the stone foundation of the house, not even a crowbar left forgotten on the dirt floor.

How long could a person live without water? Three days? Five?

Thankfully, with the coal furnace running, she wouldn't freeze. Unless, of course, she lost power in the storm. She listened to it howl outside. Over the past hour—or had it been two?—the moaning of the wind turned constant, a near wail that seeped through her, found her bones. She refused to allow that it might be coming from inside.

But as Dottie sat on the steps, the truth sank into her.

No one would be coming to save her. No one cared that she lived alone in this house, the storm brewing outside. No one thought of whether she might be alone, cold, trapped. That truth she'd learned long ago. But it hurt, just a little more, to admit it.

Once upon a time, it couldn't touch her. Not with Nelson climbing up into her lap. Or greeting her with his toothless grin over a bowl of cut oats. Or waving to her from the football field. Only in the past five years did the gossip, the rumors, the casual words serrate her until the truth turned her brittle.

God had turned His back on her. She hadn't wanted to believe it.

Had, in fact, believed otherwise, probably for too long—that instead, He had forgiven her. That He still loved her. How had she been so profoundly mistaken about that?

The wind found a crack in the door and whistled inside, sent a shiver across her skin.

She ran her hands over her skirt—why didn't she wear pants like Violet? Especially on a day like this? A few times, Dottie had heard her reading aloud to a couple of the first graders. Not a formal story hour, but something impromptu, mothering. Violet had the cadence, could do the voices. Dottie had finally found her replacement if she wanted.

Yes, if Dottie perished here in the bowels of the old Victorian, Violet would take over the reading program and manage the library, probably even better than Dottie had. Too bad Violet had never found her man—but that's what happened when you spurned the hometown boys.

Someday, Dottie intended to forgive Violet for turning down Nelson for a dance that last Fourth of July social. Most likely, Violet hadn't meant to hurt him. If Violet had known—then again, if they'd all known such a strong, capable man might be lost—

The sledgehammer. It lay against the coal bin and Dottie got up, dragged it over to the door. Maybe she could bust a hole in the door, unlatch the hasp.

She stood on the steps, hoisted the sledgehammer to her shoulder, and swung. It skimmed the surface of the door, arched down, and nearly slammed her in the knee.

She dodged and it swung out, whipping out of her hands and bouncing on the dirt floor. "Oh!"

Her hands burned.

Maybe less of a swing might help.

She picked up the sledgehammer and again hoisted it on her shoulder. Then, instead of swinging it, she tapped it against the door. The door shuddered as the hammer fell back against her shoulder.

She hit it again.

It shuddered again, this time harder.

Oh, why did her father have to make such a fortress?

With a cry—more anger than panic—she hit it again. And again. And again.

She stopped counting as she swung, finally seeing a dent in the wood. At this rate she'd be out of the cellar by Easter.

The hasp creaked and suddenly, the door opened.

Snow drifted in as she stared up at her rescuer.

"Mrs. Morgan?" Violet stood, one foot propped on the cement frame, the other holding open the door. Snow layered her dark hair, now loose and tangled in the wind. "What are you doing down there?"

"Violet!" Dottie lowered the sledgehammer to the stairs, propped it there. "I came down to free a coal jam. How'd you find me?"

An emotion she couldn't place passed over Violet's expression. "I—I heard pounding."

From the library?

Dottie climbed the stairs, out into the snowstorm, hunching down as the icy flakes hit her face. "Let's get inside!"

Her feet crunched through the accumulation of snow as she ran around the side of the house. While she'd struggled for freedom, the world had turned white, at least two inches of snow crusting the ground. She wrenched open her back door, stomped inside the mudroom.

Violet followed her. "Are you all right?"

"Of course." Dottie shrugged out of Nelson's jacket, hung it on a peg, then slipped out of the galoshes. "Come inside, warm up."

Violet shook her head. "Actually, I'm just here to ask…" She made a face, as if the words tasted sour on her tongue. "As you know, we're having the annual Frost Ball tonight…." She looked away. "The tree in the square looks so barren."

Dottie had been reaching for the doorknob into the kitchen when the realization hit her. She stilled, looked back at Violet. "You want the star."

Violet met her eyes. Nodded.

For a moment, the impulse to generosity, the old stirring of joy at seeing the star shining over St. Olaf Square, the yearning to indeed revive the old traditions, flashed inside. Quick. Bright. With a warmth that bled right through her.

Violet blew on her hands, snow caught in her dark hair, turning it shiny, like it had that night under the summer stars. When she'd turned down her son for a dance.

Her son who'd died, who'd made the star with Dottie at the tender age of five. Their star.

"No."

Dottie turned and pushed her way into her house, the flash of sweet warmth erased. No. She couldn't have Nelson's star shining bright and brilliant over the town of Frost, like some sort of mockery to her grief. No.

Violet followed her inside. "Please, Mrs. Morgan. With the storm, it's so dark out, and we thought people might need the light. Besides, don't you think it's time—"

"No, I don't think it's time." Dottie picked up a kettle, noticing that in the two hours of her entrapment the house had begun to warm. Filling the kettle with water, she put it on the stove, lit the gas flame with a match. Then she opened the icebox and pulled out the pot of yesterday's soup. "Violet, I know you mean well, but I simply cannot top the Frost tree with the star."

"But it hasn't been lit for years."

She put the pot on another burner. "Five, to be precise. I am sure you can do the math."

"I can, and I was in that war too, Mrs. Morgan. I met plenty of the Johnnies who went to war, who left behind the people they loved, hoping they would go on. I can guarantee that Nelson would have wanted you to light your—his star."

"You don't know anything, Violet." Dottie hadn't exactly intended that tone—it snapped out of her, cold and brittle. She picked up a towel, wiped her hands, softened her voice. "I know you mean well, but you're right. It's his star, and as you well know, his light has gone out. It seems inappropriate to put the star up again."

"It seems inappropriate not to."

Never in her life had Dottie been prone to violence, but in that moment, she gripped the towel with everything inside her, lest her hand lose its moorings and clock Miss Violet Hart across the face. "Please leave."

"Mrs. Morgan—"

"Violet, I fear I will not make it into the library tomorrow with our impending storm. I believe you may take the day off also—might as well just stay in for the Christmas weekend."

"But the children—the Christmas Eve reading?"

"What is it with your insistence to reignite old traditions?"

"I told a few of the mothers—"

"No. No reading, no star. No children. Please, and I'm asking you nicely for the last time, leave."

Dottie turned again, hating the effect her own words had on her, the fact that she wanted to put the towel to her face, to howl, lose herself in the noise of the storm.

When she heard Violet close the door behind her, step out, and finally motor up her car, Dottie did exactly that.

* * * * *

Please...leave.

Violet sat in her father's old '38 Plymouth and listened to Dottie's voice, dissecting it. Examining the tremor inside, the pulse of regret, the hope of rebellion.

No, probably Violet dreamed all those nuances from the crevices in her own heart. Certainly Mrs. Morgan didn't mean to be alone for the next three days, over Christmas? Certainly she had family?

Violet got out, took a board from the back seat, and scraped the heavy snow from her windshield, scrubbing at the icy layer underneath. She should have kept the car running, should have guessed that Dottie would turn her down.

A firecracker, indeed. Violet had no doubt the woman would have pummeled her way through her cellar door. It just might have taken into next year.

Please...leave.

Violet turned, peering at the entrance. Despite her tone, the woman seemed so fragile, her legs pencils in those oversized waders, her body shrunken in her son's jacket. Violet didn't know what made her think of the cellar door—how she'd even heard the pounding above the blowing of the storm. Just an impulse, maybe, but with the house so cold, and Mrs. Morgan not answering her call as she tiptoed inside her dark, cold kitchen...

Violet slid back inside the car, curling her hands around the steering wheel. She put the car into reverse, backed it around, then toward the long driveway.

If Dottie wanted to be left alone...

Violet could barely see past the giant pine tree in the yard, its furry branches coated with snow. Flakes pummeled her windshield and a shiver drove through her, despite the heat in the car.

So much for the Frost Christmas Dance. Besides the band and the committee, who might venture out on a night like this? But it was tradition. And people thrived on tradition, especially when rebuilding their lives.

Please...leave.

Oh, Dottie's voice embedded in Violet, pulsing, as if she'd looked inside Mrs. Morgan and seen something forbidden.

Besides, what if it were Violet someday trapped in her cellar, no one to call out to?

Who was she kidding? It *would* be her.

She glanced back at the house.

When she looked again to the driveway, a figure had materialized, as if from nowhere, just appearing in the darkness, etched out by her lights. A man in a long, snow-crusted wool coat carrying a case, hunched over against the wind.

"Oh!" Violet pumped the brakes, but the wheels didn't catch. "Look out!"

The man seemed paralyzed in the road, as if frozen in her headlights.

She wrenched the wheel to swerve away, to miss him, and the car careened toward the lawn. She pumped the brakes again, but they refused to answer, momentum carrying the vehicle toward the towering pine in the front yard.

No— No—

Violet saw the accident, almost in slow motion. The tree swaying above her, the branches quivering as if waving her off. The trunk rising toward her, the snow bulleting the windshield.

She threw her hands up to brace herself, and let out a scream as the impact pitched her forward.

She slammed into the windshield, bounced back into the seat, then forward again into the dash. Pain seared into her knee. She may have heard a crack too.

And then, nothing remained but stillness as she realized she'd stopped moving.

Snow covered the long hood, dumped from the defenseless tree. The car ticked, one last time, then the engine sputtered out, hissing its demise.

"Are you okay?"

The voice came at her, muffled, through the window. She went to roll it down, cranking hard twice before it came to her that perhaps she should simply open the door.

It protested, shuddering as she cracked it open. The stranger helped pry it open then bent down and held out his hand. "Are you all right?"

"What were you doing standing in the middle of the driveway? On a night like this?"

"Shh, you're bleeding." He crouched beside her as she put her hand to her forehead. He caught it. "No, wait, you have glass there." He reached up, making a face, and she winced when he pulled a shard away. "I think there's more, but we need to get you inside and clean it out."

In the light from the house, and as he cupped his hand under her elbow to help her out, she recognized him.

"You! You were at the dance hall. Aren't you a member of the band?"

"No." His other hand closed around hers, and as he pulled her up, her legs—probably from the shock—gave out on her. She collapsed like an idiot back onto the seat.

"You're really hurt."

"I banged my knee on something."

"Do you think you broke it?"

"No...I just—" But she ran her hand over her knee, wincing.

Maybe she had broken it. She at least felt the beginnings of a goose egg.

"Aw, crumb." He stood up, walked to the front of the car. "Your radiator grill is caved in, and both your running lights are crushed. Your fender is a goner. And one of your headlamps is also broken."

Oh, she could hear her mother now. *Women shouldn't drive cars.*

She watched him as he moved the branches, inspected the wheels. The snow layered his eyelashes, wetting them. He had a square jaw, the hint of russet whiskers upon it, and dark eyes— maybe blue. He wore a fedora and a gray scarf at his neck, fancy- like, as if he might be from Minneapolis, or perhaps Chicago. "You're dug in pretty well. You're not getting it out of here tonight, in this storm. We'll need some leverage to pry it off the tree."

Swell. "Are you sure it's that bad?"

He returned and, in the glow of the house, looked genuinely sorry, the way his blue eyes darkened, the furrow of his brow. In a different time, on a different day, she might have been able to forgive him. "It's that bad. I'm so sorry."

"What are you doing here? Did you *follow* me?"

His expression stilled her.

"You *did* follow me." She glanced at the house, back to the man. "Why...I don't understand. Who are you?"

"I was—am—oh, boy. My name is Jake. Let's just get you inside." He reached for her but she slapped at his hand.

"I'm perfectly capable of walking, thank you."

"I beg to differ. You're holding your knee as if it might come off, and you're bleeding from the head. I know that I am to blame for your predicament, so please relieve some of my guilt by allowing me to assist you into your house."

Jake sounded...well, not from around Frost. "It's not my house."

"Oh. Right." He leaned down, ran his arm under hers, around her back, then picked her up, cupping her under her legs.

"Oh!"

"I promise not to drop you."

"That's reassuring."

But he had strong arms, and despite the fact that yes, she could probably crawl her way back to Dottie's, an errant, even dangerous impulse inside made her sling her arms around his neck, praying he wouldn't slip as he trudged up the hill. She took a breath then leaned into him, the snow cascading into the cuff of her jacket, melting against her skin, slicking down her back.

Okay, perhaps she needed the ride after all. Pain thundered through her in the throbbing of her knee, the heat on her forehead. And the car—oh, her father's prized Plymouth. *I'm sorry, Daddy.*

He reached the door and didn't even knock, just opened it, stepping inside.

"I don't think she wants us to—" She squirmed in his arms, seeing already Mrs. Morgan's shock, hearing her voice. *Please... leave.*

This wouldn't be good.

"Hello? Anyone here?" He stamped his feet and the inner door to the kitchen opened as he barreled into the warm house.

"What on earth—who are you?"

Oh, she couldn't look. But she couldn't stop herself either as she peeked at Mrs. Morgan.

The woman held her soup ladle above her head as if she might use it as a weapon.

"It's me, Violet."

She blinked at the two of them, Violet, the man who held her, then lowered her ladle. "What are you— Put her down!"

"I need a chair for her. She's been injured."

"Injured? What on earth? Well, fine. Over there, at the table."

Jake hooked his foot around a scrolled oak straight chair, and Mrs. Morgan grabbed it and pulled it out. "Land's sakes, don't break it."

Jake set Violet down. "I need a towel and some ice."

But Mrs. Morgan was staring at her in some sort of horrified trance. "What happened?"

Violet didn't know where to start. And then, she didn't have to. A terrific crack sounded in the yard, and then a wretched moan. She stared in horror out the window as the giant white pine teetered then fell across the length of the yard. It hit the stone wall, crumbling it, and crushed the Plymouth beneath its arms.

Mrs. Morgan turned back to her, clearly having caught the demise of her tree, still holding the ladle, murder on her face. "Well, I guess you'll be staying."

* * * * *

Gordy Lindholm didn't live a life prone to panic. After forty-nine years of growing up on and running a farm, he'd seen cattle frozen to ice on the prairie and geese embedded in the bumpy surface of the marsh. After the Armistice Day blizzard nearly a decade ago, the eighty-mile-an-hour winds had ripped off the roof of his silo, and he'd lost nearly half his harvested crop. He'd been snowed in, iced in, and all but decimated in a twister back in '24 that took out his neighbor's barn.

Yet, when he heard the shot echo across Silver Lake, it made him pause in his trek back from the barn to the house, his hand on the guide wire he'd just strung.

He could make out Dottie's lights from here, despite the blinding whiteout. The kitchen light glowed out into the night, along with the front porch light. Later, around eight, her upstairs bedroom light would flicker on, stay lit for an hour.

Once upon a time, he watched the darkened pane next door—Nelson's window—too.

He never went to bed until her lights turned off. As if they were connected, a real family.

Naw, probably just a habit for an old, lonely man, was all.

Gordy listened for another report. Nothing in the howling wind, and he could dismiss it if he wanted. But an irritation niggled inside him that he couldn't shake. Her living room light, for one, came on two hours later than usual. And what if she ran out of coal or wood? Had she remembered to fill up her milk jars at the creamery? Did she have provisions for the storm?

Gordy stood on his front porch, watching the swirl of the snow against the gaslight, then finally decided on a jaunt in the truck.

Couldn't hurt to just venture out, take a drive along her front yard, catch a glimpse of her in the window. Probably, he could even pull right up into the driveway, leave the truck running, and peer in the door to the mudroom to check on the wood supply. The coal man had been around about a month ago, he thought.

As for the milk, he could leave a couple of fresh bottles on the doorstep—except they'd freeze. So maybe he'd ease open the door and slip them inside.

Even if she noticed, she wouldn't get up to greet him, fetching the milk after he'd long gone. She knew the rules, had helped establish them, keep them. The rules gave them a tepid peace.

He threw on a red wool jacket over his coveralls and climbed into his old 1925 Chevy. It shuddered twice but wouldn't turn over.

Gordy knew he should have probably replaced the carburetor, but the truck could run on moonshine if it had a mind.

Tonight, clearly, it didn't take to going out in the sleet. Fine. He piled out of the truck, returned to the house, lit a lantern, and, out of habit, nearly called to Barnabas.

He missed the spaniel looking up at him from his old blanket before the hearth, where Gordy had let the fire die to embers while milking the Jerseys, letting the oil furnace take over. Until a year ago, the old dog would have gotten up, trotted over, despite his stiff joints.

Gordy missed him more than a man ought.

He wrapped the muffler around his mouth, his nose, then pulled on a wool cap, his leather mittens. If he took the shortcut through the narrow part of the lake-turned-slough, it might take him all of ten minutes to walk over, poke around, and return.

He left his porch light on as a beacon as he set out across the marsh, through the crispy, now icy grasses, like shiny knives skewering the slough. He held a lamp, the light puddling out before him as he trekked, finally setting foot on the dirt road. Only by experience did he recognize it, the darkness folding in behind him as he traced his path along the stone wall.

Turning, he could barely make out his porch light across the expanse, a mere stone's throw on a summer day. He couldn't take too long, or he'd be stranded for the night.

Well, stranded in Dottie's barn, that is. Gordy couldn't imagine her actually allowing him inside the house.

In the buffeting wind, he imagined he could hear Nelson, calling to him from the house. *"Mr. Lindholm, are we going hunting today?"*

Of course, Dottie would be standing in the kitchen, just inside the window where she thought he couldn't see her, while Nelson bounded out of the house, down to the road.

Gordy could admit that sometimes he walked into town just so Nelson might join him for a ways, tell him about school, or football, or even—and he hated himself for yearning for these— tidbits about Dottie, her life, her work.

Did she still think about him? Wonder why he hadn't married? He listened for the answers in the nuances of Nelson's stories.

"Darren Hudson's family had beagles. I really want one, if I can talk Mom into it."

Nelson's voice found him in the cold, nudged up a smile. How could Gordy resist bundling up a puppy and leaving it on their back stoop? Nelson must have known, but perhaps that only added to Dottie's dark looks.

The boy had simply needed a father. What was he to do?

Gordy let the memories tug him along the stone wall down to the entrance. He lifted his light to follow the path up.

The glow cast over the shaggy, broken debris of a tree across the drive, and for a second, Gordy thought he might be lost.

And then the slow, choking realization bled through him.

Nelson's tree. The one Dottie planted that summer after Nelson's birth. Nelson's tree had fallen. He'd seen the decay in the low-hanging orange branches, even a few higher up that indicated disease, but never imagined it to be that weakened.

He'd heard not a gunshot but the crack of the tree.

Oh, Dottie. If only he'd pruned it, taken away the diseased, dying branches, it might have lived through the storm. He came close, brushed the snow off one of the springy, bristly arms. Glanced up to the house. The light in the kitchen still burned.

Did he see movement at the window? He couldn't tell. Lifting the lamp, he skirted the tree, heading for the barn, but the glint of metal against the light stopped him. He swept the branches aside—a Plymouth lay trapped under its icy arms.

Someone had crashed into her tree.

He looked back up at the house. Someone who could be injured or...

He'd always feared that one of TJ's old cronies might look Dottie up, land on her doorstep. The thought threaded into his brain sometimes, late at night, roused him to sit in his chair on the porch, or by the window.

Crazy old obsessed neighbor.

His last memory of TJ, however, even so many years ago, propelled Gordy up the driveway, toward the house. He'd simply sneak into the back room, take a gander inside.

Dottie couldn't blame him for caring, right?

No, that's exactly what she accused him of the last time she'd seen him. Easter Sunday, 1944. He'd begun attending the Presbyterian church in Canby shortly thereafter.

Still, this wasn't about Nelson, or TJ, or even that night he'd begged her not to leave Frost in the passenger seat of TJ's yellow roadster. People put aside old grievances during a storm, right?

He certainly would.

The light in the back room was on, and he eased open the door, intending to simply peer into the kitchen.

That's when he saw the blood. A drop on the floor, another on the doorknob.

Blood could make him panic.

"Dottie!" He slammed open the kitchen door, not caring that he carried the storm in with him—the frigid air, the violent breezes, the ice on his boots and jacket. He barreled into the kitchen.

Dottie turned from the stove, her mouth open.

A man looked up from where he kneeled before a woman seated on a chair. She held a bulky towel to her head. "Mr. Lindholm. What are you doing here?"

"Violet?" Gordy had known her for ages, of course, but had rarely seen Violet Hart since her return from the war. Maybe at the grocery store a few times. "Who's bleeding here?"

"Oh, for crying in the sink, what are *you* doing here, Gordon?" Dottie came to barricade herself between him and her guests. The man had found his feet—a young man, with army-short dark brown hair, sharp eyes, a dapper suit.

He reminded Gordy a little of TJ, which did none of them any good.

"I...well, I saw the tree, Dottie."

"You saw the tree? From your house?"

Okay, so— "I heard the tree go down. It sounded like a gunshot." He ground his teeth. "I got worried, okay?"

She threw her hands up. "Gordon, you were just looking for an excuse to come over here and we both know it."

He said nothing, desperately wishing he'd listened to his truck and the voices inside that screamed, "Bad idea!"

"Well, isn't this a fine kettle of fish. As you can see, Violet Hart has demolished my—my tree..." Dottie said it with only the slightest hiccough, but she couldn't hide anything from him, not after all these years. And the flash of pain in her eyes just might make him bleed too. *Oh, Dottie.* How he wanted to close the space between them, put his arms—

"And this gentleman here is to blame, apparently."

"He was standing in the driveway, after following me here." Violet removed the cloth, narrowed her eyes at the man, who couldn't hide a flinch at her words.

"He followed you? From where?" Gordy must have taken a step toward the man, for he held up his hand.

"From the dance hall. But listen, I didn't mean to cause any trouble. I just needed to talk to Violet. I didn't mean for her to drive into the tree."

Violet stared at him. "I don't even know you—what could you possibly have to say to me?"

The man glanced at Violet, then to Dottie and even Gordy, as if they might have some sort of answer, or aid in their postures. But Gordy just wanted to wrap the man around that fender out there for taking down Dottie's tree. And Dottie, well, she seemed to be angrier about Gordy landing in her kitchen with his melting boots than about her beloved fir.

"Well?" Violet said, voicing Gordy's exact tone.

"I have news about—about your friend Alex."

Whoever Alex was, and whatever information this cad might have about him, turned Violet white. Gordy had the strangest impulse to go and stand behind her. Or in front of her.

"What do you know, Jake?"

Jake? Yeah, a real troublemaker name. This guy had Minneapolis written all over him, with his slick suit, the thin tie at his neck. Probably drove one of those nifty new Lincoln Coupe de Villes. Gordy had seen one at the state fair last summer, all shiny chrome, slick black running boards, a sleek blue body the color of the sky.

Yes, this joker reeked of too much dapper, too much TJ, and Gordy narrowed his eyes, glad he smelled a little like the barn.

"Listen, it's not a conversation we can have here, Violet." Jake crouched before her, pressed the rag back to her head. "We need to get you back to town, let a doctor look at your head, maybe even your knee."

Gordy wanted to hurt someone at the expression on Violet's face.

"He married someone else, didn't he?" Violet said softly.

Oh boy, if those weren't words to make a man run... Gordy glanced at Dottie, wondering if she, too, could hear the past.

"Can we talk about it later?" Jake said, his gaze darting to their audience.

Violet narrowed her eyes at Jake the messenger. "What are you, his brother, here to deliver the bad news? Well, don't get your knickers in a knot. I didn't ever think I was anything to him anyway."

Oh, please. Even a man who'd spent the nearly forty-eight years of his life singing to his cattle could see through that lie.

"No, I wasn't his brother. I'm just a friend, but you meant more to him than you know," Jake said softly.

Gordy rolled his eyes.

She held up her hands. "I don't want to know, okay? It's fine, I don't really care anyway."

Yep, he should have stayed home, next to the fire, with the memories of his spaniel, because Gordy had walked right into the nightmare of his past. In Jake's expression Gordy saw too much of himself—a boy with desperation on his face, in the clench of his jaw, the rise of his chest. Gordy couldn't help but feel a little sorry for him when Violet pressed on his chest. "Please, go home, Jake. And tell Alex that I hope he lives happily ever after."

The idiot got up like he might actually obey.

Gordy shook his head. He might be a farmer, but he had years of practice reading the nonverbal communication of a wounded woman. Whoever this Alex had been, he'd broken her heart into a thousand ugly shards. And Jake was about to repeat every one of Gordy's mistakes.

Not that Dottie was any great help. In fact, true to form and just like Violet, Dottie did what she did best when people bared their hearts and stood bleeding before her.

She kicked them out.

"Stop. Enough of this blathering. I don't care whose brother you are or what Alex did or even that Violet can live without the both of you. I want you out of my house. Now."

She whirled around and pressed her finger into Gordy's wool jacket. "That includes you, Mr. Lindholm. Get out of my house. You don't belong here."

Her voice wavered, however, on the last sentence, and she didn't look at him.

Then she retreated from the room into the parlor.

And, although he could recognize the symptoms of a woman's broken heart, it didn't make him good at figuring out what to do, because Gordy just stood there.

What he should have done—twenty-six years ago, now—was to catch her, stop her...even follow her.

But he'd never been any good at catching her or at sticking around to weather the storms either.

He turned to Jake. "We'll hike back to my place and I'll fire up the truck," he said. "Let's go, before the storm traps us here."

No, he simply didn't have the courage to be trapped in the home of the woman who blamed him for the death of her only child.

CHAPTER THREE

With everything inside him, Jake wanted to run back outside, to that moment when he'd seen Violet's car careening toward him, and jump out of the way.

He just wanted to start over, to break free of his lies.

To be a man worthy of Violet's esteem. Even, her affection.

His chest burned and he guessed he might be turning pale. The hike to Dottie's house hadn't helped, not to mention the adrenaline of the crash, the cold air constricting his lungs even more, drawing out the mucus, fisting his chest muscles. He fought to breathe as he stood, in through his nose, out through his mouth.

He just had to calm down.

Why hadn't he let her drive by, out of his life, where she belonged? He had no right to stand in front of her, to deliver this news.

Or rather, this lie.

He married someone else, didn't he?

Her broken question had glued the truth inside him; he could taste the bitterness of it in the back of his throat. But worst of all was the expression on Violet's face, the hurt in her eyes. Yes, he wanted to spool back the moments, all the way back to the moment when...

When he'd read the letters she'd written to Alex and

determined to take his place. At least until the war ended, until she came home. Just to encourage her, lonely soldier serving behind the line in Europe.

Somehow, however, he'd lost himself along the way, until he ended up here, in the kitchen of some angry woman, lying round and round to the woman he loved.

Yes, loved. Because how was he supposed to read her letters and not care for her, not admire her courage, not dream up her laughter, not wish for her happiness.

Perhaps even in his arms.

Standing here, in front of her, only made it worse. Because, from the moment he picked her up, held her to himself, let her arms tangle around his neck, he'd known what a bad idea he'd harbored, nurtured, even embraced when he hopped on the Burlington-Northern and headed west to Frost.

He wanted to run his hand along her creamy white face, ease the hurt from her beautiful violet-gray eyes, tangle his fingers in her dark hair. She had a strength, a confidence about her that glued his heartbeat to his chest, made his breath tight, even without the help of his injury.

And she smelled like the faintest hint of roses, not unlike her letters. He wanted to cry with the joy of seeing her.

What a wretched man he'd become.

"Violet, it's not— Alex isn't marrying anyone else."

She met his eyes. Took a breath. "Oh. You're saying he just didn't want me in his life. What, did he send you to do his dirty work?" She gave a huff of what sounded like disbelief. "He needn't have bothered."

Her tone scraped him raw and he wanted to blurt it out—
He's dead! Alex is dead!

Before the urge could spur the words out, Jake felt a hand on his shoulder, followed by the voice of Gordon Lindholm. "C'mon, son. We need to leave if we hope to get her home before this storm hits."

He wanted to round on this man, spurt out words he'd spent most of his life censoring in his head. No. He didn't want to leave her like this—

"It's getting worse out there—"

"Go without me!" Jake shook off his hand, and winced at his tone. The entire room went quiet. And now his chest tightened. He just had to calm down. Slow his breathing before his old wounds rose up to choke him.

"Sorry. That's not what I meant. I just want to make sure Violet is okay."

"Please, I don't want to know any more about Alex, or why he sent my letter back, thank you." She turned to Gordon. "You're right. We should get going if we're going to hike out to your farm and get back to town." She stood up and he saw her wince.

"You can't walk anywhere." Jake put his hand on her elbow, eased her back down to the seat.

He tried to remain gentle as he bent down, picked up her foot, and raised her pant leg to ease off her boot. She groaned and closed one eye, and he felt the wince like a fist in his chest.

See, he'd made everything worse. Her ankle had already begun to swell. "You should have told me you hurt your ankle. I would have put ice on this immediately." He almost sounded angry, and it was too late to school it.

"I'm sorry. I guess I didn't realize I needed to report my injuries to you."

He pursed his lips. But she'd been reporting her injuries to him for two years, without knowing it. He drew in a breath.

Her voice softened. "I didn't really notice until I stood on it. If you remember, you carried me in here."

He looked at her, reeling in his emotions. "Indeed. My fault, for sure. I was so focused on your knee and your forehead, it didn't occur to me to check if anything else was injured." He put her leg down, stood. "She needs snow on her ankle. Then, we'll leave." He stood up, rounded to face Gordon. "I'll be right back."

He needed a few moments outside, anyway, just to clear his head. He took one of Dottie's towels from the counter, stepped outside, filled it with snow. The bracing air swept the cotton, the panic from his brain.

The truth will set you free. The words thrummed in his head. Yes. If only he believed them.

He returned inside, snow in the well of the cloth, folded it, and knelt before Violet. Gordon stood by the window, arms folded, watching him like he might be Violet's father.

"Just hold still." Jake lifted her ankle, pressing his thumb along the swelling as he positioned the snow-packed towel against it. She winced.

"Sorry. But I don't think you're going anywhere."

His chest burned. The few minutes outside hadn't helped, either, the cold air constricting his lungs even more, drawing out the mucus, knotting his chest muscles. He fought to breathe as he stood—in through his nose, out through his mouth.

His body had always refused to play fair.

"Thank you, Jake," she said, leaning back, closing her eyes.

Oh, she was beautiful. More than he'd guessed from Alex's descriptions. Slim, but shapely enough in those brown pants and her dark green cardigan. He could imagine her in her WAAC uniform—no wonder Alex had chased her across Fort Meade. She had dark chocolate, slightly curly hair and violet-gray eyes that had the capacity to whisk his breath away, if it weren't already lost. And those lips—heart shaped, red, and so expressive, even now as she caught her lower lip between her teeth.

He wanted to run his thumb along her lip—free it. "It'll stop hurting soon. Would you like me to bring you into the parlor, set you on the sofa?"

"No, I'm fine here. I should help Mrs. Morgan—"

"Dottie." The woman returned from her escape into the next room and now glared at Violet. "We're not at the library, Violet. Dottie will do." She glanced at Jake. "And for you too, young man."

"Jake Ramsey," he said in return. "I'm very sorry for the trouble—"

"Let's go." Gordon pushed up from the table.

Outside, the wind shook the house, and a shutter banged loose, slamming against the house.

Dottie made a noise of exasperation. "Wait, Gordon." She sighed and drew her cardigan around her. "This is a bad idea. You'll never make it across the slough in this storm. Why don't you…take my truck into town?"

Gordon looked at her, then Jake. He made a face. "Dottie, your driveway is covered by a tree."

Yes. The tree he downed. Nice, Jake.

The furnace kicked on again, the motor downstairs humming as the stoker came to life.

The shutter continued to bang against the house.

Dottie stared at Gordon, wearing an expression Jake couldn't decipher. She drew a breath, her lips puckering to a tight knot. Then, "I knew it. Just knew it."

"Knew what?" Gordon said.

The undercurrent of tone between these two told Jake more than he wanted to know. Hurt. Betrayal.

He didn't need his years of training to know that these two had once had something between them.

"I can make it back to my house, Dottie," Gordon said, almost an anger in his tone.

Her eyes sparked, although her voice cut down to a razor-sharp whisper. "And if you don't? Who's going to go out and fetch you? Is that what you think I want? To have you tromp back to your house so you can perish in the snow? Do you think I want your death on my conscience?"

Jake froze. Gordon didn't answer. Not verbally. Just let a muscle pull in his jaw, drew in a breath.

She held up her hand. "It's done, Gordon. Now, we could use a fire in the hearth." She glanced at Jake, who wanted to take a diving leap for the door.

"I'll make another batch of soup," Dottie said and brushed past them.

Gordon glanced at Jake. Jake raised an eyebrow.

"Don't just stand there. Fetch some wood," Gordon said, and thundered out to the back room.

"Wait—" Violet said. She caught Jake's arm, her hand on his wool coat. "Just tell me, is he okay?"

He. Alex. He could hear the lie, roaring to life, prowling in the back of his throat.

Jake cast a look toward the door. "I should help build the fire." His voice still sounded tight and he turned away from her, following Gordon to the back room. What if he left—right now? Just walked away from the rest of the story. Hadn't he done enough damage? His appearance had wrecked her car, banged up her face, crushed her knee, twisted her ankle, and now stranded her in the home of a woman who appeared like she might, any minute, throw them all out.

Gordon pushed past Jake as he walked into the kitchen with an armful of wood. He'd slipped off his boots, his jacket. "You're getting low out there, Dottie. Sorry."

Sorry?

Dottie didn't look at him as she rummaged around in her pantry.

They acted like an old married couple—estranged, perhaps—but with a rhythm about their relationship that suggested ancient familiarities.

Someday, he'd like to know someone so well he knew what they were thinking. And vice versa. To have someone see inside his heart, realize that he wasn't the man on the inside that he was forced to live on the outside.

You meant more than you know.

He hadn't lied, not really. Alex had filled every one of his last few letters with details about Violet—her life, her dreams. The hope he had for someday. But then again, Alex fell in love every other day, with any dame that smiled his direction. Who knew but he had a gal at Fort Benning and then again one in the hospital in Paris?

Alex had cared for her, of that Jake felt certain. But Jake no longer felt the pinch of guilt when he stamped a postcard, slipped it into the mail.

The truth was, Alex had stopped writing to her the day he'd died in the battle for Berlin, nearly a year after the D-Day invasion.

Jake had filled in after that. Mostly postcards, yes, but a few letters that might bolster her spirits, help her believe that her country cared about her service.

Did Dottie know that right in her kitchen sat a woman who could rebuild a model MB "Go Devil" military jeep engine, from flash pan to carburetor? Did she know that she had volunteered for overseas assignment, serving at S.H.A.E.F, the Supreme Headquarters, Allied Expeditionary Force first in Bushey Park, London, then followed the wave of soldiers into Normandy? That she'd probably helped repair the staff cars of General Eisenhower and seen the same war, lived through the same dangers as the infantry? Did Dottie—or Gordon, for that matter—know that she'd earned a meritorious service medal?

He did.

He also knew about her four brothers, where they'd served, and breathed with relief when they arrived home. He knew about her father's death, and her grief at hearing about it while in Berlin.

He knew that when she arrived home, she'd carried with her dreams of homecoming, hopes for a family.

And that's when he realized, fully, what he'd done.

You meant more to him than you know.

"Keep your ankle elevated or the swelling will get worse."

* * * * *

Do you think I want your death on my conscience?

Dottie's own words ran in her mind as she catalogued the supplies in her pantry. A can of tomatoes, a jar of pickles, a couple tins of processed canned ham, a container of barley. She pulled out the barley and tomatoes.

The look on Gordon's face then, a flicker of emotion, as if she'd slapped him. She drew in a quick, shaky breath.

She knew that expression too well. It could still haunt her, even twenty-six years later.

Gordy had hiked over to her house in the storm because he heard a gunshot? She didn't believe him for a second.

No, he'd been worried about her—and she wasn't so frigid inside that the truth of it didn't find her belly, warm it.

She set the ingredients on the counter then went to the back room to retrieve potatoes and onions from the bin. The chilly air tickled up her arms, down her blouse. She still wore her work attire—a skirt, long cardigan. She had a mind to go stand over the giant heating grate in the hallway, let the warm air billow her skirt up, like it had when she was a child.

Returning to the kitchen, she dumped a handful of vegetables into the sink then rooted around in her drawer for a knife. Violet sat at the table, her leg up, looking stripped.

Jake Ramsey had delivered news that turned the poor girl into a silent wreck. Dottie almost felt sorry for her.

She picked up an onion, sliced off the tail, then began to peel it, glancing up now and again at the storm billowing outside the window. In the next room, she could hear Gordon and Jake crumple paper, load in wood to the fire. Gordy, here, in her home.

How many times had she let her mind trail down dark, forbidden corridors, wondering what that might feel like? To have him in her life, instead of outside in the yard.

She would stand in her darkened bedroom, arms folded across her stomach, watching his porch light. His house sat cattycorner to hers, so that from her kitchen, her parlor, even her upstairs bedroom she could make out the glow from his yard. Sometimes, on a clear night, she even traced his dark outline as he wandered back from the barn or threw sticks to his old dog. Nelson had loved the thing—probably what made him long for his own dog.

Nelson's cranky beagle had passed away the year he'd left. Sometimes she could still see the dog, curled up in a nest in the middle of his quilt.

Sometimes she curled up with him.

A crackle came from the hearth in the parlor, the fire sparking to life. She turned back to the potatoes, her throat filling. Oh, she simply couldn't have houseguests. Couldn't let the house ring with voices again. It might stir up the dust of old, happy memories.

And then, she'd choke on them.

She picked up a rag, wiped her hands, then pressed the rag to her burning eyes.

"Mrs. Morgan? I just wanted to say I'm sorry, again, for destroying your fir tree." Violet's voice emerged soft, with a hint of fear. "I—I'll find you a new one and plant it in the spring."

Dottie steeled herself, found her librarian voice. "No, that's okay. It was dying anyway."

She'd always feared really saying that out loud. It felt easier, in a way, to stand at the cold window, staring out into the blackness, and admit it now. "It was an old tree."

"How old?"

She drew in a breath, scooping the chopped onion into a pot. "I planted it about a year after Nelson was born. So…I guess it's about—"

"Twenty-five years old. I can do the math. And that's not very old for a tree."

"No, I suppose it isn't."

She heard Violet draw in her breath, as if measuring her words.

"I remember when Nelson used to invite his football pals out here to study. My brother Johnny always came out, told us about how you'd make Snickerdoodles for them."

Dottie picked up a potato, began to curl the skin off, her movements too choppy for the long elegant curls Nelson used to steal. "How is Johnny?"

"Good. He and Hattie are expecting."

Over the past five years, Dottie had become better, more adapt at steeling herself against happy news. "That's wonderful."

"Mmm-hmm."

Out of the corner of her eye, Dottie saw Violet glance into the parlor. She wore a look of almost panic, as if the last thing she wanted was for Jake to return to the kitchen.

Dottie knew all about that. She would never look at Gordy again if she could manage it. Never have to face conversation.

They'd go to their graves separated by the marsh and the specter of the past between them.

It was just her terrible fortune that Gordy never married. Dottie might feel less guilty, less ashamed if he had.

Dottie washed the potato then cut it into bite-size cubes. "Who is Alex?" she asked, pity more than curiosity leading the impulse. She'd spent years trying to divert her attention from Gordon Lindholm.

Violet adjusted the ice on her ankle. She probably needed snow on her knee also—it looked roughly the size of a muskmelon under those trousers. "He was a solider I met at Fort Meade. We've been corresponding for years. Especially during the war. We exchanged greeting cards the last couple years. I—I made the mistake of inviting him to Frost for the holidays."

"And this Jake fella?"

"I—I don't know. A friend of Alex's, I guess. I'm not sure why Alex sent him here—especially since he already sent back my last letter."

Dottie wanted to groan, but she held it in, watching her breath disintegrate on the cold window. "I'm sorry, Violet."

"I was fooling myself…. I told myself that he was just healing from the war—I knew lots of GIs who had battle fatigue. I thought maybe if I gave him enough time, if I kept writing to him, someday he'd show up here. He stopped sending me letters after the war—mostly sent postcards. But they came almost every month, with messages like…he was thinking about me." She pressed a hand to her mouth. "I'm such a fool."

Oh, Violet. Dottie wanted to tell her that believing a man's words had been her first mistake too, but perhaps that would be too cruel. She dumped the potatoes into the pot then dried her hands. She wanted to go to her, perhaps take her hand, but for now all she could do was meet her eyes. "It sounded like he truly cared for you, from what his friend said."

"I don't know. Maybe I've been lying to myself for years. The truth is, he didn't want me—if he had, he would have hopped on a train."

"It doesn't mean he didn't care for you. Maybe he couldn't come. Maybe he was injured, or…" Or, in prison.

The word darted into her brain, and back out. Prison.

Dottie shook the thought away again.

"There is someone out there for you, Violet." The words didn't come from inside, but rather were plucked from one of Dottie's storybooks. Still, they sounded right in the moment, and as if her heart wanted to believe it, inside her pulsed the strange urge to hold Violet's hand, to clasp it between hers.

Instead, she folded her arms across her chest.

Violet shook her head. "I don't think there is anyone out there for me, Mrs. Morgan. See…I'm turning thirty in a couple of weeks."

Thirty. At thirty Dottie had already become a widow. Not that she'd told anyone about the death notice from the prison. But, by thirty, she'd stopped believing in happy endings too.

Still, Violet didn't carry the mantle of shame that hovered over Dottie. "There are plenty of good men out there."

"No," Violet said softly. "No one like Alex. He—he seemed to understand me. Or, I thought he did."

And that was the charade that wheedled a man into a girl's heart, wasn't it?

"How's your leg, Violet?" Jake stood at the door and for the first time, Dottie saw him the way Violet might—tall, broad shoulders, dark hair, eyes that held concern.

She knew a man like that once.

Gordy stepped up behind him, his mouth a tight line. "We got the fire going, but I took a gander outside, Dottie. I really think I can make it back to the farm."

Oh, how had it come to this? Her begging him to stay?

Shoot.

"No, Gordon." She sighed and stood up, drawing her cardigan around her. "It's a bad idea. You'll never make it across the slough in this storm."

The furnace kicked on again, the motor downstairs humming as the stoker came to life.

"Dottie, listen. I can make it home—"

She rounded on him. "Of course you can, Gordon. Why listen to me? I'm just a tired old woman, working my jaws to keep myself company. What do I know about storms? Please, trot out into the snow so we can stand by the window all night and worry ourselves to death. Heaven forbid you actually care what I think."

He didn't answer. Not verbally. Just stared at her, with those hazel-green eyes she could never forget.

Never really wanted to, if she were honest.

"I care about you, Dottie." He said it so quietly, with so much confidence, just like that day in the barn when the sun bled out along the prairie behind him.

She turned away. See, just an hour with this man and her past rose to strangle her. Having him all night in her home would certainly open all the old wounds.

But the thought of him perishing in the snow just might destroy her.

She looked away from him, retreating to her sink. "The storm will let up by morning. I have plenty of room here."

He caught her arm. "Would it be better if I slept in the barn?"

The barn. He would say that. And then, just like that, she saw him, peeking out from behind a hay bale, scaring her.

Gordy Lindholm, you stay away from me!

But they'd played tag, right there in the shadows of the barn until he pinned her, one hand on either side of her shoulders, against the corral. Sometimes she could still see his smile, the heat in his youthful hazel-green eyes as he lowered his lips, brushed them to hers, quick, dangerous, tasting of fresh apples and the sweat of a summer afternoon.

Twelve, she guessed, she might have been the first time he kissed her.

"No, I don't want you to sleep in the barn," she said quietly, casting a look at the two young people who clearly couldn't unravel their nonrelationship. Good. She had her own problems understanding it, and she'd been in the middle of it for nearly twenty-five years.

"Just get me two more potatoes from the bin and take off those boots. They're turning my kitchen floor into a pond."

* * * * *

Violet wanted to crawl under Dottie's floorboards and hide. So much for bringing back the star—if Violet could just make it back to town tonight, she'd never bother Mrs. Morgan again.

She could hear Gordon in the back room, rifling through the potato bin. Dottie stood at the stove, opening her canned tomatoes.

Jake had taken the cloth from her ankle and exited to retrieve more snow.

What a fool she'd been to harbor those fairy-tale fantasies that had landed her here, in this cold, ornate castle, her ankle on fire, her head burning, with Alex's messenger hovering over pitiful, rejected her as if she might crumble.

She was a soldier, after all. Okay, not a soldier, but she'd spent the night in worse situations—like that night in Berlin, when the wind dipped down to fourteen below zero, tunneling through her barracks and hollowing her out with the moan of it.

Of course, that night, she'd received the cable from home about Father's passing.

I thought maybe if I gave him enough time, if I kept writing to him, someday he'd show up here. Her own words made her cringe and turn away as Jake re-entered the room, his cheeks flush with cold. Oh, he was a handsome man, she noticed that now too. Dark brown hair, impossibly blue eyes—the kind of blue that could stop her on the sidewalk, and they bore an emotion she couldn't place as he came toward her. Pain? Regret?

On the stove, the teapot whistled to life. The kitchen dwarfed Violet's back home, twice the size, with cheerful yellow paint, light blue cupboards, and wallpaper covered in daisies and cornflowers.

Dottie had a four-burner gas stove, with an oven and two warmer slots, and a tall, two-door Kelvinator icebox. In the corner sat a round Maytag gas-powered wringer washing machine on rollers. Her large porcelain sink overlooked a window and beyond that, the snowy night.

The large oak hutch, filled with a collection of milk glass and other china, appeared built into the wall and matched the oval oak table, with the large center-scrolled legs, the eight matching chairs.

This kitchen was made to serve a family larger than Dottie's, for sure, and the feeling extended to the parlor—Violet's gaze had followed Jake's exit—a room papered in rich, velvety red, with an upright piano, a tall fieldstone fireplace, an oversized sculpted-velvet green sofa, a couple of red satin art-deco chairs, and blond waterfall side tables. A picture of Nelson's grandfather hung over the mantel, and against the wall, a glass bookshelf evidenced Dottie's career—volumes of worn books that begged long hours before the fire, the dark green afghan hanging on the quilt stand spread over her knees.

Perhaps Dottie wasn't as lonely for company as Violet guessed. Oh, why had she decided to save Dottie—and her star—from a life that seemed suddenly richer than her own?

Violet sank her head into her hands, not sure what to despair over first. Her father's destroyed car, the fact that she'd somehow become stranded here for the night, or—or the fact that, when Jake carried her into the house, for a moment, she'd very much enjoyed being in his arms.

Which made her even more pitiful.

She'd spent four years fighting off men in the US Army. And

suddenly she swooned when a handsome man showed up between her headlights?

Maybe she'd been hit harder in the head than she thought.

Especially since Jake's words continued to reverberate in her head. *You meant more to him than you know.*

It took her a second, but the verb tense finally hit her. *Meant. Past tense.* She looked at Jake, who had knelt before her, readjusting her snow packet. "I think the swelling has reduced," he said almost to himself.

"Jake...you said that I *meant* more to him than I know. Is Alex...dead?" She lowered her voice on the last word, more for Dottie than herself, but yes, for her too. She hadn't even considered it—Alex had lived through the war, after all. A man doesn't survive the battlefields of Europe only to be run down on the street by a trolley car or succumb to an outbreak of influenza.

The emotion on Jake's face definitely turned toward pity, and what looked like a light sweat dotted his brow, as if it wounded him to speak of it. He leaned back, his hands on his knees. "I didn't want to tell you this way. But, yes. I'm so sorry."

Yes. She stared at him, not able to pinpoint the strange release inside her, as if a fist had let go. A darkness careened through her, filling her empty spaces. "I can't believe it. During the war, deep inside, I feared it, of course. Even braced myself for it—but..." She shook her head.

"You were everything to him, and I needed to tell you that, in person."

She met Jake's eyes and the sadness, even compassion in them seemed to reach out, to permeate the wave of shadow inside.

"We only knew each other through correspondence, really. But…he was everything to me too."

Jake looked away, as if embarrassed by her words. Or, perhaps, hurt.

"Did you know him well?"

He made a face, one she couldn't read, and his voice emerged tight, constricted again, like it hurt. "All his life."

A friend. One who cared enough to trek across Minnesota in a blizzard to tell her the terrible news.

Alex. She looked outside, at the storm buffeting the window. She could still remember him—mostly. Curly brown hair, hazel eyes, a smile that lit up as he leaned over her changing a tire, retiming an engine. Once, he'd wiped grease off her face with his thumb, told her she looked pretty in oil.

The compliment had clung to her bones, seeded too many fantasies late at night as she lay on her bunk at Fort Meade.

He'd written her nearly every week for a year after he shipped out—he'd only been at Fort Meade for a few days, really, en route to Normandy. He told her of the cities he visited—London, Paris. She'd hoped that they might cross paths over in Europe, but he'd been shipped home long before her.

She lowered the cloth from her head. Her forehead ached. Pulsed, really, like her heartbeat, a fist pounding on the inside of her head. But the bleeding had stopped. Oh, her mother would be thrilled with her appearance tonight for the—

"The dance."

"I think we're long past the dance," Mr. Lindholm said. "Dottie was right. There's no getting the truck out in this wind." He was looking past her, however, his gaze on Dottie. She'd been rather rough on Mr. Lindholm, and the look he settled on her hinted at pain.

I care about you, Dottie.

Those words had touched Violet, so softly spoken from this grizzled farmer that they wheedled under her skin. But as far as she knew, Dottie had been single since...well, yes, apparently she'd married, but under every polite conversation about Dottie Morgan ran the undercurrent that no, she'd run off to marry some handsome gangster, gotten herself pregnant, and skulked back to Frost in shame.

Maybe Frost had simply become a good place for the brokenhearted and lonely to hide.

Dottie.

Gordon Lindholm.

Violet.

She whisked her hand across her cheek. "I'm sorry...I just need to know." Her voice fell. "How did Alex die?"

Jake didn't look up at her, his breath coming slow and long, almost as if he forced it through a web of pain, and she hated, suddenly, that she'd asked. "It was awhile ago. I—I should have come sooner."

"It was kind of you to come at all. I received a Return to Sender from his address today—I appreciate knowing that he didn't just reject my mail."

"Oh, no, Violet. He would have never done that. He lived for your letters."

That seemed a little over-the-top, but Jake betrayed not a hint of sarcasm.

"He hasn't written to me but a greeting card and postcards in the past four years. Nothing of emotion or dreams, like his letters during the war."

"Perhaps…he felt like he might be leading you on."

She looked back at him, frowned. "I thought you said I was everything to him."

"You are—were." He flushed, set her foot down. Looked away from her. "I'm sorry, Violet. Alex did care for you." He rose but still didn't meet her eyes. "I'm going to see if I can get my suitcase out of the snow before it's completely buried out there."

She drew in a breath as she watched Jake leave, the opening of the door allowing a draft into the warm room.

If Alex had cared so much for her, why had he never hopped a train from Minneapolis, taken the half-day journey west to Frost? Why had his letters dwindled to postcards after he'd shipped home? Why had he stopped writing about his life, his fears and hopes?

Maybe because he'd never seen her as more than a friend. More than the woman who wore grease on her face, knew how to turn a wrench.

She tightened her jaw against the pulsing pain in her head, her ankle. She just wanted to get home, climb into bed and, at least until the throbbing stopped, forget that she'd ever believed in a happy ending for a girl like her.

Dottie came around the counter, wiping her hands. "Let's get you bandaged up, shall we?"

CHAPTER FOUR

Gordy could make it home, he knew it. He had calculated the trail home the entire time he'd crafted her fire. He'd even stood at the window after he got the fledgling blaze going, the darkness swelling the room, his eyes on the dimming glow of his porch. He could follow the stone fence to the marsh. From there he would follow his porch light to the yard. If he needed, he'd aim for the barn, then follow it around to the guide wire.

He'd made it home plenty of times during a whiteout. He'd even lived through the Armistice blizzard back in '40. It had caught him while out hunting, dressed for the remarkably warm weather in a lightweight wool jacket.

Then again, he'd had Nelson in tow, and the thought of the boy curled into a frozen ball in some field had fueled an inner fire that kept them both alive.

He would have died for Nelson. Sometimes, now, he wanted to die without him.

The fire had caught on the dry pine and birch logs, crackling, curling up the bark as it bit into the wood.

If only he'd stocked her porch with firewood before today. He knew Dottie's supply had dwindled—he'd simply been negligent. If he had stocked it, he'd be sitting at home, cozy, warm.

Alone.

And Dottie wouldn't be simmering in the next room.

Once they survived the storm, he'd restock her firewood for the bitter January winds. But tonight they needed to keep the fire lit to ensure the blizzard winds wouldn't blow down the flue, into the house. He tromped through the kitchen for one more load of wood then returned to the parlor and fed the blaze. They'd need it hot to propel the smoke up the chimney instead of into the house.

Would it be better if I slept in the barn?

He heard his words as he returned to the kitchen, watching Dottie stir the soup. She had a meager supply of potatoes—he'd found four still-firm spuds for her to add to the remnants of her soup. He'd be surprised if the contents filled each bowl to half. She didn't look at him as she worked, her back stiff to him.

I care about you, Dottie.

For a second in her eyes he thought he saw something break inside, a fissure of the wall between them, memory flashing through. Maybe a glimpse of the time he'd driven her home in his father's Chevy then parked just inside the barn, where they could lie on the bed and count the stars.

Do you ever wonder what the stars might look like in Africa? Or China? She asked it while chewing on a piece of hay, the starlight in her eyes. Those beautiful eyes could stop his breath in his chest when they caught his. That and her straw-blond hair, the way it fell over her shoulders. Sometimes, in school, he sat behind her and just imagined running it like water between his fingers.

"No. Never. Not once." He'd rolled over, propped his head on his arm. "I'm happy here."

"In Frost?" She looked at him, and for a moment, indeed, he lost himself.

"No," he finally whispered. "Right here, with you."

She giggled, but not a hint of humor embedded his tone. Funny, she never believed him. Not then, not later.

Not even now.

With everything inside him, he wanted to stay. Wanted to be in her world, just for a night, even if he had to share it with Violet Hart and this stranger, Jake Ramsey.

Truth be told, Jake's presence was the only thing keeping Gordon from walking out the door.

But he wanted to stay with her blessing. Not... *Please, trot out into the snow so we can stand by the window all night and worry ourselves to death.*

This could be a very long night.

"Take your jacket off and sit down, Gordy," Dottie said, not looking at him.

He glanced at Violet. Someone—probably Dottie—had bandaged her head.

"I think I'll just check on those shutters," he said, glancing at Violet. And where, exactly, did her friend run off to? The man smelled highfalutin, as if he'd never done a proper day's work in his life. Something about him—his store-bought suit, those fancy shoes. His expensive coat...

Jake dredged up memories of TJ.

Another good reason for him to stay and keep watch.

Gordy buttoned up before stepping outside. The snow pelted his face, the wind biting his ears. In the last hour since he'd trekked over, probably five inches had accumulated. Lighter, fluffier snow than what fell before, and he sifted right through it to the crusty foundation below. The light glowed from the house, barely pushing back the night, but he saw movement, down by the tree.

What was that kid doing? He was on his hands and knees, under the tree, rooting for something.

Gordy tucked his head, hunching his shoulders against the wind, and slogged through the snow down to him. He braced his hand on a branch as he started to slip.

Jake sat up, caught his hand.

He hadn't needed help. "What are you doing?" He had to shout above the wind.

"I lost my suitcase!" Snow frosted Jake's dark hair, his upturned collar. "I need it!"

Gordy grabbed him by the collar. "What's so important you have to find it tonight?"

"It has letters in it. From Alex to Violet. I want to give them to her."

He just didn't get this kid. First, he'd traveled all the way from Minneapolis to Frost, just to tell her that some pen pal had died, and now he dug around under a tree to deliver the man's letters? Talk about pitiful. At least Gordy had known when he couldn't get the girl, when to walk away. This chump had all the makings of lovesick fool written on his reddened face. And, he didn't handle weather well, the way he doubled over, started to cough.

"C'mon—we'll find it in the morning!"

"But it's important!"

"So's not freezing to death."

He wrangled the man to his feet, catching him as he doubled over again. They struggled back up to the house, but before Gordy could deliver him inside, Jake slammed his hand against the door-jamb. "Just...a second."

He seemed to be wheezing, his face whitened.

"Are you okay?"

He shook his head.

Gordy reached for the door handle.

"Not...yet." Then, as Gordy watched, he pulled out a pack of cigarettes.

"Are you serious?"

Gordy had never been a serious smoker—just when he wanted to relax—but he knew those who had to have a pack a day. With that cough, this kid might want to slow down.

Jake pulled out a cigarette, dropped the pack in his pocket, then tried to light the smoke. The match flickered out. Another.

"You'll never get that lit in this wind. You don't need it!"

But Jake shook his head, tried again.

Gordy grabbed him by the shoulder then turned around and dragged him in the direction of the barn. Twelve steps—he knew the count exactly to the corner—then dragged his hand to the door, found the handle, and flung it open.

He pushed Jake inside, followed him in, and shut the door behind him.

Jake stood in the darkness, coughing, his breath wheezing between bouts.

Maybe he had some sort of disease. A match struck, then

Jake's face glowed as he managed to light his smoke. He inhaled deeply. Held the smoke in his lungs.

Gordy watched him all the way to the exhale before he shook his head and walked over to the electric light, flicking it on.

Jake stood, his eyes closed, breathing in through his nose, out through his mouth, slowly, deliberately. He'd take a drag on his cigarette and do it again.

"What's wrong with you?"

Jake glanced at him. "I'll be fine in a moment here. It was the cold. And the wind."

Gordy frowned.

Jake took another pull on his cigarette. Breathed that funny way again. Finally, "I have asthma. I'm smoking for medicinal purposes."

"If that's what you want to call it." Gordy stuck his hands in his pockets, his gaze roaming past Dottie's father's International Harvester truck to the stall where they'd—

"It's true. It's almost entirely comprised of stramonium. There's very little tobacco. It calms my lungs, helps slow my breathing. I've got a tin of Elliot's Asthma Powder in my suitcase if it gets worse."

Jake sounded like he spoke the truth.

"Huh," Gordy said. "Never heard of it."

"Asthma? It's a disease of the lungs. I had it as a child, after a bout of influenza, but I grew out of it. I even made it through the army's medical inspection. Didn't give me a problem until I picked up pneumonia while over in Belgium. Now, when I exercise or get a cold or even get overly excited, anytime I breathe hard, really, my lung starts to swell. It produces mucus, which makes it difficult to breathe."

"Then what are you doing out in the cold, if it's so bad for you?"

Jake leaned against the truck, pinching the cigarette between his fingers and taking another drag. He looked at Gordy. "Trying to figure out a way to get Violet to forgive me."

Gordy raised an eyebrow.

"It's a long shot, really. But...I did this stupid thing."

Gordy liked hearing that—confession—out of Fancy-Pants's mouth. Gordy folded his arms over his chest.

"My...friend Alex was writing to Violet during the war. But he was killed in action, and they sent all her letters to me, as his beneficiary." He looked away, lifted a shoulder. "I read them. And I liked her."

His words made a fist form in Gordy's gut. "And the stupid thing was...?"

"I wrote to her, pretending to be Alex. Or, a version of Alex that resembled me."

Gordy shook his head. "And I thought I was in trouble."

Jake didn't look at him.

"I got home from—from visiting a friend just this morning. My mother informed me that Violet's letter had arrived, and that, since it was addressed to Alex, she returned it to sender."

"So you naturally hopped on a train to intercept it."

"I wanted to tell her the truth, face to face."

Gordy raised an eyebrow. "That's a dandy pickle there, son."

Jake winced. Gordy almost felt sorry for him. He wanted to say something profound, even encouraging, but his own mistakes rose up to silence him.

Jake had his gaze on him when Gordy looked up. "What?"

"Why do you look at Dottie like that?"

"Like what?" He reached over to turn off the light, but Jake stopped him. Gordy glared at him.

Jake smiled. "What trouble are *you* in?"

Gordy considered him. Now he wanted a smoke too. Could even feel his lungs tightening, a little.

"I taught her son how to shoot. She blames me for making him want to go to war."

"Every boy wants to go to war," Jake said quietly.

"No, every boy wants to be a hero. And Nelson was. He became a sharp-shooter for his unit. Even earned a bronze star before he died. They awarded it to Dottie posthumously."

"I'm so sorry for your loss."

He'd never had anyone say that to him before. Sorry. For Nelson's death. Like he had lost someone. His throat burned as he drew in a breath. "He was a good boy."

"Why didn't his father teach him to shoot?"

Gordy shook his head. "His father was a no-account Dapper Dan who swept through town and took Dottie with him. He never returned for either of them after she came home."

He tried to deliver those words without judgment, but by Jake's raised eyebrow, he failed. Gordy lifted a shoulder. "I asked her to marry me first."

Jake stared at him, too much pity in his face for Gordy to bear.

Gordy shoved his hands into his pockets. "She refused to talk to me after she came home. Too ashamed, I s'pose."

"Did you try to court her?"

Gordy frowned at him. "Of course not. She made her choice. I asked once. I wasn't going to ask again."

Jake seemed to be breathing better now. "I'm not real swell with women, Gordon, but I think if you love someone, you don't give up."

"That why you were digging around for your suitcase, those letters from your buddy?"

Jake lifted a shoulder. "Could be."

Gordy recognized his type, all right. He'd looked at him in the mirror for the last twenty-six years. Hopeful. Foolish.

Brokenhearted.

"Listen, Dottie's entire life was her son. When he died, so did she. All Dottie wants is her son back. I can't give her that. Which means, she'll never forgive me. So you can put aside your love talk. Me and Dottie—we're never coming in from this cold."

Gordy reached up again and flicked off the light, grabbed Jake by the collar, and stepped out of the barn. "Stay close!" he yelled as they headed back out into the storm. "You get lost, and no one will find you until spring!"

As he trudged toward the house, he noticed that he could no longer see his porch light glowing through the storm.

* * * * *

If only Dottie had given Violet that confounded star, she wouldn't be serving up four bowls of watery tomato beef soup and hoping the biscuits would puff up enough to suggest a hearty portion.

Why didn't she pick up the Cornish hens? Or even finish her marketing?

Because who knew she'd have houseguests? Not even the girl scouts had knocked on her door for over five years.

Tomorrow. They'd all leave tomorrow and she'd trudge back out into the snow and pick up what the market had on sale. Game hens or not, it didn't matter. She could open a can of processed ham for Christmas for all the celebration she had in her.

Dottie opened the cupboard in search of more bowls. She'd only used the one—washing it over and over again for the past five years. Pulling down her pottery, she hiked back to the sink to wash the dust off before ladling in the soup.

"I'll set the table," Violet said, rising from her chair.

"Stay put," Dottie barked. If the girl injured herself more, she just might camp out here through the weekend. Although, she had to admit, the girl seemed fairly stoic with the news of Alex's death.

Dottie had seen the way she looked at the newcomer, Jake. Recognized the second glance, the spark of interest.

Perhaps she hadn't really loved Alex. Or perhaps she'd been in love with the attention of a handsome man.

Dottie knew that confusion well.

She carried the bowls to the table then went in search of silverware, cloth napkins.

"Johnny always said your kitchen smelled like fresh-baked bread. I agree."

Johnny had an overactive imagination. "Doesn't your mother bake bread?"

"Of course. But more often we buy it now. She has no time for domestics, what with all her volunteer duties. And, with Father gone, it's just her and me." Violet reached down, picked the towel off her ankle. Tried to move it in a circle. It elicited a wince.

"Put the towel back on."

"It's dripping onto the floor."

"It'll clean. When did your father pass?" Funny, she should know that, but Dottie hadn't exactly been abreast of Frost news. She simply couldn't bear to read the paper, with the updates of the war, and since then, the boys returning home. She pulled out a stepstool, reached the soup tureen from the top of the china hutch.

"He had a heart attack in 1946. I was still overseas." Violet readjusted her towel. "I never made it home for the funeral."

"I'm so sorry." Dottie grabbed a hot pad then poured the soup from the pot into the tureen. "Where were you stationed?"

She expected something like South Dakota or Iowa—she'd heard of the military sending women to training camps in Aberdeen or Des Moines. For a split second, right after Nelson signed up, Dottie had nearly followed him into battle. The WAAC enlistment allowed for women up to age fifty, and the vision of staying behind while her son galloped off to war nearly strangled her. Perhaps, also, she could attribute it just as much to the stirring of an old reckless impulse, the kind that caused her to jump aboard TJ's roadster, tuck herself into his arms, ready to see the world.

Dottie glanced at Violet. She hadn't tried to know her over the past year since the city hired her to assist Dottie in the library. The woman—nearly thirty, which qualified her as more than a reckless young girl—had an energy about her that could infect Dottie, if she let it. Dottie recognized the energy, however, and retired to her office—running down errant subscribers, ordering new stock, filing court records—and allowed Violet to take over the promotion of new circulation. Since Violet's arrival, the children's reading nook hosted fresh new books and a steady stream of youngsters who longed to hear a story. No wonder Violet had suggested the revival of the Christmas reading.

In fact, Violet should do it. The last thing the children of Frost needed was a Christmas story told by a woman who didn't even believe in Christmas—or rather, the magic, the grace, the healing of it—anymore.

Indeed, she should have passed on that star to Violet. She'd never light it again anyway.

"I started in Des Moines then went to Fort Meade, in Maryland."

See, just like Dottie, Violet had returned home, her dreams of seeing the world shattered—

"Then I volunteered for duty at SHEAF, and I went to London. We were there for the retaliation of D-Day, when the Germans bombed Bushey Park. After that, they sent me to La Havre, France, and I finally ended up in Berlin. I was discharged in 1947."

"You came home after your brothers?"

"We were busy processing the soldiers headed stateside. And taking care of the POWs, helping the military keep order. It was a mess over there, and we just couldn't leave."

Which meant she'd missed the parades, the celebrations. The appreciation. Perhaps, really, there hadn't been any for her. Dottie remembered the gossip—how Frances Hart had forbade her from going, how her daughter most certainly did not have "the questionable morals of the ladies of the WAACs," and that she would not be going to "keep up the morale of the soldiers."

Worse, a few blamed Violet for sending their boys to war by moving them from secure stateside jobs to combat.

If Nelson hadn't been proficient with a rifle, if he hadn't earned his excellent marksmanship medal, been tagged as a sniper during basic training, Dottie might have accused Violet of the same.

Not a fair—or accurate—indictment, to be sure. But accusations rarely were.

Dottie pulled out the biscuits. They'd puffed up with the addition of extra baking powder. She dumped them into a basket and added them to the table.

If only she had milk. But no, she hadn't stopped by the creamery either. They'd manage with tea.

She found a jar of leaves, added a spoonful to the teapot to steep.

In the mudroom, Dottie heard the stomping of the returning men and steeled herself against Gordy's entrance.

He had divested himself of his jacket, his coveralls, his boots, even his hat when he entered. She hadn't seen him close-up, without his outer clothes, for years. Now, he wore a pair of wool pants and a blue-checkered flannel shirt, rolling the arms up to his elbows as he wandered in. He still had those wide farm-worked shoulders, the sinewy forearms, those strong milking hands. His age showed only in his dark brown hair—whitened around the edges and needing a cut, although it lay tousled by the stocking cap—and his white-flaked golden-brown goatee that accentuated his strong jaw.

He might still be the most handsome man in Frost, should a woman be assessing. But a woman of her years was long past noticing.

"Smells good in here," he said. He glanced at her with those hazel eyes that could take her apart, second by second if they lingered. Her mouth dried and she looked away from him before they could scour up more of the past, or worse, send a dormant flicker of heat through her and really do damage

"Stop trying to flatter me and sit down."

He rolled his eyes and pulled out a chair at the table.

Jake, too, had divested himself of his wool coat, his soggy shoes, and entered in his stocking feet. He wore a white cotton dress shirt with a thin tie, a pair of black dress pants, and, like Gordy, he'd rolled up the cuffs of his shirt. If she were younger, she'd label him handsome, with his dark hair cut army-butch short on the sides, the shank of hair that fell over his eyes, the rough edge of dark whiskers upon his chin, those blue eyes that moved to Violet as if caught in a magnetic pull.

Jake drew in a breath, and Violet looked up at him.

Oh yes, Violet couldn't figure out her allegiances—her poor Alex, cut down in his prime, or this young man, who wore his emotions on the outside of his body.

A woman would have to be blind not to see the man was sweet on her.

Jake pulled out the chair opposite Gordy and sat down. "I'm ravenous."

A smile that started deep inside Dottie came out in a smirk. He sounded just like…

See, this was why she shouldn't have houseguests. She picked up the teapot, filled the cups. "I don't have any milk."

"I'm not surprised," Gordy said, then looked up, eyes wide, as if he hadn't quite meant to say that.

She glowered at him. He raised one of his eyebrows, clearly not sorry.

"I'll get to the creamery tomorrow, thank you very much."

"If it abates. A man can barely see his hand in front of his face out there."

She looked at Gordy, a sort of horror whisking through her. "It most certainly will abate, Mr. Lindholm."

He tightened his jaw.

It *had* to abate. They'd starve, at the least, and who knew what manner of emotional destruction might be wrought. She and Gordy could barely speak to one another, the specter of Nelson hanging between them, and Violet and Jake just might combust, both of them harboring their own unspoken longings.

Yes, they all needed to flee as soon as the storm abated.

Dottie sat, picked up her napkin, set it in her lap.

Her houseguests stared at her, as if waiting. Gordy, hair askew, looking tired, if not crabby. Violet, glancing at Jake out of the corner of her eye. Jake, his head down, peeking at Violet with those terrible blue eyes.

The fire in the next room crackled, the smell of the soup— beef, onions, tomatoes—lifted into the air. Outside, the blizzard howled, shaking the house, and for a second, a whisper of warmth threaded through her.

Foreign. With a hint of ache.

"Perhaps we should say grace," Violet suggested.

Grace. Of course. Dottie nodded, folding her hands.

Violet reached out as if to take Gordy's hand, but he didn't notice.

Jake had already folded his hands, although Dottie saw him hesitate, as if he might have reached out, taken Violet's offering.

Too quickly, Violet pulled her hands back, clasped them.

Dottie bowed her head. A prayer. She knew many, but the words stuck in her throat, inaccessible.

The owl clock on the wall ticked. Again. Her heartbeat swished in her ears. *Pray.*

Then, in the tick of silence, she heard a small voice in the back of her head, a memory, sweet and swelling through her. *Come Lord Jesus...* She repeated the words. "Come Lord Jesus...be our guest."

Gordy joined in, his voice strong. "And let these gifts—"

Violet added on her voice. "...to us be blessed."

"Amen," Jake said.

"Amen," Dottie echoed softly.

Outside, the wind gave a long, shrill moan.

★ ★ ★ ★ ★

If only Arnie's mother had allowed him to take his sled to school, he might have been able to use it to slide home, or maybe even hide under, and escape planet Mungo.

But she hadn't been in the mood to listen to his pleading this morning, that he'd need the sled for his interplanetary trip to outer space, to fight Ming the Merciless. And now, without it, Flash Gordon had crash landed, his ship buried under an avalanche. Thankfully, he had his ice suit and heat gun. He had to be on the lookout for snow dragons, perhaps kill an ice bear and use its carcass for warmth.

Anything to survive this storm and save his true love, Dale

Arden, who was held captive by Queen Fria in the ice kingdom of Frigia. He just had to make it to the castle, hide there, and gain his strength. There, he'd wait for Dr. Zarkov and Prince Ronal to join him so they could attack the ice brigade.

He refused to cry, it would only alert the winged serpents. They would swoop down, maybe even gouge out his eyes.

He tripped, fell into the icy drifts, and his schoolbooks scattered, out of his reach. Already, the darkness, the mourning wind, and the brutal snow had turned him near blind. He may have cried out when he fell, but the howl of the blizzard ate it.

He shook now, the feeling in his toes lost, his body nearly numb. He just had to make it to the castle. To Dr. Zarkov. He had a penetro raygun to unfreeze him.

Crawling now, he listened to other voices.

One hundred times, Arnie Shiller. "I will not daydream in class."

I will not daydream in class.

He could still hear the screech of the chalk on the board, the smell of the dust in his nose as he clapped out the erasers. By the time he finished, the rain, like the pecking of the Hawkmen at the window, had turned to the bullets of Ming the Merciless, piercing his invisible ice suit. He still had to stop by the creamery and fill the bottles, and with the rain pummeling his wool hat, turning his mittened hands soggy on the school steps, he had nearly run out of daylight.

He'd run inside, grabbed his coat and his stack of books, and left before Mrs. Olafson could order more disciplinary chores. Without a doubt, he'd have more lines to scribble tomorrow, or even after Christmas vacation.

The creamery had closed for the night, the window dark when he arrived. He pressed his nose against the glass in case Mr. Gunderson still worked the counter. The sleet only slithered under Arnie's collar.

He'd carried the bottles in their wire basket out of town, pressing through the storm, until a gust of harsh wind yanked them from his hand. He heard them shatter but didn't turn back.

Night unleashed then, poured down upon him in a torrent of icy powder. He balled one hand into a fist in his mitten, the other holding the strap of books.

His father would want him to make it home, to be the man of the house. Of course, he didn't actually remember his father speaking these words, but his mother said so, and he believed her. She needed him, Flash Gordon, to haul out the clinker so the coal stove wouldn't jam, and to secure the shutters against the storm.

She needed Arnie to return home because his father hadn't. He'd perished in the soil of Europe, fighting them Germans.

Sometimes Arnie heard his mother at night, sobbing.

In the morning, she'd smell of the whiskey she kept in the cupboard.

Arnie had passed the community center and the Catholic church, his eyes falling on the nativity scene, wrapped in plastic, yet still lit up. It beckoned for a moment, the manger appearing warm in the midst of the storm. But he pressed on, past the ball field and even over the bridge. He recognized the bridge because he heard the Frost River rushing under the hum of the storm, and he ran his mitten along the stone walls until he reached the end.

His storm house lay ahead, somewhere in the biting darkness.

They assigned every child in school who lived on the farms beyond Frost a "storm house," a shelter in case of blizzard.

Because his farm lay a mile out of town, on the Third Street extension, he'd drawn Mrs. Morgan's place. He'd walked by it a thousand times, every day to school and back. The big green house on the hill, with a tower for archers and a balcony where someone might leap to their death. Ogres and dragons guarded it, hiding Hansel and Gretel and the witch who waited to eat him.

Only the waist-high stone wall protected him from his fairy tale nightmares of Mrs. Morgan's Storm House.

He saw her sometimes, at the library. She had straw-dry, bristly hair, pulled back in a bun, and dark, almost stony eyes. She issued him his library card, handing it to him with scaly hands, her mouth a tight line of disapproval as he formed his name.

He'd walked—or even run—by it, yes, a thousand times, a prayer on his lips that he'd never have to run there for refuge.

But the cold pressed into his bones tonight, and his feet had become anvils.

If he kept going, perhaps Queen Fria might ski by, take him prisoner. How he'd relish banishment in the atom furnaces right now. He'd even work as a slave for food, although he'd stopped feeling the clench in his stomach long ago.

Dragging forward, he dreamed of the Hawkmen, shrieking from the sky, and the roar of Thun, Prince of the Lionmen, hunting for him, his ally in the storm.

He slammed into something, so hard he bit his tongue. He couldn't feel it anymore but tasted the blood. He reached out and pressed his icy mittens on the something, barely feeling the bumps.

Mrs. Morgan's stone wall.

Now, he just had to find the castle. But fatigue turned him inside out, and he wanted to rest, just a little. Just—

"Flash, don't give up!"

But the mountain stretches high to the clouds. I can't find the top.

He pulled himself over the stone wall, crumpled on the other side.

Flash fights his way over the wall of doom and into the icy fields of Frigia. He claws his way up the hill, as the winged serpent's hairy arms grab at him, douse him with the flash-freeze powder. He struggles through, hearing Dale call to him.

"Save me, Flash Gordon!"

Displaying super-strength, he breaks free and climbs toward the light.

His hand banged against something smooth, hard, and he ran his arm up, found a handle.

Not the castle, but safety, all the same. An ice cavern built in the hills around the castle. He opened the door, rolled inside. Found a spaceship inside. Not warm, but enough to keep him dry and out of the wind.

He climbed in and shut the door.

Safe from the icy breath of the winged ice-dragons, Flash Gordon has no idea that he's stumbled inside the lair of the wicked Queen Fria. What exciting and terrible experiences await our friend? Be sure to listen in again next week for the continuation of the Amazing Interplanetary Adventures of Flash Gordon!

CHAPTER FIVE

Friday, December 23

Dottie awoke to the nostalgic smell of butter frying in a cast-iron pan, the nutty sweetness saturating a wintery Saturday morning. She kept her eyes closed, drawing in the fragrance of it. Nelson, making flapjacks.

He would be downstairs, wearing her frilly green polka-dotted apron around his waist, that cockeyed grin on his face, wielding a spatula as he coached the pancakes to a golden brown.

She didn't want to imagine the mess—the broken eggshells in the sink, flour dusted on the floor, the cinnamon shaker over-turned on the counter, the batter dripping on her Formica counter.

She simply allowed the image of Nelson, his tawny brown hair tousled, his broad shoulders sculpting out his white undershirt, his jeans hanging low on his hips, to saturate her mind, fill her with a tangy warmth she could taste. He'd probably be barefoot, and when she walked into the kitchen, knotting her robe at her waist, he'd turn and grin at her, his blue eyes sparkling with mischief. "Mornin', Ma."

"Making a mess again, I see, kid." She'd slide onto one of the oak chairs at the table—she should probably take out the leaf, make it smaller, but she and Nelson did just fine taking up one end—dressed in the red silky robe he'd given her on his fourteenth Christmas, and wait for breakfast.

Saturday mornings she lacked for nothing, her charming son stacking his fork with pancake, slippery with syrup. He'd grin at her as he spoke with his mouth full, chewing over his day.

"Mr. Lindstrom and I are going to check on the cows out in the far pasture, then I'm going down to the school for the Saturday afternoon basketball program. Is it okay if the guys come over for the Green Hornet tonight?"

When wasn't it okay?

Behind her closed eyes, she got up, pressed a kiss to his head, bussed his empty plate, and piled it into the sink. He'd join her, then, wiping the two plates, cleaning up his mess, reeling out stories of the dance the night before, or perhaps his newest theory on how to get her father's old 1929 Ford roadster to run again. Something about the fuel line, or a water pump, or...she could never keep track of it.

She had no doubt he'd get it running, someday.

How she loved wintry Saturdays.

The walnut double bed squealed as Dottie rolled over. She opened her eyes. Stared out the window.

Snow buffeted the window pane, ice edging the inside of the sash, lacy frost scrolling patterns across the pane. And, as she lay there huddled under her quilt, Nelson and the taste of joy dissipated, leaving only the hollow ache inside.

No Nelson in the kitchen making flapjacks. No team of fellas sprawled in her parlor, listening to the Green Hornet on the Silvertone.

Reality rushed back at her as she stared into the murky gray morning. Instead, strangers—okay, not exactly strangers, for she'd known two of them for most of her life, but one stranger and two...interlopers...invaded her home.

Dottie closed her eyes again, wishing away last night. The stilted conversation around the watery soup, the dry biscuits. She'd made up the bed for Violet in her parents' old room and given Jake the bed in the narrow spare room. She supposed she might offer him Nelson's room, but she couldn't bear it, and besides, the room needed dusting, an airing out. To Gordy she'd given—well, she'd wanted to give him the barn, but no, she gave him her father's den on the main floor, tucking a blanket into the leather divan. If he didn't fit, the floor would work fine for him.

Oh! See, she didn't *really* want him to sleep on the floor, but she needed someplace to store all her anger. Her grief.

She pushed the covers back. Hopefully the storm had abated and today her houseguests would trudge back to their own homes. She slid her feet into a pair of worn gray slippers, pulled an old green velour robe around her, cinched it, and went to the window.

Her breath caught. She couldn't see ten feet beyond her house, the world white—or rather gray, in an almost sickly pallor. If the sun had risen, it couldn't temper the storm. Maybe twenty inches had fallen, perhaps even more. The accumulation already reached a quarter of the way up the sill of her bedroom window, clogging out the light.

No, unless the storm abated soon, she had another day of houseguests.

Hadn't she suffered enough?

She went to the bureau, ignoring the old woman in the mirror, and ran a brush through her pale hair before tying it up in a tight bun. Then, trying to decide on the decency of emerging from her room in her bedclothes, she reached for a pair of jean trousers and a white collared shirt.

She added a red scarf and knotted it at the nape of her neck as she headed to the bathroom.

The white ceramic tile collected the cold and she ran the water for a couple minutes before it turned lukewarm. Splashing her face, letting the water drip off her chin as she stared in the mirror and inspected the new wrinkles around her eyes. Probably it didn't matter. She brushed her teeth, then tried out a smile.

It seemed foreign on her face.

Was that humming? Directly below her, in the kitchen, and through the grate in the floor, she heard an ear-bending rendition of "Jingle Bells."

That Gordy. Not only had he invaded her kitchen, but now he was humming?

Still, she sank onto the edge of the claw-foot tub, listening to the male voice, letting it churn up memories. Her father, chopping wood with five-year-old Nelson, handing him one log at a time to add to the pile in the mudroom. A dusky memory of her mother, rolling out pie crust, cutting off a piece for her to make her own pie, dusted with cinnamon and sugar.

Dottie pulled back the eyelet curtain and stared outside. The snow pummeled the window, thick, bulky flakes, and she could barely discern the fir tree outside her window, weighted with the burden of snow. Somewhere, in all that whiteness, her giant white pine lay toppled, but she couldn't make it out. Small mercies, perhaps.

In a different time, she might have been beguiled by the magic of the season, of a Christmas season blizzard. A white, merry Christmas, with a houseful of friends and family making memories.

But who did she have to make memories for?

She let the curtain fall. Gordy needed to stop singing or she'd throw him out into a snowbank on his britches.

She opened the bathroom door, and the aroma of breakfast rushed up at her. What right did the man have to invade her kitchen too? He had some nerve, that Gordy Lindholm, digging into her food stores, helping himself to her hospitality duties. But he'd always acted like what was hers belonged also to him.

Her anger seemed a live coal in her chest as she gripped the oak railing and padded down the stairs. The fire in the hearth had died—the stoker humming in the basement. And from the kitchen the humming had switched to "I'll Be Home for Christmas."

Of all the songs to choose…

She skidded to a halt under the arch between the rooms, her heart choking off her breath.

Not Gordy, but Jake stood at the stove, in his undershirt and trousers, a flour cloth tied around his slim waist, holding a spatula. Humming. And making…

"What on earth is going on in here?"

He whirled around, his mouth open, eyes wide. "Oh, good morning, Mrs. Morgan—"

"What are you doing?" She couldn't shake the anger now

sputtering to life inside her. Who did he think he was, to just—
"You just help yourself to my kitchen?"

He stared at her as if her tone had stripped the words from
him. "Uh…I get up early…I thought…"

She didn't know what to make of it, or the blush on his face,
the way he swallowed then finally turned back to the stove and
flipped the pancake before it burned.

She stared at her counter. No spilled flour, no broken egg in
the sink, no cloud of smoke.

He slid the pancake onto a plate.

She stared at it—flat, and crispy. "I think you forgot the baking powder."

"It's blini. It's Russian. You serve it with jam. My housekeeper taught it to me. Takes just a couple eggs, some flour, a scant
amount of sugar and salt. I used some of your powdered milk,
although I cut it in half…" He stared at her, what looked like apol-
ogy on his face. "I'm sorry. I was trying to help." He stared at the
blini. Back at her.

He had such remorse on his face, she didn't want to be angry
with him. It was just…the smells, the song on his lips. The fact that
she liked seeing a young man in her kitchen, stirring up mischief.

She picked up the plate. "Jam, you said? I think I have some
apple butter in the pantry."

He nodded like he already knew that.

She set the plate on the table, retrieved the butter, then opened
the drawer and found a couple forks, knives.

A pot of coffee perked on the stove.

She poured the coffee into a cup, found another, and set him a place. Then she slid onto the chair and stared at the thin pancake. It curled, crispy on the edges, but otherwise cooked to a perfect brown. "How do I eat this?"

He turned, a smile darting up his face. "I'll show you." He took his own plate to the table, sat down beside her, in Nelson's place. Spreading a thin layer of apple butter across the blini, he then folded it in half, then half again to make a triangle. When he cut it through and pierced it with his fork, it resembled a stack of flapjacks.

He stuck the pile in his mouth and smiled at her. "Yum."

She buttered her blini, folded it, and filled her own fork. Yum, indeed. "Do we have enough for the others?"

"Why should we keep breakfast to ourselves?"

She didn't answer. Good thing he'd made the coffee too strong, because she needed something to blame for the sting in her eyes.

He looked past her to the window as he reloaded his fork. "The storm doesn't seem to be letting up. We may be stuck here all day today."

If God was merciful, He'd send a sudden spring thaw.

* * * * *

Call him a pitiful man, but Gordy had always dreamed of waking up in Dottie's house. Always dreamed of smelling breakfast frying in the kitchen, always dreamed of sitting down at the large oak table, having her join him, asking him what his plans for the day might be.

"I'm going to get the Ford Ferguson running, and then maybe clean the barn." Not exciting conversation, even in his head, but it didn't have to be. In his head, they were an old married couple, so

comfortable with each other, they didn't need to speak. He might slide his hand over to hers, wrangle her sweet elegant fingers between his, despite the roughness of his work-worn hands, and meet her beautiful blue eyes.

And then, their son would bounce into the kitchen from the barn, wearing his work jacket, carrying in a bucket of milk. "Hey, Dad."

The image had the power to turn his chest into a knot as he stared at the brown paneled ceiling of Dottie's den.

But he'd never been *Dad* to Nelson. Just Gordy. And, most of the time, that felt like enough. More than enough, really. Because as Nelson got older, he spent nearly as much time at Gordy's farm as he did with Dottie. And it never seemed that she resented it.

He remembered the day she waved to him from the porch, smiling. As if she might invite him in. Nelson, about sixteen, had even suggested it.

"Ma always makes too much food anyway."

But, like always, whenever he got too close, the hurt would rise to strangle him. "Naw. I have chores."

He couldn't ever quite erase from his memories the look of disappointment on Nelson's face.

Gordy had managed to sleep the entire night on the dark leather sofa, warm enough under a wool blanket. Now, as he sat up, clad in his thermals, the cool room shook him awake. Back to reality.

He had a farm to run, a cow to milk.

And if he stayed much longer under the roof of Dottie Morgan, his longings might devour him whole.

He stood at the window, gauging the weather, and shook his head. He couldn't even see Dottie's barn across the drive, the snow heavy and blinding. And, in the night, a thin veneer of ice filmed the window, pasted the cracks.

So much for milking. Harriet was nearly dry anyway, and skipping her milking would seal her fate. Maybe by this afternoon…

He pulled on his wool trousers, then his flannel shirt, buttoning it before he opened the door, peeking into the hall. He heard voices in the kitchen—so Dottie had already risen, probably to make breakfast. He tiptoed up the stairs to the bathroom. Last night she'd issued them all toothbrushes and towels. At least he could make himself presentable.

It took an eternity for the hot water to reach the shower. He washed up, wishing he had clean clothes, then scrubbed his hair dry with a towel, staring in the mirror.

He didn't usually care about his appearance, but this morning, in Dottie's oval mirror, he appeared ancient. Saggy around the jowls, his beard grizzled, like an old hermit, his eyes tired. Once upon a time, in that visage had been a man who had made Dottie laugh, who had coaxed her onto his Ferguson tractor for a drive out to the back forty, who had believed she'd say yes to his proposal of marriage.

He drew his hands down his face. He needed a shave. He needed a haircut.

He needed the last twenty-six years back.

What if—what if this were his one chance to remind Dottie of what they could have had? What if—what if today he wooed her back into his arms?

He stared at the old man with his schoolboy longings, and shook his head. No. He'd never been enough for Dottie. Sheesh, twenty-plus years of her saying no, in word and deed—and he hadn't yet figured that out?

He brushed his teeth and exited the bathroom. He heard singing in the kitchen now—a duet of voices—male and female.

"Oh, the weather outside is frightful…"

Dottie?

He hung on the banister, listening. The impulse returned to him. What if today, trapped in her home, the one built for family, he could stir up the past, the *good* memories? The ones where he wasn't a specter of guilt or shame. The ones where he'd been enough, or even more than?

"Can I have this dance?"

The memory shook him through, and for a moment, he clung to it.

He'd learned to dance especially for her, for that night. The lights twinkled, tacked around the perimeter of the Germanic hall and on a Christmas tree in the corner. The band played something jazzy, new, and he'd gotten his hair cut. She wore her blond hair in waves, as if she'd tied it up in rags the night before, and he longed to touch it. He liked it shorter, although it scared him, the way she'd changed in three months since graduation from high school. She didn't need makeup, but she'd painted her lips anyway, her eyes darkened too, like the other girls at teachers college. She wore a long red dress that clung to her curves too much, but he didn't mind. He'd missed her so much this fall, her absence drilled a hole right through his chest. When she arrived home, he'd barely waited an hour before he strolled by her house.

He planned to ask her to go skating with him on the pond. And then, under the crisp moonlight, with their mingled breaths in the air, he'd get down on one knee and beg her to stay in Frost, to build a life with him.

But first, they had to dance.

He'd held out his hand, and she smiled into his eyes. "Why, Gordon Lindholm, when did you learn to dance?"

In the kitchen with his mother, the yard with his dog, and even a rake in the barn. "I promise not to step on your toes," he said, barely able to form words.

Once upon a time, it had been so easy with her, her laughter like sunshine on his heart. He'd head over to her house after he finished his chores and they'd spend hours exploring the creek or stealing apples from the Nystrom's orchard, or just walking in the tall field grass. She wanted to see the world, and that had frightened him a little too. But he dismissed it. Probably too easily.

Definitely too easily. He held her in his arms, silently counting out the foxtrot, smelling her silky hair—apples, cinnamon—and dreamed up their future. He'd build them a house, and she could teach at the school until they had children. They'd have a passel of boys and he'd teach them how to farm and hunt. And every night he'd come home to her, hold her in his arms, and yes, dance in the kitchen if she wanted.

"Did I tell you that the girls and I are going to Minneapolis right after Christmas? One of my dorm mates has invited us for New Year's Eve."

He frowned, met her eyes. "But…I thought we could go skating."

She smiled at him then leaned her forehead to his shoulder. "You're a wonderful dancer, Gordy." He might have dreamed it, but he thought she'd pressed her lips to his neck. "I promise to be back in the spring."

He drew a breath, leaned his head against hers. "I'll be right here, waiting."

But she hadn't returned then—not until summer. And a week later, Dapper Dan had arrived.

Gordy had proposed all right. But not under the moon, with the words like magic, caught in the air. No, his proposal had emerged almost angry and desperate, in the back stall of the barn, in a moment neither of them probably wanted to remember.

But he could change it all today. Hadn't he spent over twenty-five years showing her he'd wait? That he'd forgiven her, if she could only forgive him back? That they could start over?

He just needed one day to show her that she needed him, that he'd been here all along. That he wasn't going anywhere.

One day to bring warmth, even Christmas, back into her life.

"As long as you love me so, let it snow, let it snow, let it snow."

He caught the song, humming the tune as he hit the landing and headed toward the kitchen. He'd fetch her fresh wood and start a fire, maybe even pop some corn.

He stepped into the kitchen expecting to see Dottie with her hands in sudsy water, Jake, perhaps holding a towel, adding his tenor to her song.

But, no. Violet sat on the counter, wiping dishes and singing as Jake stood elbow deep in the suds at the sink, matching her tune. No Dottie in sight.

The song died inside as Jake turned. "Good morning. We saved you some breakfast." He gestured to the table, where a cloth lay over a plate.

Good grief, since when was he the last one to rise? "Where's Dottie?"

"She's out in the barn getting more wood."

"It's a whiteout—why did you let her go alone?" He didn't care that his tone made Jake jerk, or that shame flashed in his eyes. Well, he should feel ashamed. "What kind of man are you?"

He stormed past Jake, into the mudroom, pulled on his boots, his wool coat, hat, and mittens, and headed out into the cold.

Where, apparently, he and Dottie belonged.

* * * * *

What kind of woman was she? Twelve hours after Alex's death and all she could think about was Jake. She'd wakened with the feeling of his arms around her, the smell of him as she'd hung onto him through the snow, those devastating blue eyes in hers as he'd packed her knee and ankle in snow.

She liked him too much for a girl supposed to be grieving for her long-lost love, and the shame of it could fill her throat if she stopped to consider it.

Only…the thought continued to pulse at her: Even if Alex had cared for her, even if she had been "everything" as Jake claimed, Alex still hadn't come for her two years after the war ended. She'd even written, telling him when she was passing through Minneapolis on her way home from Europe. Had looked for him as she pulled into the station, ready to disembark, hoping.

No Alex.

Maybe the silence of the cold room—the way she'd shivered the night away, huddled under the covers, then risen early to wrap herself in blankets and sit on the settee, watching the storm cover the earth, had helped her hear the truth.

Alex hadn't really loved her, despite her fantasies.

Her mother's voice found her as she shivered the night out, the darkness turning to gray. *Sweetheart, no man is going to marry a gal who can change her own tires. Men need to feel needed.*

Like, perhaps, when she'd clung to Jake's neck last night, and even let him help her up the stairs to this frigid room? He'd wished her good night, a sort of tug in his gaze she couldn't quite figure out.

He seemed like a good man. She should have asked him more questions about his life, but Dottie shooed them all off to bed so quickly after dinner, as if she wanted the night to hurry its way along.

But, by the looks of the storm, they weren't headed out anywhere today.

She hoped her mother and sisters had figured out that she'd been stranded at Dottie's. Weren't worried sick for her, believing her stuck in a snowbank. But there was nothing she could do until the storm abated. Which meant that today, trapped in this house, she could be the kind of girl men wanted. A man like Jake might want. Needy and sweet. A girl worth taking a train to see, even to deliver bad news. He deserved it.

So, she'd dressed, then limped down to the hall as soon as she saw Dottie vacate the bathroom. Her leg ached, but the swelling had diminished, and she could hobble enough to get around.

Or maybe—maybe that was too independent? But she certainly couldn't call Jake up here to carry her to the bathroom.

She hung onto the banister, finally hopping on one foot into the bathroom. She'd never been so thankful for a toothbrush in her life as she scrubbed away the night then finger-combed her dark hair. It hung long and loose, not a librarian style in sight.

She heard humming as she took the stairs to the kitchen, sitting on her backside to scoot down. She island-hopped from one piece of furniture to the next, finally putting weight on her ankle as she reached the door. The pain didn't curl her over. She even took another step.

Dottie and Jake sat at the table.

"No, those aren't the words... Good morning, Violet." Dottie smiled up at her as if she actually belonged there.

Jake turned. "What are you doing walking around? You could injure yourself."

I can take care of myself. The words edged her mouth, but she bit them back. "I'm sorry, it just smelled so good down here."

Jake got up, slipped his strong arm around her waist. He smelled good—freshly washed, with cinnamon on his skin. This wasn't a terrible trade-off. She reached out, braced herself on the table, slid into the seat.

Okay, her leg did hurt.

"I'll get you some breakfast." Jake picked up a plate, slid a skinny pancake onto it. "This is called blini, it's Russian." He slathered it with apple butter—so that was the cinnamon smell—folded it twice, and handed her the plate.

"Did you make this?"

He grinned, and it could probably stop her heart. Oh, that Alex, why did he let her pine for him for so many years? "My Russian housekeeper taught us."

"Alex told me he had a Russian housekeeper too."

Jake looked at her, raised an eyebrow, like that news caught him unaware. Then, "Right. That's right, he did." He smiled at her, but it seemed polite.

She skewered the blini, tasted it. "This is good."

"Of course," Jake said, his real smile back. He stood at the sink, filling it with water.

Dottie rose from the table. "We need a fire. I'm heading out to the barn to get some wood."

"I can do that—" Jake started.

"Heavens to Betsy, I'm not an invalid here." She patted him on the shoulder, and Violet just stared at her as she headed out to the mudroom.

"What did you do to get adopted?" she asked when she heard the door outside close.

Jake looked at her. "What?"

"I haven't seen her smile for…well, it's been a few years."

He frowned and turned back to his dishes. "Did you sleep okay?"

"Froze to death, thank you. I can't wait to sit by a warm fire. Maybe play a game."

"Chess?"

Oh, she could kill him in chess, and wouldn't that be fetching? "How about checkers?"

"Ever play Monopoly?"

He might stand a fair shake. "If Dottie has the game, you're on." She got up, began to hop toward him, carrying her plate.

He frowned again as he met her and took the plate, her hand on his arm. "Listen, you need to stay put."

"I'm not an invalid either." Oops. Wait, should she be?

"I know that. But let's pretend you are, just for today."

I know that? What was that supposed to mean?

"How about if I sit on the counter, dry the dishes? Would that make you happy?"

"Not as happy as letting me carry you to the sofa, but I know you wouldn't go for that."

He did? She frowned and for a second, his eyes widened.

"Alex used to say that you were pretty independent."

Why, thank you, Alex. She knew it. No wonder he hadn't rushed out to the train station to meet her. He considered her just one of his chums, just like every other fella she worked with in the motor pool. "Not that independent. I'll let you carry me to the sofa after we finish the dishes."

Had she really said that? The words just spiraled out, nearly on their own. But, she liked that smile—would trace her finger up it, get caught in his whiskers, if she could. "Let me help with the dishes."

He considered her a moment before he put his hands to her waist and lifted her to the counter. Then he walked over to the table, lifting a napkin and settling it over the remaining blini.

"What were you and Dottie arguing about this morning?"

"We were trying to figure out the words to that new Dinah Shore and Buddy Clark song, 'Baby, It's Cold Outside.'"

She'd heard it on the radio. She found the tune. "'I've gotta get home…'"

He laughed, "'But baby, you'd freeze out there…'"

"It's a little…naughty."

"It's funny," he said, his blue eyes too full of trouble.

"The song is all about seduction. He wants her to stay. He even makes her a drink," she said, liking how Jake looked with his hands in sudsy water. She wanted to pick up some suds, blow them at him.

The thought startled her.

"He's a red-blooded male. Of course he wants her to stay."

"But he's a bad boy. He's just trying to finagle a kiss from her."

"It's about desire. And the games men and women play. Listen to her words, to the tone. She's *hoping* he'll talk her into it. A gal is supposed to play hard to get, it's part of the game."

It is? Oh, she just didn't know any of these games. "My mother would most definitely not approve of that song."

He handed her a plate. "Your mother isn't here. And besides, you don't live for the approval of your mother, do you?"

She slowed her drying. "Why would you say that?"

He made a face, shook his head, returned to his washing. "You just seem…more independent than that."

There he went with that independent word again.

"Well, I guess you win, because you're right, it's a blizzard out there." She put the plate on the counter.

He handed her another plate. "'Oh the weather outside is frightful…'"

She grinned, adding onto his song.

He had a nice voice, a rich tenor, and she had to like a man unafraid to sing, with his hands in dishwater. His strong arms rippled the edges of his white undershirt, stretching along his back, his slender waist and hips.

The memory of being in his arms, her arms around his strong neck, made her nearly lose her place in the song.

Steps fell on the stairs and the song died as Jake turned. "Good morning."

Gordy stood in the kitchen in his bare feet, his hair poorly combed, as if he'd just towel-dried it. He was a handsome man, with a farmer's build, hazel eyes with flecks of gold. He must have been a catch back in his day, before the stern look set in.

"We saved you some breakfast," Jake said, gesturing to the table with his sudsy hand.

"Where's Dottie?" Gordy said.

"She's out in the barn getting more wood."

Something flashed in Gordy's eyes, and even Violet flinched.

"It's a whiteout—why did you let her go alone?"

Ow, his tone could take off a layer of skin.

Beside her, Jake jerked, and something that looked like guilt, or even shame, hued his face.

"I—" Jake started, but Gordy had already pushed past him.

"What kind of man are you?"

The kind of man who made you breakfast, Violet wanted to snap. But instead she looked down, at her swollen ankle, willing herself not to make a scene. Jake could fight his own battles, right?

But he said nothing as Gordy banged out of the house, slamming the door.

Jake washed the dishes in silence.

"You offered to help. Why didn't you tell him that?"

"It doesn't matter." He handed her another plate. "He's right. I should have insisted."

"I believe her exact words were, 'I'm not an invalid.' Were you supposed to argue with her?"

"Yes. Probably. I don't know." He took the stack of plates, walked over to the hutch, and loaded them in. "Maybe Gordy's right. A real man would have."

"I think a real man accepts that a woman can carry in wood if she says so. Letting her doesn't make you less of a man...or her, less of a woman."

"Well, you would say that, wouldn't you?" he said, stalking back to the sink.

"What's that supposed to mean?"

"Help!" The door to the mudroom banged open, and a second later, Dottie flew into the kitchen, running through the house. "Get a blanket, and start a warm bath running!"

Behind her, in his arms, Gordy carried a body, limp and crusted with snow. "We found a kid in the barn," he said, running behind her. "He looks dead."

CHAPTER SIX

"Don't put him in the bath!" Jake followed Gordy through the house, catching up to him. He laid his finger against the boy's neck. Yes, a pulse, but bare. "Give him to me."

Gordy had the boy in a death clench, his eyes fierce with the horror of finding him. "Why?"

Upstairs, Jake heard the water running in the tub.

"He needs his body core heated first. If you warm his extremities, the cool blood will rush to his heart, cause a cardiac arrest." He reached for the boy. "Give him to me."

Gordy might have been more shocked than willing, but he handed over his bundle to Jake.

Jake set the boy on the velvet divan in the family room. "Stoke the fire."

He looked about ten years old, caught in the pallor of death, his skin gray, his rabbit shopka encrusted with ice, his wool scarf frozen to his cheeks. Curled tight into a fetal position, his frozen posture made it nearly impossible for Jake to start shucking off his snowy boots, his icy pants.

"What are you doing?" Violet had hobbled into the room behind them—now crouched beside him.

"Get his jacket off him." Jake tugged off the boy's stiff pants.

His legs appeared nearly white. Violet worked on the buttons of his coat, frozen solid to the cloth.

"Dottie, we need scissors!" He pressed his warm hands to the boy's cheeks. "Where's the blanket!"

Dottie appeared, shoving the blanket at him. He tucked it over the boy's legs, for now, and, because Violet still hadn't wrestled free the buttons, he grabbed the jacket, took a breath, and ripped it open.

Buttons popped off as he yanked the jacket down, off the frail body. The boy wore a wool sweater under the jacket. Violet was unwinding the scarf from his neck.

"How did you find him?" Violet said, tugging it free.

Dottie had returned with scissors. "I went to the barn for wood and saw that the door was ajar. I thought maybe an animal had gotten in—and then I saw the door to the truck was open. I couldn't believe it when I saw him, lying there on the seat, all balled up. Why didn't he come to the house?"

"Maybe he didn't see it. Or couldn't make it," Violet said.

"Do you know him?" Jake asked as he took the scissors and began to cut off the sweater. He did the same to the frozen undershirt.

Dottie shook her head. "I don't know. He looks familiar."

"What are you doing?" Violet said. "He's going to freeze."

"He's already frozen. He needs warmth, right now. Get another hat for him."

"I ran a bath," Dottie said as she ran toward the mudroom. Gordy bumped past her, carrying wood.

"No—it's not fast enough." Jake stood up and only hesitated a moment before he shucked off his undershirt. He didn't look at the rumple of scar tissue across his chest as he reached out and picked up the boy. He pulled him against his chest, the chill of the child's body shuddering through him, raising gooseflesh. Then he lay back on the sofa, cradling the boy against him. "Tuck the blanket around us, Violet. Then get more. We have to warm his core."

"Is he alive?" Gordy said, stirring the coals in the hearth to life.

"For now. We need more blankets."

Jake had been thirteen that day when they'd fallen through the ice. He remembered the trick Svetlana used to keep Alex alive.

He wrapped his arms tighter, willing his heat into the child. Coaxing each breath from him. *Please God, don't let this little one die.* Alex had been colder— and underwater—and he'd lived. Although, after that, just like Jake, he'd become even more prone to bronchitis and pneumonia.

Dottie returned with a hat and shoved it on the boy's head. When she met Jake's eyes, he saw the mother in them.

"Pray, Dottie," he said softly.

She pressed a hand to her mouth, her eyes wet.

"Dottie, where do you keep your blankets?" Violet said, gripping her arm.

Dottie met her eyes. "Yes, blankets. They're upstairs in the closet."

Violet limped toward the stairs, but Dottie stopped her. "Put on some tea." She took the stairs up, two at a time.

Violet glanced back at Jake. The boy seemed no warmer, but the chill of his body had begun to shiver through Jake, making him shake. "Yes, we need tea. *I* need tea, to keep warm."

He watched Violet hobble to the kitchen, getting stronger, it seemed, with each step.

Gordy's fire crackled to life, and he fed it to a robust blaze. Then, slapping off his hands, he left for another armful of wood.

Just Jake and the boy remained, cocooned in blankets on the sofa.

"Where did you come from, kid?" Jake said into the boy's hat. He closed his eyes, found himself back at Lake Calhoun.

The sky a crisp, pristine blue, it had coaxed his attention away from his lessons, and when he returned home from school, he found Alex in the back room, behind the kitchen, holding their skates.

Alex always was trouble—his mother said so with a glint in her eyes, but she shooed them both out the door.

They'd lost count of the warm days, this crisp late-March snap of cold charming them to see only the shiny layer of ice. Deep under the smooth surface, however, water channeled through tunnels of warmth. Pressure from the top would add cracks, weaken their skating rink.

They hiked out on their blades, across the street to play knights, fighting with sawed-off poplar branches, then raced around the shoveled rink, the snow like blue diamonds. His toes had turned numb by the time the sun began to drift to the horizon, casting perilous shadows upon their playground.

He grabbed a rock, used his sword to knock it around. Alex headed back to the bench.

Jake heard the crack as he rounded the far edge of the snowbank.

Probably, the snow had warmed the ice underneath, weakened

it, and the cracked webs grew in front of him as he watched them, mesmerized for too long.

When Jake sprinted toward shore, the ice collapsed beneath him.

The water was a thousand icy needles, searing him whole. He opened his mouth to scream and water filled his lungs.

He went down in his heavy wool jacket, tried to kick to the surface, but banged his head on the ice. His eyes burned when he opened them, his lungs on fire. He slammed his mittened hands against the ice.

Then, he was being dragged through the water, out of the hole, his head cresting the surface. He breathed in, coughed, but managed to grab the jagged side of the ice.

Alex had him by the scruff of his coat. He scooted back as he pulled Jake from the water, then rolled him away from the hole. Jake found his knees, coughed out more water, but began to crawl, scrambling away from the hole.

He heard it crack again, a shot splicing the twilight, then Alex's shout as it crumpled under him. He turned just as Alex splashed into the dark water.

"Alex!" The cracking spider-webbed beneath him, and he scrambled back as it dissolved just beyond him.

Alex hadn't surfaced. "Alex!" He scrambled to his feet, still coughing, his coat saturated, already shivering.

The water had sucked him under.

Alex was strong, wasn't he? A Russian boy, a year older than himself. He'd survived the Bolshevik revolution with his mother, escaped, and started a new life in Minneapolis. "Alex!"

Jake turned and fled for his house on his skates, banging into the back entrance, screaming.

Their butler, a burly man from Ireland, had finally pulled Alex out, almost ten minutes later. Gray and not breathing. They pushed the water out of him, and Jake's father blew oxygen into his lungs as Alex's mother undressed him and held him to her chest in front of the fire.

Jake had turned himself into a corner, shivering under his blanket, and wept.

Dottie tucked another blanket around him as Violet returned from the kitchen. "Tea's ready."

Dottie went to fetch it and Violet sank down on a chair. She gave him a strange look. "Alex told me once that he fell through the ice, and his best friend saved him. Said he came onto the ice after him and nearly died when he fell in himself. Said his best friend was a real hero."

She had eyes that could swoop every word from his chest, but this time, her story held them fast.

"That was you, wasn't it?"

He tried to hide the horror from his eyes. Dottie came into the room carrying a cup of tea. She sat next to him and lifted it to his mouth. He sipped it, the heat traveling to his chest, where the boy had begun to shiver.

He didn't look at Violet.

Oh, Alex, what did you tell her? "No," he said finally. "That wasn't me."

But she got up, pulled the chair toward him, and sat close enough to put her hand on the boy's cheek. "I still think you're a hero."

* * * * *

Dottie set Jake's empty cup in the sink, rinsing it. The spray rounded in the cup, hit her face, and she jerked back. But perhaps the water would hide the way her eyes burned, filmed with tears. She lifted a towel, pressed her face into it.

Oh, God simply wasn't going to let her forget her sins, was He? He was going to make her watch this little boy die.

"Dottie."

She didn't lower the towel at Gordy's soft voice. She couldn't let him see her cry. Ever. She turned back to the sink, tossed the towel on the counter, then added soap to the water and began to clean the cup.

Gordy stepped up behind her. Too close. She could smell him—a hint of the barn, yes, but woodchips and smoke from the fire, and so much of that comforting masculine aura that she knew as well as she knew the color of the dawn over the eastern fields behind his house.

She drew in a breath. He couldn't see her anyway, couldn't see her hands shaking, the way the cup rattled as she set it on the counter.

He reached around her and touched her wrists. Held them. "Dottie, are you okay?"

She drew in a breath, seeing his hands holding her arms. Strong, steady hands. Hands that she trusted.

Not that she'd ever tell him.

But, in reality, he probably knew.

She shook his grip away and reached again for the towel.

"Yes, of course," she said, and her voice nearly backed her up. She turned.

If she took one step, she'd be in his arms. She could almost see herself curling her arms up around his, folding herself against his chest, lifting her face to meet his. She'd let herself have this moment too many times over the past twenty-plus years. Powerful moments when she tucked herself in the comfort of memory, now even more dangerous when he hovered so close. She pressed her hand on his chest to back him away. "I'm just worried about him."

"Jake seems to know what he's doing."

"Someone needs to tell his mother he's here."

"Do you know him?"

She nodded. "I think his name is Arnold Shiller. This—this is his storm house."

"His storm house?"

"They send me a notice every year. I threw out...I never dreamed—"

"No wonder he came here."

She pinched her lips tight then went to stand by the door, peering in at Jake. Violet sat next to him, pressing her palm on the boy's frozen cheek. "Do you think he'll live?" Oh, he had to live.

Her eyes burned again, and she drew in a quick breath.

When she turned, Gordy had poured her a cup of tea, was handing it to her. She took it without meeting his gaze. "I think his father was in the war with Nelson. I see his mother around town. She's—she's not well." Dottie slid onto a chair, staring out the window.

After a moment, Gordy pulled out the chair opposite her, sat down. He set his tea on the table, ran his wide thumb over the handle. "You're remembering the Armistice Day blizzard, aren't you?"

She closed her eyes. Why, thank you, Gordy, for dredging up that horror again."

"Three days, by yourself, wondering if I'd bring Nelson home safely."

"Of course you would bring him home safely," she snapped. But yes, she'd sat right here, for three days, watching the world turn white and bury them all alive. "It would have been...well, maybe I wouldn't have gone out of my mind if I'd known you'd made it back to your place safely."

A tick of the clock.

The thunder of her heart.

Then, "I know," Gordy said quietly. "I should have brought him straight home. I'm so sorry."

She glanced up at him. Really? And all these years, she'd thought he'd grabbed his one opportunity to pay her back. To make her sit by the window, waiting, just like he'd done all those years earlier. "So many people died. You saved his life."

Her own words, emerging softly, startled her as much as they apparently did him. He frowned at her, as if words had abandoned him.

"I never thanked you for that."

"What was I going to do, Dottie. Let the boy freeze?" He turned away, toward the window, his voice sharp.

Right. She should have known better than to offer up gratitude, even forgiveness. After all, this was Gordy Lindholm. He didn't know how to forgive.

She glanced back out to the parlor. Then outside. "I've got to get word to his mother that he's okay." She got up. "The Dersheids have a telephone. Maybe I can—"

"Stop thinking with your heart and use your head. You can't go out there in this storm—you'll get yourself killed. Besides, I can guarantee you that the Shillers do not have a phone, so unless you're prepared to hike out to their farm—"

"Maybe I am." She found her feet, leaving her teacup. "Maybe that's exactly what I'm going to do."

"Oh please." He skidded his chair back, following her. "Just stop, and think this through for one second. Why do you have to always be so impulsive!"

She turned on him, her finger at his arrogant chin. "Me? Impulsive? I haven't been impulsive for over twenty years."

"Once was enough."

"Oh, for cryin' in the sink—I make one impulsive decision and you can't forgive me for it—even twenty-six years later."

"Your one impulsive moment cost me my family!"

She stilled, his words shuddering through her. His jaw tightened and he looked away, closing his eyes as he shook his head. "I didn't mean that."

"Yes you did. "

"You should have married me."

"You should have asked."

"I did!" His eyes were reddened now. "I did, Dottie."

"Was that what that was? Because it seemed more like a tumble in the hay, and a command, issued by a desperate boy."

Oh, she hadn't meant to make that moment sound so sordid.

And, when he swallowed, the hurt filling his eyes, she was right there, back in the barn, startled by the force of his ardor, as if he had something to prove to her. Her heart turned to fire as he lifted his eyes to hers, his voice low and tunneling through her. *Don't leave Frost. Marry me, Dottie. I'm the one you want.*

She gritted her teeth against the memory. How his words had stirred her ire.

He'd been correct, of course, but she couldn't allow him to be.

She pushed past him, grabbing her father's parka, his rabbit-furred hat.

"You're not going out there."

She ignored him.

"Fine." He grabbed his coat off the peg, that flimsy wool one, and shoved a stocking cap on his head.

"You'll freeze in ten minutes," she said.

"Fear not, I'm angry enough to keep me warm for the next year!"

She shook her head, shoved her feet into her boots. They were still soggy from the jaunt out to the barn, but she didn't care. She zipped up the parka, grabbed her mittens.

Gordy wound a muffler around his neck. "You're going to get us both killed."

"No one asked for your help."

He winced at that, and she hated her words. But it was too late now, wasn't it?

She wrenched open the door. The wind blew her back in, but she righted herself and stepped out.

Oh, a person could slip into the frothy white waves and be

buried in a minute. She blinked back the ice that hit her eyes. She should grab a scarf.

No, she should turn around.

But Gordy stood, blocking her path. So, she stepped out into the whiteness, put her head down, and hiked down the driveway. If she followed the stone wall that would bring her to the road, she could just…

The wind ate her breath, the snow knives on her exposed flesh. She'd get lost and perish and prove Gordy right. Again.

She was impulsive. And she did think with her heart. And she did…

She did cost him his family. Their family.

Her eyes filmed, began to freeze. *Gordy, I'm sorry.*

She turned, almost ready to say it, when her feet slipped on the ice below the snow. She grabbed out for Gordy as her feet lifted, her arms windmilling.

He grabbed at her, tried to right her, but the force of her fall skidded his legs out from beneath him.

They landed hard in a pile of parkas and icy drift. Snow tunneled down the neck of her jacket, into her mouth. But Gordy had cushioned most of her fall with his body. She lay half on him, her head on his shoulder, his arms around her.

"Oh," she said softly as the snow drifted around them.

He rolled over onto his side, meeting her eyes. He had snowflakes in his lashes, collecting on his goatee. "Are you okay?"

She drew in a breath. Shook her head. "I used to believe that even though I did it wrong, everything turned out right." She closed eyes. "Please, just leave me out here in the cold."

But he didn't move, and when she opened her eyes, they were again in the hay mow, heat radiating from his gaze, right to her core. His hazel-green eyes ran over her face, her eyes, then stopped at her lips.

Then, suddenly, as if they were teenagers again, he touched his lips to hers. Sweetly, reserved, even tentative, although she knew behind that touch lay a hunger she had once loved to stir. He tasted of toothpaste and smelled of the soap in her shower, and she closed her eyes and let the years drop away.

Yes, Gordy, I'll marry you.

Around them, the wind moaned, shivering the pine trees.

But...wait. No. He'd had his chance. Then, he'd sneaked into her life and stolen her son. Had practically sent the boy to war armed with the skills of a sniper.

More than that, this wasn't Gordy forgiving her. It was him using his devastating charm to derail her, to have his way and keep her from trekking out into the storm.

She opened her eyes, pressed against his chest. "No, Gordy. No..." She scooted away, shaking her head.

He wore panic in his eyes, not unlike so many years ago. His voice dropped, low, husky. "Dottie, c'mon. Haven't we fought long enough?"

The question stilled her, and she waited, her heart in her throat, for more. For a simple, *I still love you.*

It would have been enough.

Then, he drew in a breath, his jaw tightening. "Stop being so stubborn."

Stubborn.

Same old Gordon. She should have expected it. She untangled herself from his arms, climbed to her feet. Stared at the blizzard. It seemed to be only growing more violent. "Stay away from me, Gordon Lindholm."

She turned, left him in the snow, and hiked back to the house.

* * * * *

He'd been wounded. Violet tried to wipe the image of the scars on Jake's chest from her mind, tried to see him again as whole, and the harbinger of bad news.

Tried to remember that just twenty-four hours ago, she'd been pining for his friend Alex. But Alex wasn't here. Alex hadn't wanted her, and this man had just bared his wounds to the company of them to save this little boy's life.

She knew she shouldn't look, had felt shame the moment her gaze landed on his chest. He had the toned muscles of a soldier, despite his scars. She might forgive herself for the way her heart leaped to life inside her.

But, first, she had to know how much Jake really knew about her.

Had Alex told him about her job with the WAACs, in the motor pool? How she had changed tires and replaced radiators throughout the duration of the war? Had he mentioned that her mother hadn't once written to her, how she'd received mail only from her father, until his death? Had Alex told him how she'd felt like a misfit on Saturday nights when she'd rather be out in the barn with her father, overhauling the truck, than spiffing up for a dance?

Jake had said some cryptic things in the kitchen that had her curiosity buzzing. Like saying she didn't care what her mother thought. Or calling her independent. Except, on his lips it didn't seem like criticism.

No, back then, when her emotions had a firmer grip on her resolve, she hadn't cared what her mother, what the people of Frost said. She just hadn't wanted to be left behind. She wanted to fight alongside her brothers.

Be a heroine.

However, she didn't want to be the motor pool girl to Jake. The thought pulsed inside her, gaining power. Not with him lying on the sofa, holding this frozen boy in his arms, like he might be his father. Jake had closed his eyes, shivering, and she tucked the blanket up around his shoulders, making a little well for the boy to breathe. He'd begun to shiver also, but he hadn't wakened.

Getting stranded at Dottie's house—with Jake here—just might have saved the boy's life.

Maybe Jake was a doctor.

But first, "What did Alex tell you about me?" she asked.

He kept his eyes closed. His chest rose and fell and for a moment, she thought he might be sleeping. "Enough," he said finally.

What did that mean? But he answered her before she spoke.

"He told me that the day he met you, you nearly ran him over."

"I did not!"

He opened one eye. "I now can relate to his words."

"Funny."

He smiled at her, and she felt it deep inside. "I was chauffeuring a general, and Alex was in the way. I honked my horn—"

"Calm down, Sergeant, I was just kidding."

She stilled. "You know I was a sergeant? Did Alex tell you what I did?"

He met her eyes. "I suppose it had something to do with driving?"

So, maybe he didn't know. "Go back to sleep."

"I'm not sleeping. I'm concentrating on staying warm."

"You're shivering."

"I'll be fine."

"He's really shivering too."

"I know, and it's going to get worse. He'll be in pain when he wakes up."

She ran his hair from his face. "Poor kid."

"Brave kid, to make it all the way to the barn in the storm. But then again, people don't really know what they have in them until they face something like that." He opened his eyes again. "The war made a lot of heroes out of people you'd least expect to be."

Like him? Her gaze flickered to his chest, although the boy and the blanket covered it. She didn't want to ask, but it seemed almost rude not to. "Were you hurt in the war?"

He didn't open his eyes. "Belgium. I was transporting some wounded; we were hit with artillery fire."

"You were a medic?"

He drew in a breath. "I did a lot of things. Not all of them am I proud of. And none of them were very exciting."

She frowned. But Roger didn't like to talk about the war either, so much of it still in his eyes, or his dreams. Sara told her too many stories of him waking in the middle of the night, shaking.

"Alex was in the infantry," she said, not sure why. "He stormed the beaches at Normandy."

"I know. Alex was a real hero." Jake's tone sounded tired, however, almost with a shade of remorse.

Maybe she was talking too much about Alex. Babbling, in fact. She could hear herself, blathering on about the love that wasn't. She looked around. Couldn't she be doing something useful?

"He told me, after the war, that he wanted to build airplanes. Or maybe cars."

Jake had opened his eyes again. "He said that?"

She *had* to stop talking about Alex. She got up, stoked the fire. "What do you do, Jake?"

He was quiet again and she returned to him. "Jake?"

"Right now? I work for the army, traveling." He opened his eyes, however, and met hers. He had a self-deprecating smile. "What do you do?"

From the mudroom, she heard feet banging into the house. She turned, and in a moment Gordy stormed into the room, ice caked in his goatee.

"Where were you?"

"Don't ask." Gordy looked at Jake. "How's the boy?"

"Still alive, thank God."

Gordy turned away and crouched down before the large Silvertone radio. "Maybe we can get a weather report."

But when he turned the dial, nothing happened. He got up, checked the plug.

"It hasn't worked in about three years." Dottie appeared at the door, looking shaken, her cheeks red.

Gordy turned around, his mouth in a grim slash. "Of course it's broken." He stormed past her and returned in a moment with a tray of tools. He yanked the plug from the socket, turned it around.

"What are you doing?" Dottie came toward him.

"I'm fixing it."

"You're going to break it."

He looked up, narrowed his eyes. "More than it already is?"

She threw her hands up, as if she might strangle him, then turned away. "Do you two need tea?" She nearly barked it, and Violet shook her head. Dottie stormed back into the kitchen. This Dottie, she recognized. The one seated at the table this morning... perhaps the Dottie she'd only hoped to see.

"She's quite angry," Jake said. "What did you do, Gordy?"

"Just keep your trap shut, Dapper Dan. If it weren't for you, none of us would be in this mess."

Jake met Violet's eyes, raised an eyebrow, making a face. "Mommy and Daddy are fighting."

She opened her mouth then shut it. But a giggle emerged.

Still, she couldn't help but turn her gaze to the back of the Silvertone. Even from here, she could see the dark dusting of one of the four radio tubes. It needed to be replaced if they wanted to listen.

Instead, Gordy wiggled the fuses on the main board to make sure the connections were solid and not blown.

She held her tongue. Gordy didn't need her mechanical skills. In fact, no one needed her mechanical skills.

That thought sifted through her. She glanced at Jake.

If she never said anything about the war or her job, he'd never know. And then he wouldn't have to look at her with the stigma of her military service in his eyes.

"The FM radio tube is broken," Gordy said finally. He sat back. "Dottie, do you have another radio tube?"

"Oh sure, I keep one in my apron pocket," she barked from the kitchen.

But what he could do is swap one of the radio tubes from the AM slot to the FM slot. Violet stared at the flames flickering in the hearth, eating at the logs, willing herself to stay quiet.

Jake had moved his hand atop hers on the boy's cheek. He had sleek, strong hands, and she wouldn't move hers all day if it would help the boy stay warm.

"Maybe if I switch them out…" Gordy unsnapped a tube from the AM connector, replaced the FM tube.

He turned the radio back around, plugged it in. Fiddled with the dial. Static, then a voice came through.

She recognized the deep tones of J. Anthony Smythe, as Henry Barbour and his family's soap opera escapades filled the room. Gordy flipped the stations, perhaps searching for the weather.

Dottie came out of the kitchen holding a spatula. "I wanted to hear that."

The weatherman came on, his voice cut with static. "The wind chill is down to thirty below south of Canby and—"

The voice cut out as all the lights in the house clicked off, leaving only the crackle of the fire behind.

"Never mind," Dottie said.

Gordy ran his hand down his face. Stared at the radio as if he'd like to throw it—or something—against the wall. "Do you still have that old generator, Dot?"

"It's in the barn. It hasn't worked for years."

Gordy got up, as if heading out to the barn. Violet stilled the urge to follow him. She may have even started to draw her hand away.

Jake's tightened over hers. "Stay. He needs a woman's touch."

She met his eyes and smiled. A woman's touch.

Gordy could fix the generator just fine on his own.

CHAPTER SEVEN

What did Dapper Dan over there have that Gordy didn't? Gordy had hauled the generator back into the house—his hands turning stiff in the cold, and now worked on it on the dining room floor, much to Dottie's consternation.

"You're going to get gasoline all over my carpet. And not to mention asphyxiate us."

"I won't start it in the house, Dottie." But she stomped back to the kitchen.

Perfect. So much for helping them remember the good old days.

His gaze kept returning to the clasped hands of Violet and Jake and he just wanted to throw something.

Like Jake.

Out the window.

And lock the door.

What was it with some fellas who knew exactly what to say, when and how to say it? Twelve hours the man had been here. He'd caused Violet to drive into a tree and wreck her car, delivered the bad news of her friend's death—not to mention the gigantic lie he toted around about said dead man and the subsequent corre-spondence—and perky Violet sat there, holding Jake's hand and giggling?

The generator hadn't a spark of life, although he'd checked the diesel fuel. Could be a clogged fuel line, perhaps even a blown spark plug.

Who was he kidding? He didn't know where to begin to repair the engine. Sure, he could putter around the farm, coax the Ferguson to life, but diagnostic mechanics still had the power to elude him.

He got up, walked over to the fire, picked up the poker, and stabbed at the logs in the hearth. Sparks spiraled up the flue.

With the electricity out, the stoker wouldn't run, which meant they'd have to keep feeding the fire, not to mention close off the other rooms.

Which meant they'd have to stay in this room or perhaps the kitchen to keep warm.

The house was getting smaller by the minute.

He could still feel Dottie's lips on his—the taste of cinnamon from the apple butter, and coffee—it rushed him back in time, stirring the hope of their tomorrows in his heart. He'd lost himself in that brief moment, lost the man he'd become.

And, in that flash of time, he became the man he'd wanted to be. The man who loved Dottie back to herself.

Then, she'd pressed her hand into his chest and stopped his world from spinning. Still, he hung onto her, desperate, just like he'd been in the barn that day so long ago.

"Dottie, c'mon. Haven't we fought long enough?" he'd said it softly, with pleading.

But, as if time had cruelty, he saw her change in his arms, just like before. Her mouth closed into a tight line, her eyes sparking. And his mouth, as usual, decided to break his heart.

"Stop being so stubborn."

What was wrong with him?

Outside the snow had begun to cake upon the windows, and the occasional sky-rending crack evidenced the weight of icy accumulation upon the trees. He had no doubt there'd be trees littering the roads when the storm lifted.

The boy moaned in Jake's arms.

"Gordy, could you ask Dottie for a thermometer? I'd like to take his temperature," Jake said.

"I'll get it," Violet said, and Gordy noticed how he squeezed her hand before releasing her. She caught his eyes, a softness in them, a moment before limping from the room.

Gordy stared after her. His words emerged almost in a growl. "What are you playing at, Dapper Dan?"

Jake caught his eyes, frowned. "Stop calling me that. And I'm not playing at anything—"

"You're holding her hand."

Jake made a face. "I know. It just…it felt like the right thing to do."

"What are you trying to do—break her heart? Or yours?"

"I don't know, okay?"

Gordy slid into the chair. "You know perfectly well that when she finds out you wrote to her, pretending to be Alex, she'll never speak to you again."

"You're killing me here." Jake shifted the boy, repositioning him. "Keep your voice down."

Gordy lowered his voice to a whisper. "You gotta tell her the truth."

"I know that!" He glanced toward the door, schooled his voice down to low. "Don't you think I'm sitting here, calling myself a chump? She's Alex's girl, except…" He shook his head.

"What?"

Jake glanced at the door. "Something's not right. Alex told her this story about when he nearly drowned…only he had it backwards. He saved me, not the other way around. Why would he tell her that?"

"Maybe he wanted to sound bigger in her eyes."

"Trust me, Alex wouldn't trade his life for mine. Until I was twelve, I couldn't play sports. I spent half the winter in bed. He would have never wanted to be me."

"What's so wrong with being you?"

Jake shook his head. "Trust me, I'm no hero, Gordy. I…let's just say that I never picked up a gun to fight, I never saved any lives. She deserves a guy like Alex."

"Why doesn't she deserve a guy like you?"

He looked up, at the ceiling. "Because I'm not the man I should be. Because…I spent the last four months of the war in a hospital in Minneapolis. Trust me, I'm no hero."

"You went to war, didn't you?"

Jake closed his eyes. "I went to war, yes. I watched my buddies die. And I came home, broken."

The urge to throttle the man had passed. Jake seemed like a real straight ace, the way he'd rescued the kid, the way he held him as he shivered.

Gordy stirred the coals. "If you want to win this girl, you have to tell her the truth. Alex has been dead for two years. It's time she knew that. Then you can start with a clean slate."

"Oh, and like you've got the corner on truth. You're so sick in love with Dottie, you can't see straight to form a decent sentence."

"Watch yourself, kid."

"I see the way you look at her—and the way she looks at you."

Gordy gave a harsh laugh, full of grit and pain. "Dottie can't stand to look at me."

"Well, right now, sure. But yesterday—"

"It's too late for us, kid. We had our chance, and blew it."

Jake narrowed his eyes.

He didn't want to tell this kid, but... "I kissed her."

"Just now? Good grief, Gordy, what's going on with you two?"

"Keep your britches on. She nearly slapped me and told me to stay away from her."

Jake made an appropriate face. "You got a real way with women, mister."

"I don't know what her problem is. I come over here almost three times a week, make sure her woodpile is stocked, drag out her clinker, drop off fresh milk. I rake out the storm gutters, I change the oil in her truck, I cut the grass."

"You sound like you're married to her."

He did, didn't he?

"Why do you do all that?"

Gordy stared at his hands. Too rough, too big. "Because maybe if I'd asked her to marry me the right way, she wouldn't have run off, got married, and come back pregnant."

Jake just stared at him, Gordy's words reflected in his expression.

Gordy looked away. "This is all my fault."

"What way is the wrong way?" Jake's words emerged soft, almost kind.

Gordy flinched, but the image came anyway. Him, catching her before she escaped in her father's Model T, all gussied up and pretty for a trip to the soda fountain in town to meet TJ. She wore the yellow dress, the one with the tiny blue flowers, and had her hair in pin waves around her head. *"Gordy, what are you doing here?"*

He'd hooked her by the elbow, pulled her back into an empty stall, where they'd piled the fresh straw. "Stopping you from doing something foolish."

Her smile dimmed. "I don't know what you're talking about."

"You're going to deny that you're going down to see TJ? That last Friday you let him bring you home at three a.m.?"

"Were you watching me out your window?"

Yes. But he had the brains not to let that issue from his mouth. "He's trouble, Dottie, and a gal like you is going to get hurt—"

"A gal like me?" She yanked her arm away from him. "What kind of gal is that?"

A sweet gal. A gal who, despite her bobbed hair and firecracker spirit, needed to stay in Frost. A gal who made him feel smart, and handsome. Or, at least, once had. "A small-town gal."

But those hadn't been the right words. She put her hands on his chest, pushed him away. "I'm not a small-town gal!"

"You are—and I'm a small-town guy. And we belong together. We've always belonged together."

And then—then his desperation turned him into a man he didn't recognize. A man who pushed her back into the straw and kissed her. And not a tentative, sweet kiss like so many he'd stolen before. No, this one bared his heart.

He didn't know if she kissed him back—maybe she had, but certainly by the time he raised his head, met her eyes, he'd wounded something between them.

She was breathing hard, a strange emotion in her eyes. He didn't want to think it might be fear.

"Don't leave Frost," he'd said, his heart right in the middle of his throat, choking off his voice as he leaned away from her. He swallowed it down, cupped her face with his work-roughened hand. "Marry me, Dottie. I'm the one you want."

His world stopped then, right there, in that moment. In her intake of breath, the way her gaze roamed his face. Please.

Then she shook her head, wriggling away from him.

He'd wanted to pin her there, to hold her fast until she agreed with him, but for all his desperation, he couldn't be that guy.

He didn't want to *make* Dorothy Wilson love him. Or maybe he just didn't know how. He gritted his teeth, feeling the heat stoke in his chest, clog his throat as she dusted off her pretty yellow dress. As she backed away from him toward the truck, leaving him there in the stall.

"Stay away from me, Gordy Lindholm. Just, stay away."

He closed his eyes against the image of her leaving him. She returned six months later, with a new name and expecting Nelson.

So, he'd stayed away.

"I'm not good with words," Gordy finally said to Jake.

"That's apparent. You and Dottie are constantly barking at each other."

"I don't bark."

"You're an old hound dog, Gordy. But even the old hounds can win a gal with a little wooing."

"I don't woo."

"That could be your problem. She's not your wife, and if you keep on barking at her, she never will be. Woo the woman. Say kind things to her."

"She doesn't want me to be kind to her."

"What kind of malarkey is that? Every woman wants kindness. Besides, it's only for a day. We're trapped here. What else do you have to do?"

A gust of wind shook the house and the flames flickered.

"Are you going to tell Violet the truth?"

Jake sighed, leaned his head back. "Just for a day, can't I be the hero?"

Gordy pressed his hand on the boy's head, hating how the kid shivered.

Yeah, maybe.

Maybe today they'd all be people they weren't.

* * * * *

Something about Jake seemed so familiar. Violet knew she'd never met him before, but being with him felt so…easy.

Like she'd known him for years.

Her hand still tingled where he'd touched it—she felt like she had when she was thirteen, that day when Robbie Larson had told her she was the prettiest girl in school. Not that Jake had said as much, but…

He needs a woman's touch.

Violet caught her hand, held it to herself. When he'd looked at her, she felt beautiful. He didn't have to say it.

But why did he lie about being the rescuer in Alex's story? Of course he'd rescued Alex—Jake was just that type.

"Can you hand me those potatoes," Dottie said from the stove. Violet had made her way to the kitchen, where Dottie stood opening a can of meat. She dumped it into the soup, juice and all.

Violet lifted a colander with peeled, cut potatoes from the sink, handing them to Dottie.

"What are you making?"

"Kitchen cabinet soup. I found some canned cabbage and a jar of carrots and a can of pork. I hope it's not too old. I should have picked up that hen. How's Arnie?"

"Arnie?"

"I think that boy is Arnie Shiller."

"I know that name. He's on the overdue list for a Flash Gordon Little Big Book." She leaned against the counter. Funny, her ankle had stopped throbbing. "Jake needs a thermometer."

"What is he, a doctor?"

"I don't think so. He just…well, I think he rescued Alex a long time ago from drowning."

"He's a real hero, isn't he? I mean, leaving out my tree, of course, he doctors up your knee and then makes us all breakfast. Now he's saving that little boy. Are you sure you want to keep grieving for Alex?"

Dottie's question caught Violet's breath. "Alex deserves to be grieved. But yes, Jake…he seems like the real deal. And I don't think he knows about my service in the WAACs." She lowered her voice. "I'd like to keep it that way."

Dottie glanced at her. "What on earth for? Serving your country is something to be proud of."

"Not according to my mother and most of the fellas I've met."

"Pshaw."

"I just want him to see me as a regular lady, not with grease on my face."

"I would think you'd want him to see you as a lady, even with grease on your face."

"Please, Dottie? Just for today. Don't tell him, okay?"

Dottie sighed. "I don't like charades, but...perhaps we'd all like a fresh start."

Violet looked more closely at her. Dottie's eyes seemed reddened. Had she been...crying?

"Dottie, are you all—"

"I'm fine." She took the colander from Violet's hands, dropped the potatoes into the pot one by one. "I just hope this is enough. Guests, I never planned for guests."

"I'm sorry. I shouldn't have come over hoping to get the star."

"You can have the star, Violet." Dottie dropped the colander in the sink. "You can have it and keep it. I'll never hang it again anyway." She turned away, ran water into the sink.

Oh, Dottie... Outside, the snow blew against the window, piling on the windowpane. It seemed lighter outside, as if the sun managed to slice through the storm, although it still appeared as twilight out. Still, the snow whitened the world, covered it with a fresh grace.

They'd have a white Christmas after all.

The thought stilled her. "Tomorrow is Christmas Eve."

"Indeed," Dottie said, but her voice sounded tight, stilted.

"Are you sure you're okay?"

Dottie nodded, but her shoulders betrayed her. Violet didn't move. "I just don't understand why he's still here."

"Who—Jake?"

"Gordy."

"He's stranded—"

"No, I mean, why does he persist in driving me to my last nerve?" She turned, pressing a towel to her face. She shook her head. "He just can't help but torment me. Everything, from filling the wood bin to his little gifts of milk on the doorstep. He's always hovering. And then…"

She looked at Violet, pressed her hand to her lips. Whispered. "He kissed me."

Violet stared at her, nonplussed. What? "Mr. Lindholm?"

"No, Santa Claus. Yes, Mr. Lindholm. He kissed me, right out there in the snow. Like we were teenagers."

Perhaps they were. Violet had to hide a smile. "Clearly he cares about you. He even said so."

"He's just trying to remind me of my mistakes."

Violet frowned. "Dottie, don't be silly."

"It's true." Dottie picked up a long wooden spoon. "He knows I wished I'd said yes that day he proposed."

"He proposed to you?"

"Twenty-six years ago."

"Why didn't you say yes?" Gordy had proposed? Violet *knew* something simmered between them.

Dottie's mouth pursed into a tight knot. "I was a stubborn, silly girl. I wanted him to tell me he loved me." She shook out some dried herb from a jar above the stove, added it to the soup. "TJ told me he loved me the first day he met me. Why would it take Gordy over twenty years?"

"Dottie! He says he loves you every time he fills your wood bin."

"No. He says, *see what you could have had.*" She faced Violet. "And I could have. I—I came home, and I—I could have apologized. But he never came over, and…I was ashamed."

"For over twenty years you've been ashamed? Of Nelson?"

Dottie shook her head. "No, never of Nelson. Nelson made me believe that God had forgiven me. That He still loved me despite my impulsiveness." She gave a despairing laugh. "Apparently, I was wrong about that too."

"Dottie—"

"You know, there was a time when I thought Gordy had forgiven me." She went to the window, stared out, as if seeing something beyond the billowing snow. "He and Nelson…they had something special. Nelson started helping Gordy on the farm when he was about seven, I guess. I didn't stop him—my father had passed, and I thought it would be good for Nelson. Gordy, after all, was a good man. And they started hunting together. Gordy taught him how to shoot, and we had venison every year. I started to think—to hope—that Nelson might help us find a way back. I remember one day as he headed out, I suggested that Gordy could come in for dinner that night. I even…I even went outside to greet them. I stood on the step and waved."

She lifted her hand, as if back in time. "Gordon just stood there, on the edge of the property, beyond the stone wall."

"He didn't come in."

"Not once." Dottie turned around, folding her arms across her chest. "Until last night, of course."

"So you two have never spoken of your loss."

"Our loss?"

"Nelson. If Gordy loved him like a father, then he's grieving—"

"He wasn't Nelson's father."

"But..." Violet turned her voice to low. "Don't you think he wanted to be?"

Dottie looked away, but a muscle pulsed in her jaw.

"He's here now. Maybe—maybe God is giving you another chance to make things right between you two."

Dottie held up a finger, her eyes sharp. "Don't you talk to me of God and second chances. God took my son, and I deserved it. There are no chances left for me."

Violet stilled, Dottie's words landing in the back of her throat, scraping it raw. She found her voice, kept it gentle. "Dottie, the point of Christmas is second chances for all mankind."

"I don't celebrate Christmas anymore." She shook her head. "There's nothing left in it for me."

"Except, of course, Jesus."

Dottie turned away. "You'll find the thermometer in the bathroom cabinet."

"We're trapped here for a reason. What was it we prayed last night? 'Come, Lord Jesus, be our guest'? Isn't He here with us?"

Dottie stared out the window. "I hope not. He's done enough already. He's had His say in my life."

"I don't think God is ever done speaking into our lives. Even when we don't want to hear it. Even when our hearts are cold."

"Violet!" Jake's voice rose from the next room, ringing of urgency. "Dottie!"

Gordy appeared at the door. "The kid is waking up."

* * * * *

Arnie's wails poured through Dottie, clear to her bones, settling there with a hot ache as she watched him struggle in Jake's embrace.

His moaning seemed to hold the rest of them captive. Gordy looked stricken, his eyes wide, as if he'd never seen suffering.

"What's wrong with him?" Violet said, her arms curled around herself.

"Now that he's warming, the blood is flowing into his extremities, and it hurts." Jake sat up, holding the boy against himself. "This is what happens when you're cold too long. Warming up is excruciating."

Arnie did appear warmer, his ghostly gray cheeks now a shade of pink.

Jake clamped his arms tight around the boy, holding him as he thrashed.

"Oh, for Pete's sake, hand him to me." More an impulse than a desire, Dottie sat down on the sofa and reached for the boy.

Jake pushed Arnie onto her lap. He wasn't a large child; perhaps if he'd been husky, he might not have suffered so. Dottie felt his bones through the blanket as he shook. His crying fell to whimpers then back to wailing.

But he curled against her, and she held on. "Shh."

Gordy turned back to the fire, added a log, then just stayed crouched, staring at the flames.

"Is he going to be okay?" he finally said to Jake.

Jake had risen, grabbed his shirt. "I don't know." He crouched, reached for the boy's white toes. "They don't look frostbitten." He met Dottie's eyes. "Where do I find some socks?"

She spoke without thinking. "Upstairs, in Nelson's room, top drawer."

He ran up the stairs as Gordy glanced at her. She gave him a look. "What am I to do—let the boy freeze?"

But instead of barking back at her, his face softened. "No."

She tucked her head against Arnie's, whispering, her tone warm. "It's going to be okay. Once, when my boy Nelson was about six, he went ice skating. When he came in, his feet were nearly ice blocks. We thawed them in the tub and he cried for an hour. But then it was over, and he was warm again, good as new."

She didn't look up as she spoke. But she wondered if Gordy heard her, remembering those days when he'd watch them skating on the pond, back before the marsh overtook it.

"I'll get tea for him," Violet said.

"Make sure it's not too hot," Gordy said. And then, to Dottie's surprise, he pulled up a chair across from her and took the little boy's toes in his big hands.

This could have been their grandson. The thought pulsed inside her. They might have had more children, a daughter, perhaps. Well, no, probably Arnie was too old, but the thought wouldn't leave her.

This could have been their life.

Maybe God is giving you another chance to make things right between you and Gordy.

She glanced up, but Violet hadn't yet returned.

Gordy sat so close, his expression tight against Arnie's whimpering. He smelled of the smoky fire, had rolled up his sleeves past his elbows to reveal his amazing farmer's forearms.

She had been in those arms, and pushed him away.

Arnie continued to squirm, almost falling off Dottie's lap.

"Let me take him," Gordy said, moving to sit beside her, as if she would simply acquiesce and hand the boy to him.

Dottie tightened her grip, almost an instinctive move. But the tenderness on Gordy's face as he looked at the boy loosed her hold. Maybe Arnie did need someone stronger than her to hold him.

"Be careful," she said as she released Arnie into Gordy's arms. He held the boy as Dottie tucked the blankets around him.

Arnie immediately curled into Gordy's chest as Gordy wrapped his strong arms around him.

Dottie had to turn away, focus for a moment on the flames in the hearth.

"I found the socks." Jake returned down the stairs and handed them to Dottie. She crunched them in her hands a moment, warming them before working them onto Arnie's feet.

His cries had subsided to a persistent moan. She cupped his cold cheek. "It's going to be okay, Arnie."

He chose then to open his eyes. And for a second, just stared at her. She tried a smile, but it seemed too late because, gaze still glued to hers, he pushed away from her, kicking at her. "No! No!"

"Arnie, you're safe." Gordy's voice cut through the boy's panic. He leaned down, guiding the boy's gaze to his own. "You made it to the barn. You were very brave."

Dottie's eyes filmed.

Arnie looked up at Gordy. "I wanna go home."

She expected some snippy remark, even under his breath, from Gordy, but he surprised her again by softening his voice into something kind, even fatherly.

"I know. But the storm is too bad. I promise, we'll take good care of you. You're at your storm house."

She stared at the fire again, blinking against the heat.

"No—I have to go home," Arnie said.

"You're going to be okay, Arnie. It'll stop hurting when you get warm. Look, Mrs. Morgan's here. You remember her from the library, don't you?"

Arnie's eyes widened. Dottie turned back and offered a smile.

"And there's Miss Hart—"

Dottie turned, and Violet had entered, carrying the tea. She, too, grinned at Arnie.

Arnie turned and buried his face once again in Gordy's chest.

Dottie had the strange urge to do the same thing. In fact, she might know exactly how this little boy felt.

Yes, Jake's prediction of the pain getting worse before it stopped seemed accurate. Because, as Jake stood back, by the fire, and Violet sank down in a chair, holding the tepid tea, Gordy tucked the child under his chin and began to sing.

It came out husky and even roughened, not so much a lullaby as something he might sing to his cows.

"I'll have a blue Christmas...without you."

And wouldn't you know it, he looked up at her, meeting her eyes. "I'll be so blue, just thinking about you..."

Yes, this was really going to hurt.

CHAPTER EIGHT

Jake had to give Dottie and Gordy credit for being able to handle Arnie's cries without flinching.

He, for one, just wanted to run from the house at top speed. How he hated the crying.

It only made him feel helpless. How he hated helpless.

He'd prayed, however. That, he could still do.

Dottie and Gordy had worked together, slowly warming Arnie's extremities, first with tepid water, then adding warmer water as his body thawed. At least he could move his toes now.

The child would live.

But, with the wind swirling the snow outside, Jake couldn't tell if it had stopped snowing, or if it might just be the wind stirring to frenzy—they wouldn't be breaking free anytime soon.

And deep inside, Jake didn't want to leave. Not yet.

No, for one day he'd like to live in this icy wonderland where Violet looked at him like he might be more than he knew he was.

Gordy's words had tolled in his head all afternoon, but he pushed them away. He couldn't tell her the truth. Not yet.

He'd worked it out in his mind for the better part of four years, but had lost it the moment she said, *I still think you're a hero.*

Yeah, a hero who had lied to her, led her on.

"It's your move, Jake."

Violet had found a wooden Aggravation board and some marbles, and she had just whittled his arsenal down to one, with three in her home base.

"I'm a little afraid," he said, not lying in the least.

"Chicken."

He smiled and rolled the die. It clattered on the board and he advanced his marble four spaces. He needed a one or a six to rescue a new marble from base.

Violet scooped up the die. "Poor kid. I remember him now. His mother comes into the library sometimes to pick him up after school. She works at the flour mill. I think his dad died in the war." She advanced her marble three spaces. "Christmas hasn't been the same since my father died. It seems like I'm always waiting for him to return home, that at anytime, he'll walk through the door with a giant tree."

He rolled again, nearing home with a count of five. At least one of his marbles would be safe from the Great Aggravator.

"I'm sorry about your father, Violet."

"It's been three years. And at least I had a childhood with him. It would be terrible to be Arnie's age. If it's just he and his mother, then Christmas must be pretty quiet."

"I had a few quiet Christmases when I was young—just me and my parents. I remember one year, my father was treating patients with influenza, and my mother wouldn't put up a tree. So, Christmas went by without even a present."

He didn't add that it was the year his brother died, of that very same influenza.

She looked up at him, holding the die. "Alex told me about this Christmas where he snuck a bag of oranges from the house-keeper's pantry and gave them to this little boy who lived with him—a child of one of the servants. They sat in a closet and ate the entire bag." She tossed the die on the table. "He said what he missed most in the military was oranges."

Jake watched her move, his breath caught in his chest.

He'd given Alex those oranges.

More than that, Alex had been the servant boy, the son of their Russian housekeeper. The cold edge of horror sank deeper. Had Alex...stolen his life? His identity, his past?

Maybe she just had the story mixed up. He picked up the die and shook it. A three. Apparently he was stuck here.

"Christmas Eve is tomorrow." She rolled again and moved her fourth marble into home. "Sorry. Want to play again?"

"I'm too bruised, I don't think I can take it." He grinned at her as he collected the marbles. "Why is Dottie's house so...there's not one decoration up. Not a hint of Christmas cheer."

Violet tucked her hair behind her ears, slid her folded hands between her knees. "She hasn't decorated for Christmas since her son died."

"Is that him, holding the football in that picture?" He pointed to a framed shot on the piano.

"Yep. Nelson T. Morgan. Everyone loved him, he didn't have an enemy in town." She got up, picked up the picture. "I even had a crush on him, although he was a couple years younger than me."

"Where was he stationed?"

"He was a sniper with the 4th Infantry."

"That was Alex's division."

She nodded. "I saw Nelson when he came through Fort Meade. Even introduced him to Alex at the canteen. I hope they became friends."

Gordy had wrapped Arnie in a blanket after his ordeal in the kitchen and now brought him to sit before the fire. Arnie closed his eyes, curling against the man.

Gordy looked up and met Jake's gaze with a raised eyebrow, his eyes darting to Violet.

Jake turned away from him. "I have an idea. Where do you think Dottie keeps her Christmas decorations?"

"I don't know. The attic?"

"This house needs some cheer." Jake leaned close to her, cutting his voice low. "And that child needs a Christmas. If we don't get out of here tomorrow, there'll be no Santa coming down the chimney, no stockings, no tree, no oranges. Just a bunch of crabby grown-ups—"

"Speak for yourself."

He grinned. "Okay, three crabby grown-ups and one beautiful woman."

Violet held up a hand. "You're right. He...we all need some Christmas cheer." She glanced toward the kitchen, as if she included Dottie in that assessment. "C'mon."

She stood up then gestured with her head for him to follow her. "I think I know where the attic stairs are."

"Don't move so fast there, champ." He watched her as she settled weight on her foot, tucked his hand under her elbow.

"It's really much better." She glanced at him, a smile tugging up her face. "All that doctoring."

Oh. Well.

Dottie was in the kitchen, humming something as they moved past the door then up the stairs. The steps creaked, but Gordy didn't betray them. Violet shuffled down the hallway, toward her bedroom. "I saw a door in the ceiling." A cord hung down from it, and Jake snagged it, drawing it down. A stairway unfolded onto the floor.

The cool breath of the attic sifted down into the hallway.

"We need our jackets," he said.

"We'll only be up there a minute."

Dust mites. Cold. A lethal combination for a man with only one lung, and that one prone to infection. He willed his breathing steady as he climbed up behind her, making sure she didn't fall. Her ankle must be improving. And, so far, despite the stress of the day, he'd managed not one moment of labored breathing.

This attic, however, might just suffocate him. Dust lay on the boxes, the room frigid despite the gray batting stuffed in the rafters, the only daylight from the floor below.

"It's hard to see up here without the electricity."

Boxes, most of them marked, filled the room. Violet had found one and opened it. "Lights, and this one is Christmas bulbs."

Jake opened one, holding his breath, and pulled out table linens, a tree skirt, and a stocking, the name "Nelson" embroidered at the top.

"I wish we had electricity," Violet said.

"Gordy dragged in an old generator from the garage, but he gave up on it." Although, Violet might be able to fix it, couldn't she? Jake glanced at her, but she betrayed nothing of curiosity about the project.

"How about we just bring down the advent candles."

"No." He got up, moved over to what he thought— "It's a crank Victrola." He ran his hands over the sides, started to crank it, felt the tabletop turn. "What we need is music. I'll bet Dottie has something cheery."

Violet had joined him. "Do you think it still works?"

"Let's try it." He hoisted it up. "Think I can hand it down to you?"

She nodded and hiked down the steps, reaching up to take it. He placed it into her hands and followed her down.

In the fading daylight, the antique Victrola seemed in good shape. Dusty, yes, but with the gramophone in place and the needle still intact. He grinned at her and brought it downstairs.

Dottie came out of the kitchen and froze. "Where did you get that?"

"In the attic. We need some Christmas cheer."

She drew in a breath but, miraculously, didn't argue. He set the Victrola on a table in the parlor. "Do you have any records?"

"They're in the bookcase."

As Jake dusted off the Victrola, Violet opened the bottom of the bookcase and pulled out a stack of records. "You have Glenn Miller—'Chattanooga Choo Choo' and 'At Last.'"

"I also have Dinah Shore, and that new crooner, Frank Sinatra. Nelson left his records with me for safekeeping."

Jake didn't have to look at her to see the expression on Dottie's face. He saw it reflected in Violet's eyes.

Grief left its handprints everywhere he looked.

"Let's play one," Dottie said, suddenly, almost too brightly. She walked over to Violet and took the stack from her hands. "How about something...cheerful. Here's the Andrews Sisters, 'Don't Sit Under the Apple Tree.'"

Her eyes were shiny as she handed the record to Jake. He took it and she walked past him without another word as he unsheathed it and put it on the Victrola, then cranked the handle and set down the needle.

He watched as Dottie sat opposite Gordy on the velvet sofa, her hands folded in her lap. She glanced at Gordy like she might be in grade school.

Gordy didn't notice, apparently. "So, dance with her already," he barked at Jake.

Dance. Jake glanced at Violet. She'd stood up, but peered at the floor, as if they might be thirteen. What was it about music that seemed to paralyze some people? Well, dancing he could do. He got up and extended his hand to Violet. "I'd like to ask you for this dance, but I'm worried about your ankle."

She stilled. "My ankle is fine. But...I don't know how."

Out of her periphery, he saw Dottie look up at her.

"I never attended any of the dances in town."

He took her hand. "I'm a great lead. Trust me." He pulled her into his arms. "It's just like walking. Step, two, three, rest..." He showed her the footwork then counted it out.

She kicked him in the shin. "Sorry."

"Your first step is back. Really, trust me."

She made a face. "I—I can't."

"Sure you can. Listen—close your eyes. Feel my hand in yours, and on your back. I'll move you."

She closed her eyes. "Don't let me run into anything."

"Please." He counted again, more of a whisper, then moved her forward, over, then back, in a foxtrot square.

"Alex told me once that he learned to dance from his mother. His parents would have grand parties, and he'd sit on the top of the stairs, mesmerized by the food, the music, the lights. He said his favorite part was watching his parents waltz. His mother would close her eyes, and he wanted to be able to lead like his father did." She opened her eyes, and he steeled himself against the expression that wanted to crest over him. "I think there was a latent romantic inside Alex."

He studied her face, looking for tease, but found none. His heart hammered. "When did he tell you this?"

"In one of his letters. I can't remember. He told me a lot about his childhood—how his brother died when he was seven, and how it destroyed him. How he made friends with the Russian house-keeper's son and taught him to read. How the housekeeper died of TB, and he wished he could have helped her, maybe even become a doctor. He was a good man."

A good man. Jake could hardly breathe, a vise circling his chest. "Uh…I…"

"Are you okay?"

He stumbled then, lurched forward, and she stepped back, falling. Her hand flared out, brushed a milk glass lamp, and it flew off the table, crashing to the ground.

"Oh!" Violet said.

He let her go. Stared at the curls of white glass on the floor. "Dottie, I'm so sorry."

"It's my fault," Violet said, bending to pick them up. "I told you I couldn't dance." She got up, brushing past him, stalking toward the kitchen.

Jake stood there in the middle of the room, feeling the idiot as Dottie followed her out.

He'd had his life stolen from him by the housekeeper's son.

"Are you okay, Jake?" Gordy said from across the room. Jake glanced at the door. Shook his head.

"I—I can't believe it. Alex stole my life." He didn't really expect Gordy to understand. He stepped closer, cut his voice low. "All those things Alex told Violet—they happened to me. He was the Russian housekeeper's son. I was the one who shared my oranges, I was the one who taught him to read."

"You were the one whose brother died." Gordy's eyes widened. "Oh."

"Yes, exactly. So, how am I supposed to tell her that everything Alex wrote to her are lies?"

"Not to mention the other lie you're carrying around."

"Shh!"

Gordy groaned, his hand on Arnie's head. The boy had sunk into slumber, his lips askew on Gordy's chest.

Jake sank down on the sofa opposite Gordy. "It's sounds desperate, and petty. What would I say? 'Alex is me. He took my identity.' Right." He closed his eyes, leaned his head back against the sofa.

He got it. Really, he did. Alex, a poor immigrant's son, would leap to create a new identity. Jake almost didn't blame him for the ruse.

It almost exonerated him of his own guilt.

Almost.

* * * * *

Violet had told him she couldn't dance. She stood at the window, her fingertips pressed against her eyes. What did he expect, Judy Garland?

Oh, she'd been a fool to think that she could pull off dainty and beautiful. And now Dottie's beautiful lamp lay in shards on the floor.

Violet just wanted to keep running, straight out into the storm, lose herself in the whiteout.

"Violet?"

She heard the voice and didn't turn, just opened the pantry door, searching for the broom. Finding it, she pulled it out, but Dottie put her hand on it, stopping her. She expected the librarian's tone.

"It's okay, it's just a lamp."

"First your tree, now the lamp."

"There's no electricity anyway. And the tree was dying." Dottie smiled at her, an expression of kindness so rare it caught Violet's breath and held her fast.

She looked away, past her, feeling a tear tickle down her cheek. From the next room, the music died. "I can't dance."

"No, you can't."

She glanced at Dottie, who wore a strange look. "I have to apologize to you, Violet. You probably don't remember the last Christmas ball we had, but Nelson was eighteen and about to ship off to war. I was there—and you were there. Sitting in a chair, watching everyone dance. Nelson asked you to dance…and you turned him down. I thought, how can she turn my boy down when he's going off to war?"

"I didn't want to embarrass him."

Dottie patted her cheek. "I forgive you for not dancing with my boy."

"I would have, if I had known—"

"He had plenty of other girls to dance with. I just know he thought you were pretty."

Violet didn't know where to begin to sort out Dottie's words. Nelson Morgan had thought her pretty. She attempted a smile, but she knew it emerged pitiful.

She looked past Dottie, to the owl clock hanging on the wall. A wind-up model, it ticked away the minutes. Darkness would be falling soon. "My mother hated the fact that I didn't attend the town dances. She would send my brothers into town, and I'd be out there in the barn, helping my father with the tractor or the baler or some other piece of machinery. She'd storm out of the house and scold him for turning me into a boy."

She drew in a breath, her memory on her mother, silhouetted by the fiery sunset bleeding out behind her, and on her father's soft reply. *"Violet's more useful to me than all my boys put together."*

Violet ran her thumb under her eye. "I guess she was right. I am a boy."

"Oh, for Pete's sake, Violet, you're not a boy. Far from it." Dottie turned Violet around to see her reflection in the window. "I see a beautiful young lady who is trapped in this house with a man who likes her enough to ask her to dance."

"Trapped is the operative word here." Violet turned back around. "He's just being kind because he's Alex's friend. If he knew I served in the military, that I knew the inside of my father's Plymouth better than he did, he—"

"Why should you be ashamed of what you're good at? Why are you trying so hard to hide your spark?"

"Because I don't want to end up..." She looked away.

Dottie drew in a breath. "Like me. Like the widow librarian, alone at Christmas."

Violet looked at the floor. "I'm sorry, Dottie."

Dottie shook her head. "Nope, you're right. But what you don't know is that I liked my life, very much. Sure, there were a few holes..." She drew in a breath. "But I had made my choices, and because of Nelson, I was glad for them." She tucked her hand under Violet's chin and raised it to meet her eyes. "You did a brave thing for your country. You should be proud of that. It doesn't make you less beautiful or less of a woman because you did what you felt was right and honorable."

"Alex told me once that I looked beautiful with grease on my face."

"I'm sure Alex was right. But Alex isn't here, is he?"

Violet made a face. "I'm talking about him too much, aren't I?"

Dottie nodded.

"It's just that Jake is so easy to talk to. There's something about him that makes me feel like I know him. And, it's so strange—I actually had this crazy hope that someday Alex and I would dance together. I might have even told him that, once.

And, I invited him to the Frost ball this year." She shook her head then frowned. "You don't think Alex told Jake about that, do you?"

"What kind of man would Alex be if he told Jake your secrets?" Dottie shook her head. "I'm sure it's simply providence." She took Violet's hand, and Violet saw something in her eyes—distant, yet familiar.

A younger version of Dottie, back when the storyteller believed in happy endings. "What was it that you told me? That Christmas hadn't given up on me? Maybe it hasn't given up on any of us." She squeezed Violet's hand. "Give me that broom. And go find some candles. It's getting dark outside."

* * * * *

The nostalgia of the candlelit parlor had gone straight to Gordy's head, as if some other hazy past that he hadn't lived crept forward to lasso him, drag him back to a snowy winter night. In that past, Nelson was curled up against him, Dottie crocheting on the sofa. The fire crackled in the hearth, and outside the blizzard tremored the house.

Sometimes when Gordy sat at his house, watching Dottie's light, he dreamed of this image—Nelson between them, a silence that felt comforting and not at all stiff.

Gordy's leg had long ago fallen asleep where Arnie braced his head on it. The boy had finally stopped shivering, and now a fine line of sweat glistened on his brow. They'd shut off the doors to the rest of the house, and the room had cooked to a toasty warm. He'd have to stay awake and tend the fire. Now, Jake sat near it, poking the blaze.

Poor guy had too many lies piling up against him to sit still, frustration playing over his face.

If he'd been Jake, Gordy would have found a soft mound of hay in the barn to wait out the storm.

Arnie shuddered in his sleep, as if he might be dreaming.

"He had a rough day," Dottie said, looking up from her crocheting.

"I still can't believe he found the barn in that storm."

"His mother must be frantic."

He ran his hand over the boy's hair. "I heard him mumbling in his sleep. I think he said something about Flash Gordon."

Dottie shook her head, gave a chuckle.

"You're thinking about *Jack Armstrong, All American Boy*, aren't you?"

She met his eyes, an enigmatic look on her face. *Yes, Dottie, I knew him too.* Finally, she nodded. "Nelson would sing the theme song when he did his chores."

"Didn't he send away for wings?"

"Oh, those were from Captain Hawks Sky Patrol. For three box tops from Post Bran Flakes, he could earn gold wings. He dog-eared the pilot's manual."

"Didn't he get a model airplane kit too?"

"Yes. Thirteen more box tops for the balsa wood model kit of a Pan American Airways China Clipper. It's all he ate for an entire summer—bran flakes."

"He had quite the imagination. I'd find him over at my house, hiding out from bandits or German soldiers or some other villains."

"It was those shows—*The FBI in Peace and War, Edgar Bergen and Charlie McCarthy, Fibber McGee and Molly*—they put adventure into his head."

He gave her a look. "Dottie. Hardly. *You* put adventure into his head. You filled his life with stories—not just from books, but the ones you told him about his grandfather. And even your travels. And, he was the son of the woman who couldn't wait to leave Frost and see the world."

She stilled, drew in a breath. "Are you saying his desire to go to war is my fault?"

Oh no, he hadn't meant it as an insult, or even to tear open old wounds. He kept his voice calm despite the panic that wanted to choke him. "No, of course not."

"I'm not the one who taught him how to shoot, or let him listen to those bloodthirsty Joe Lewis fights—"

"Dottie, please, that's not what I meant."

Her jaw tightened, and she looked away from him, back to her crocheting. She might stab herself if she didn't slow down.

Gordy watched the fire flickering, the silence turning to fingers that clawed into his chest and squeezed. Jake glanced at him from the corner of his eyes.

Certainly Dottie would have to forgive him sometime, right?

On his lap, Arnie sighed then rolled over. Probably Gordy should restock the woodbin for the night.

He glanced at Dottie again. She wouldn't look at him.

"I just meant that it takes a hero to raise one," he finally said. Then he got up, setting Arnie on the sofa. "C'mon, Jake. We need to fetch more wood."

Jake followed him out to the back room. Without the heat from the house, ice filmed the inside of the windows, snow seeping under the sill of the door. The little room shook with the fury of the wind.

They'd used most of the stack he'd hauled in this morning, and they wouldn't survive on what remained.

"Bundle up," he said, tossing Jake a muffler. Jake wound it around his head, grabbed an old hat from the shelf. Gordy recognized it as Nelson's wool work hat but didn't say anything.

Pulling on a pair of gloves and his boots, he glanced at Jake. "Stay right behind me."

"I'm not a child."

Gordy held up a hand, as if in surrender. "I don't want to blow away either. Besides, it's dark out there."

Although, when he wrenched open the door, the force of the wind nearly careened him back into Jake. "There are exactly twenty-four steps to the barn!" he hollered as he pulled up his collar and dove out into the blizzard.

The night soaked into his eyes, the snow burning them, the wind stealing his breath. He fought for each step, calculating the distance. Why hadn't he run a guide wire to her house from the barn? He should have. Now, with the wrong steps, they could veer wide of the barn, end up in a field, frozen stiff.

The wind chapped his skin, piled snow into his collar. Gordy couldn't tell if it was still snowing or just blowing. At any rate, the wrath of the wind stirred up the drifts, like waves against the house, the barn. They might have to dig their way out in the morning.

He could barely make out Jake when he glanced behind him.

Good thing the man ran smack into him when they reached the barn.

Gordy opened the door and made to reach for the light when he remembered the electricity had gone out. Jake shuffled in behind him, breathing funny, as Gordy went in search of a lantern. He knew this barn nearly as well as his own, and found it in the utility room. Taking off his glove, he searched for the little box of matches and lit one.

The fire illuminated the lantern, and he lit the wick then turned it up.

Jake was standing by the doorway, doing his funny breathing. "You okay?"

He shook his head and pulled out one of those asthma cigarettes, his hands shaking as he stuck it between his lips, fumbling in his pockets.

Gordy handed him the matches.

Jake lit it, leaning against the door, eyes closed, drawing the smoke in.

Gordy took the lantern, went over to check on Ollie. The farm horse seemed to be surviving the storm, although his water had a sheen of ice over it. Gordy chipped it out then added grain to the feeder.

Jake had come up to join him, folding his arms over the top of the stall door.

"Better?"

"I used to have a horse. My father bought it for me, thought it would be good for me to learn to ride. An Arabian—beautiful animal. I was about nine years old."

Gordy threw a blanket over the horse, buckling it under its girth.

"He threw me and I broke my arm, and my mother made him sell it."

"That's part of learning to ride."

"I know. But my mother was overprotective after my brother died. No one could blame her."

Gordy backed out of the stall, closed the door.

Jake followed him to the woodpile.

"I saw the scar. Is that from the war?"

"Yeah. I picked up some shrapnel and then my lung collapsed. It only made things worse when I picked up pneumonia. I lay there in the hospital, unable to breathe, feeling as if a horse lay on my chest, day after day, listening to the moaning around me. It dug into my soul. Now, I stand near a draft, it nearly takes me out for a week. These seem to help keep my lungs clear."

"They ship you home?"

"Not for that." He threw down the cigarette, ground it into the soil of the barn. "No, I came home because…I lost myself out there." He stared at the crushed cigarette.

Gordy read his face, saw in it something he'd always worried about for Nelson. That the boy would return broken in his head, his heart. In his spirit. "Battle fatigue is nothing to be ashamed of. I saw it happen to the best of soldiers." He began to load Jake up with logs.

"You served?"

"The great war, just one year. I didn't see any action, but I knew some of the guys in town who did. They came back different."

There was a cord of long-burning oak on the bottom, and he wriggled some logs out.

"I was ashamed of myself." Jake grunted as Gordy added another log.

"Your friend Alex didn't seem to be ashamed of you, or why would he pretend to be you?"

"I'm sure he left out that part."

"But you really don't know how much Alex told her."

"How's it going to sound? My telling her that everything Alex told her was really about me? That he wasn't a hero. If I were her, I wouldn't know who to believe."

"Then don't tell her anything." Gordy loaded the last of the logs in his arm. He'd need one hand free for the lantern. They'd have to come back for another load. "The way the storm is blowing out there, we just may be trapped here another day. The way I figure it, you have a day to show her who you really are. Forget about Alex. Be Jake."

"I thought you said I needed to tell her the truth?"

"That is the truth. Don't tell her, show her. She'll figure out the real you."

Jake shook his head. "What if I haven't figured out who the real me is yet?"

Gordy stared at him. Then he grabbed the lantern and kicked open the door. "One step at a time. Stay behind me and don't lose sight of the light."

* * * * *

When last we checked in with our intrepid interplanetary hero, Flash Gordon, internationally renowned American athlete, he was on his way to rescue his beautiful sweetheart Dale Arden when he and his cohort, scientist Dr. Zarkov, crashed on the planet Mongo. Fleeing the terrible Emperor Ming the Merciless, he met up with Thun, Prince of the Lionmen, who joined the band of rescuers to journey through the terrible icy land of Frigia. With the winds thrashing him, he managed to find the snow cave and hide inside while the terrible ice bear of Frigia stalked him. Unknowingly, he'd stumbled into the lair of the hated ice-queen, Fria, who took him captive.

Enduring excruciating torture at the hands of the Hawkmen, Flash resisted their attempts to break him, to surrender the location of his companions.

Now, he lay, resting in the dungeons of Fria, the lava fires of the mountain of Blizzaro raging deep within. Caught within his bounds, he dreamed of Dale, and his Doctor Zarkov.

They'd pushed Arnie's cold feet into ice water, and a thousand knives serrated his flesh. He hated the whimpers that emerged from him, and the way he'd cried into the big man's chest.

Flash, I am here to save you!

Hark, it was the voice of Princess Aura, drifting down some vast corridor. Deeply in love with Flash, the Princess vowed to keep him in her clutches.

Suddenly, Prince Thun appeared, working at his bonds.

Flash, art thou all right?

Flash is thrilled to see his Lionman friend. *I am wounded, but must find my beloved Dale. Hurry.*

You are almost freed, Flash. Let me untie thy bonds.

Flash pushes himself to his feet, despite his wounds, feeling new strength.

In his mind, Arnie saw himself springing away from the hands that held him, venturing back out into the cold. Run!

Thun turns around at the sound of soldiers' feet. *Hark, I hear Queen Fria's guard. Run, Flash! You must run.*

Flash sprints down the corridors of the great halls, but each leads to an icy dead end. Turning, he faces his captors, the soldiers of Queen Fria. The smaller one, with the ice-blue eyes, chases him, and despite Flash's mighty strength, captures him first, around the chest. He thrashes in his grip, and the soldier is aided by the wide hairy man of the ice-bear tribe. He captures his legs with a terrible laugh.

"I have him, O Queen!"

Flash closes his eyes against the image of the wicked Queen Fria, her icy hair like serpents around her head.

No, no you will not take me!

Arnie shifted in the arms of his captor, letting the fire in the hearth heat him. His lungs burned, and his stomach roared, but fatigue kept him from complaining. They lead Flash away, back to the dungeons, but he will never quit searching for his beloved Dale.

And yet, he cannot resist their powers as they feed him the queen's elixir of great slumber.

"Arnie, how about some more soup?"

Arms lifted him upright, and he allowed the heat to find his belly, soothe it.

He'd sleep a little, and then, when they weren't watching, he'd sneak away and escape.

What is happening in the icy chambers of Queen Fria, buried five thousand feet below Planet Mongo's icy crust? Will he awaken to rescue his beloved Dale? What exciting experiences await our friends? Stay tuned for the continuation of the Amazing Interplanetary Adventures of Flash Gordon!

CHAPTER NINE

Saturday, December 24

The way I figure it, you have a day to show her who you really are. Forget about Alex. Be Jake.

The words rumbled around in Jake's head all night, shifting with the wind. He finally told Gordy that he'd tend the fire. It didn't do either of them any good to sit and brood in front of the crackling frames while the blizzard voiced the howl inside him.

Jake had finally fallen asleep in front of the hearth, as he might have as a child. When he awoke, the flames had settled in a bed of glaring coals. The morning streamed in the windows, lighter, although the wind still buffeted the panes, rattling them as if trying to break in.

Jake stirred the coals with the poker then added the last of the logs. *Be Jake.*

He could murder Alex for writing all those pieces of his life to Violet, but in truth, wouldn't he have made up a life for himself, if he could? Replace all the dark places with something bold and heroic? Alex had grown up sleeping on a cot in his mother's tiny room in the Ramseys' attic. He'd had no father, a legacy of poverty. He'd been the servant.

No, Jake didn't blame him for wanting to be the owner's son.

He'd bet, however, that Alex never mentioned the asthma that sidelined Jake most of his childhood.

Stop worrying about the guy you aren't, and be the guy you are. Gordy's words edged into his mind.

The man should hardly be giving out romance advice when it had taken him twenty-six years to tell the woman across the street that he loved her.

Yesterday had felt downright agonizing, watching Dottie and Gordy long for more. Poor Gordy—he just didn't know how to woo her.

Or maybe…maybe the farmer had been doing it for years. It didn't go unnoticed with Jake that Gordy seemed to know Dottie's house and her barn better than she did. And, from the way they talked, he'd spent as much time with Nelson as she did.

Dottie and Gordy shared him, each clinging in their own way to him. And now, with his absence, they just didn't know how to bridge the gulf.

Maybe, despite his own failures, Gordy had a point.

Perhaps, today, he'd simply be Jake. Without a past. Without a future.

Just, Jake. And if he could woo Violet just a little, she might forgive him for his lies.

He heard banging in the kitchen and looked up. Dottie, probably, because she'd vacated the velvet sofa. Gordy had made a bed on the floor, near the radio, making another bed close by for Arnie. Violet had curled up on the chaise lounge.

A chill brushed the air. They needed a hotter fire to leverage warmth back into the room.

Perhaps he should stop worrying about being anyone—himself *or* Alex—and just focus on surviving. He got up to fetch more wood.

As he entered the kitchen, an acrid odor tinged the air. It smelled of burning sugar, reminded him of Svetlana's old-fashioned homemade candy. Maybe Dottie—

No. Violet stood at the stove, stirring a sugary syrup that foamed up around the pan and spilled onto the stovetop. He reached around her, turned down the heat.

"What are you cooking?"

"I found a jar of peaches and some dried apples. I thought I'd heat them up, make a compote." She glanced up at him. "You made breakfast yesterday. I thought it was my turn."

Oh, she was pretty. Those violet-gray eyes, that dark chocolate hair. She'd left it down again today, and he resisted the urge to push it back from her face. Instead he placed his hand over hers, stirring. "You want to keep the heat on low because sugar boils quickly. I think I saw some dried cranberries too."

But he didn't let go, just kept stirring. She could fit perfectly into his arms if she only took one step closer. Or perhaps he should just tuck his arm around her.

And then what? Kiss her? He could imagine that she might taste of coffee, her cup half full on the counter. She might kiss him back too, molding herself into his embrace. He'd lose himself in the smell of her....

He'd forget who he was altogether, probably.

Jake backed away from her, found a smile when Violet looked up at him, and then he retreated to the pantry.

It took him a moment for his brain to focus on the contents. He found the jar of dried cranberries and then also did a mental calculation of what remained.

Two cans of ham, a jar of olives, another of whole tomatoes, a bag of old sunflower seeds, a tin of crackers, a can of sweetened condensed milk, a bag of pasta, and a box of baking soda.

They'd eaten the last of the potatoes from the bin, and not an onion or carrot remained, although he had found a half head of dried garlic on the bottom of the bin.

In the canisters on the counter, he'd found oatmeal, farina, flour, and a dusting of sugar.

Dottie needed to learn to take better care of herself. Although, for a woman living alone, she would have managed just fine through the storm.

He closed the pantry and returned to the stove. Unscrewing the jar, he dumped the cranberries in the pan. "Just keep stirring."

Pulling out another pan, he set it on the stove and grabbed the canister of farina. Dottie had thawed and boiled a pot of snow yesterday for fresh water, and now he dipped his cup into it, filling up the pot.

He let it heat up then poured the farina in, stirring until it thickened.

"You're a good cook," Violet said.

The cranberries in her pot had plumped up, along with the apples. He took the compote and poured it into the farina. "It's a Russian trick."

"How did you learn so much about cooking?"

"I spent a lot of time in the kitchen as a child. It was the

SUSAN MAY WARREN

warmest room in the house, and my mother was gone a lot. Our housekeeper liked to try out her English on me."

"Can you speak Russian?"

"Da," he said, winking. "A little. But mostly I can understand it. I know angry, get-your-muddy-feet-off-my-clean-floor Russian very well."

She laughed. "Were you a bad boy?"

"No," he said. "I was a lonely boy." A sick, lonely boy. "With a big imagination. I spent a lot of time listening to the radio, to *Fibber McGee and Molly*, and the *Green Hornet*."

"I liked the Green Hornet too. He had amazing gadgets. I wanted the sting gun."

"Oh, I'll take Green Hornet's Secret Compartment and Transmitter Ring."

"Fine, give me the explosive Belt Buckle."

"The Gold Transmitter Pocket Watch." He grinned at her.

"All right, then I get Black Beauty."

"You want the car?"

"I'm going to have to replace the one in the tree, aren't I?"

He made a face. "Ouch."

"Sorry." She wrinkled her nose at him. "Seems like a year ago, doesn't it? That you were standing in the middle of the snowy driveway? And today's Christmas Eve."

He watched her pick up the pot, ladle cereal and compote into five bowls. Christmas Eve.

"I would be at home, trying to figure out what to get my mother for Christmas," he said.

She laughed. "Me too. My mother is impossible to shop for.

183

I think she hates gifts. I usually give her a new brush, or even per-fume." She'd barely given her poor mother a thought over the past two days. She dearly hoped that her mother knew she was safe and warm at Dottie's. Perhaps her brothers would trek out to Dottie's when the storm died.

"My mother prefers donations to charity, although she never minded when my father 'surprised' her with a string of pearls."

She grinned at him, blowing on the spoon, then taking a bit of the remains before dropping it in the sink. "And what girl wouldn't?"

He hid his frown. But...uh...*her*? Hadn't she written in one of her letters that she found jewelry and perfume a waste of good money? That she'd much prefer something practical?

She put a towel over the bowls to hold in the heat. "Poor Arnie. It's not much of a Christmas celebration here. And although the snow seems to have lightened, the wind chill could freeze a man's nose off his face. Listen to it—I think it's trying to blow the house over. There's no going out in this."

"I wish we had electricity. We could at least put up those Christ-mas lights." He moved toward the door, glancing at the mudroom. "I need to get some wood." He wrenched open the door, bracing himself for the cold.

Indeed, the room felt like an igloo, chill brushing off the walls. Last night's woodpile run had netted enough wood for last night, but they'd need a fresh supply for the day.

He grabbed his long coat, the wool hat and muffler, as well as Gordy's gloves. He'd just take a quick run out to the barn.

He nearly plowed into the door when it didn't open. He shoved it again, but it only creaked, the sound of snow crunching against it.

Violet had come into the mudroom, rubbing her arms. She reached for her boots. "I'll help you carry in a load."

He tried the door again, adding some oomph. It didn't move. "What's holding it shut?"

"Snow. Last night it was drifting over good. We may be trapped."

Her eyes widened. "Trapped?"

"Don't worry, Vi. We'll figure this out—"

"Where is he?"

The voice came from the parlor—Dottie's voice, crisp, with the sharp edge of panic.

Violet turned, but Jake brushed past her, clomping through the kitchen in his boots. Dottie came into the kitchen, wearing a wool sweater over a pair of pants, her blond hair down, tangled. "He's gone. Arnie is gone."

* * * * *

Dottie had awakened with the conviction that Gordy was trying to torture her.

She had spent the better part of the night listing all the reasons why she'd never forgiven him for not knocking at her door, for not barging his way into her stubborn heart.

Although, he seemed to be doing a fairly good job of it over the past twenty-four hours, without even trying. Like him calling her a hero. At least, that's how she interpreted his words. *I just meant that it takes a hero to raise one.*

His words had stolen hers, churned her thoughts together into a hot ball.

Maybe *Gordy* had been the hero. For sure he'd been Nelson's hero. How many times had Nelson come home, brimming with stories of hunting or fishing or working the farm with Gordy?

She should forgive him. Dottie couldn't pinpoint the source of that impulse, but the thought wound through her brain, startled her awake numerous times to stare at the crackling fire.

Jake, too, seem bothered, because every time she woke, it seemed he sat in his chair, mesmerized by the flickering flames. He finally fell asleep in the wee hours. And not long afterwards, Violet rose and tiptoed to the kitchen.

If Violet could scrape together something for breakfast, then miracles could happen. Since Arnie'd arrived on Dottie's door-step, she'd kept flirting with creative ways to use canned ham to craft a holiday meal. Some Christmas Eve.

Forgive Gordy. She couldn't escape the thought, it seemed.

Forgive him for not knocking at her door. Forgive him for teaching her son how to shoot.

Forgive him for making Nelson want him for his father.

She could hear him, even now. *"I sure wish Mr. Lindholm was my daddy."* Nelson's words were an arrow, piercing her as he'd shuffled into the kitchen for the second time, after peeling off his muddy boots. Dottie had kept her face stoic, her breathing calm.

Nelson slid onto one of the oak chairs at the table. She poured him a glass of milk from one of the bottles he'd brought home from Gordy's farm. "Mommy, how come you and Mr. Lindholm don't get married?"

This answer came easier. "I'm too old to get married again." Except, thirty-two wasn't old, was it? Even now, forty-four didn't seem so old. Until she looked at the trail of the past.

"But Mrs. Olafson at school got married again, and she's old." The milk left a mustache as he downed it.

"Well, if Mr. Lindholm asks, then I'll consider it." In the well of her heart, Dottie had hoped Nelson might pass that tidbit of information along, but perhaps it left his head the moment he ran upstairs to his room.

What if she did forgive Gordy? She'd lived so long with the anger burrowing inside her, she might just collapse in on herself, nothing to keep her warm when her visitors left. When Gordy returned home and they went back to keeping track of each other's lighted windows.

Dottie had finally untangled herself from her memories, her what-ifs, then tiptoed upstairs to dig out a wool sweater, long johns, and a pair of wool shoes. The house contained a hovering chill, and she feared that the blizzard would freeze her water pipes. Oh, the mess, come spring.

She stopped by the bathroom and spent way too long in front of the mirror, considering her hair up, or down, the wrinkles around her eyes, the loosening jowls around her jawline.

On a whim, she put on lipstick, a little face powder. A dash of perfume, just because it was there. It raised gooseflesh on her skin. And, she left her hair down.

On a whim.

Returning downstairs, she could hear voices in the kitchen, then the back door opening. Jake had vanished from his perch by the fire. She smelled something cooking in the kitchen, peeked in and saw Jake and Violet by the stove, stirring some concoction.

They could be a cute couple, what with Jake's broad shoulders, his kind blue eyes, the way Violet laughed at his jokes, her eyes shining. Dottie had watched them dancing together last night, and for a moment, she saw herself and Gordy, that Christmas before she returned to teachers college in Mankato.

Why hadn't he asked her to stay home that New Year's weekend? She told herself for years that she would have stayed if he asked, but as the memory dusted over her, perhaps she'd been too headstrong. Maybe she'd simply wanted an escape from her quiet, brooding father, so solemn after her mother died, spending his money and time on gadgets and new inventions. Too many evenings as she'd grown up, the only sound between them was the fluttering of pages from his vast book collection.

Regardless of her reasons, she'd had her taste of freedom.

Gordy had learned to dance that year, and stepping into his arms felt like stepping into home. He smelled clean and fresh, with a dash of cologne, and in his suit appeared a real gentleman. She remembered tucking her face close to his neck, smelling him.

She may have even kissed him.

When she'd caught his gaze, however, the heat, the desire in it had frightened her. She wasn't ready for the world he wanted for them.

She just needed more time. So she'd told him about Minneapolis.

It was only the first of her mistakes.

The second was thinking that TJ Morgan might truly love her, that the words he crooned into her ears might be enough.

It hadn't been Gordy's fault she didn't say yes. She understood his proposal well enough, had even, for a moment, surrendered to his touch, had wanted him to continue.

She'd never been kissed like Gordon Lindholm had kissed her in the barn. But, she hadn't wanted the adventure to end.

Probably she needed his forgiveness too.

She had no idea, however, how to ask.

Or, perhaps, offer it.

She stepped into the kitchen, noticed that Violet and Jake had slipped into the mudroom. Probably to get more wood. The ice frosted the window completely over, letting in only wan light. She couldn't see outside, although the wind howled.

Today, maybe, the storm would die. They could all be back in their homes by Christmas. She wasn't sure why that thought rattled her, hollowed her out.

Bowls of breakfast cooled on the counter, covered with a towel. She went over, carried two to the table.

Maybe she'd invite Gordy to eat breakfast with her, while the kids were out fetching wood.

Tiptoeing back into the parlor, she glanced at him lying on the floor by the Silvertone. He'd propped his head on a sofa pillow, his legs drawn up, her mother's wedding ring quilt over him. Strange that he'd sleep so long—in fact, yesterday he'd risen last also.

And that's when she noticed it—the empty blankets near him, where Arnie had slept. Where—

She ran into the kitchen. No Arnie. Back to the parlor.

"Where is he?"

Gordy roused at her voice, but she didn't stay, just ran back to the kitchen.

Jake came through the door, bundled in his jacket, his boots.

"He's gone. Arnie is gone."

189

"How could he be gone?" Gordy said, leaping to his feet so fast, she could doubt he'd slept at all. "Where could he go?"

"All yesterday he cried about going home. Maybe he left this morning?"

"We're snowed in," Jake said. "The door's frozen shut."

"What about the front door?"

"I haven't used it in years." But Dottie headed into the front hall anyway. She unbolted the door, turned the handle.

It didn't budge.

"Let me try," Gordy said.

"If you can't open it, I can guarantee Arnie wouldn't be able to," Violet said, but Gordy tried anyway.

He peered out the window in the parlor. "These are covered in snow. He didn't get out."

"Search the house." Jake shucked off his jacket, heading back to the parlor.

Violet opened the door to the sewing room, the arctic blast from the closed room chilling the house. She hadn't set foot in her mother's sewing room since before Nelson left for war.

Dottie headed upstairs, first stopping at her room, then the bathroom. She was striding by Nelson's room when she heard it.

The faint sounds of a train.

She heard the little-boy-made *choo, choo* sounds of the engine, breath huffing through puffy cheeks, and steeled herself against what she'd see.

Quietly, she eased the door open.

Arnie sat on the floor, the worn box to the Hafner wind-up train on Nelson's twin bed. And, in the middle of the floor, in the center of the rag rug, Arnie had assembled the track into an oval. Around and around went the wind-up train, all four cars—the engine, the green grain car, the black coal car, and the shiny red caboose with the word PENNSYLVANIA scripted on the side.

Dottie pressed her hand to her chest as she listened to the boy make the sounds. He'd also set up Nelson's old farm set, with the painted wooden tractor Gordy had given him on his fifth birthday.

The engine died and Arnie picked it up, inserting the wind-up key in the engine, and cranking it until it started rolling again. When he set it back on the track, he looked up at her, stilling.

The engine continued its trek around the oval as he drew in a breath.

Why was this child so afraid of her? She couldn't erase the way he looked at her yesterday when he'd awakened in Gordy's arms.

She kept her voice soft. "It's okay, Arnie. You can play with those."

The room bespoke the smell of mustiness, age. The fact that she hadn't opened it to air out, receive the warmth of the house since Nelson shipped out, evidenced in the dust mites under the bed, the scent of age embedded in the bed linens. Nelson had cleaned out most of his childhood mementos, packing them in boxes in the closet. The train set, and other toys, he must have shoved under the bed, because one end of the blue bedspread was flung up.

How had Arnie found this room, these toys?

And not just any toys. These were the toys Gordy had given Nelson over the years. Her gifts—Monopoly and Sorry, the many Hardy Boys books—he'd packed away in the closet. But Gordy's toys he'd packed separately, made them accessible.

As if he knew that someday, some other little boy might need them.

Oh, being trapped in this house had turned her all soft and sentimental.

"You found him."

Gordy's voice, behind her, and she glanced at him. Smiled. "He's just playing."

But Gordy was staring at the boy as if he'd seen the ghost of Christmas past. "You kept it."

"Kept what?"

He looked at her. "I gave that to Nelson when he was ten. And that farm set—I left that on the stoop."

"Like Santa Claus. Thank you for that. Nelson was a believer until he was twelve because of your many midnight visits." But nothing of resentment hued her words. She looked at him, smiling. "You nurtured the magic of Christmas for him."

"I always wondered if he liked them. I…never knew."

She drew in a quick breath. Of course. Nelson thought Santa had brought them, had probably never thought to thank Gordy.

And she, of course, couldn't bear to acknowledge that Gordy's gifts to her son had made him feel loved.

Made her feel loved.

No—no… Gordy loved her *son*. Not her.

Still, as she watched Arnie sacrifice a cow to the terrible train monster, she couldn't help but lean over to Gordy and whisper into his ear. "Thank you, Santa."

He smiled, and she saw a blush spread up his neck. "You're welcome."

* * * * *

Who was Violet kidding? Jake had about as much interest in her as he had in a can of ham. For a moment there, standing in the kitchen next to the stove, Violet had thought…well, she'd thought he might kiss her, which only attested to the fact that three days cooped up in Dottie's too-large-for-its-own-good house had gone straight to her head. She'd heard of cabin fever. What about old-Victorian-on-the-hill fever?

Storm house fever. That's what she'd call it.

And now, with the snow piled over both doors and probably halfway up the house, they really were trapped.

At least they had breakfast. Because Jake the Soldier had saved breakfast from the clutches of the gal who could wrestle a head-gasket back into place but couldn't figure out how to heat up peaches.

His breakfast—this Russian concoction—could roll her eyes back into her head with joy. And she wasn't the only one—Gordy seemed especially loud with his eating this morning. And Dottie kept closing her eyes, as if in praise of such glorious food.

"Can I have more?" Arnie said, his bowl empty.

Jake got up. "Sure, kid," he said and grabbed the pot off the stove. He spooned more into the bowl and met Violet's eyes.

She could nearly reach out and take a hold of his relief. Carry it with her. She hadn't realized how afraid they'd all been that Arnie could die. Or, that he might have taken off in the middle of the night for home.

Dottie and Gordy had hauled the toys into the family room

and set up the railroad track there. No one wanted to lose him again.

"Can I go home today?" Arnie said between bites.

"The wind's gusting pretty hard out there. And it's hard to see what we're facing. How far do you live?" Violet asked.

"Out past Gundersons', where the road T's, and then a jog up from there."

Violet guessed about three miles from town. What was he doing walking home? "Where's your mama? Why didn't she pick you up after school?"

He shoved another spoonful into his mouth. "She works at the mill, on the late shift on Thursdays. But I'll bet she's home by now."

Violet met Dottie's gaze. Probably not. "Gordy, I think your mama would want you to stay with us until the storm blows over. We'll get you home as soon as we can."

He put the bowl down, considered her with those fetching brown eyes. "But tonight's Christmas Eve. How will Santa know where to find me?"

Dottie touched his hand. "Oh, don't worry. Santa always knows where to find good little boys."

Violet frowned as Arnie's head tucked down into his chest. "I'm not a good boy."

"Arnie, why would you say that?"

His eyes flitted over to Dottie, then back. "'Cause I daydream."

Dottie hid a smile, catching Violet's gaze. "Is that so?"

"I had to stay after school and write 'I will not daydream in class' on Mrs. Olafson's blackboard."

"Oh," Dottie said. "That is fairly serious."

Arnie bit his lower lip.

"But I think that can be solved. See, daydreaming is allowed here at Storm House. You can be anyone you want to be. Make up an entirely new life, if you want." Dottie looked at Violet, raised an eyebrow. "Right?"

Violet looked away. She noticed Jake playing with his spoon.

"In fact, at Storm House, you can even pretend you live here, that it's your house," Gordy said. "Like a secret house where only you belong."

"It's *my* house?"

Gordy nodded. "But you have to dream it up to make it come true. Can you do that?"

Arnie nodded, but his smile dimmed as his gaze fell again on Dottie. "But what about Santa? We don't have a tree, or stockings, or…will he still come?"

"You let the grown-ups take care of that, Arnie," Jake said. "Santa will be here in the morning, I promise. Right, Gordy? Dottie?" He looked at Violet.

"Right," she said. *Right?*

Arnie slid off his chair, scampering into the parlor. The puttering sound of an engine derailing seemed to put a smile on Dottie's face. She glanced at Gordy.

Who looked at Jake. "And how are we supposed to give this child a merry Christmas?"

"We do have a big fir tree outside in the yard."

Gordy raised an eyebrow.

"And a generator, for our lights."

"It doesn't work," Dottie said.

Why did Jake look at her? Or maybe Violet just imagined it.

"And a feast in the cupboards."

"Son, are you ill?" Dottie said.

"Gordy, let's see if we can figure a way out of here and fetch that tree, not to mention more firewood. Violet, why don't you and Dottie scrounge up more decorations?"

Jake pushed himself up from the table. "We have work to do, people, if we want Santa to show up tonight."

He gathered up his bowl and set it in the sink then marched out of the room.

"What was that?" Dottie said, staring after him. "He can't possibly think I'm going to make Christmas dinner out of a couple cans of ham?"

Violet saw Gordy's hand land on Dottie's, squeezing it. "If anyone has the imagination to pull it off, you do, Dottie." He winked at her and followed Jake out.

"Is it something they ate? Maybe gas is leaking through the house?" Dottie said.

Violet heard footsteps on the stairs. They weren't going to climb out the bathroom window, were they?

Dottie must have read her face.

"In the blizzard of 1940, I was snowed in, just like now. Gordy and Nelson were holed up at his place. He knew I was worried sick, so as soon as the wind died enough for them to get across the pond, they hiked over. The drifts had piled up to the second floor, and Nelson climbed the drift to the bathroom window."

"They're going to kill themselves."

"Gordy knows what he's doing." Dottie bussed the bowls,

dropping them into the sink. "Let's head up to the attic, see if we can find some decorations."

Violet delivered her bowl to the sink then followed Dottie up the stairs. "You stay here, Arnie, okay?"

Arnie had built himself a fortress with the sofa cushions, the radio, a table, and one of the bedroom quilts.

Dottie pulled down the attic stairs from the ceiling then climbed up. Even with the daylight sneaking in the cracks, the place needed light. Violet climbed down and returned with a candle.

Dottie had dragged a box near the stairway, now began pulling out ornaments wrapped in paper. An acorn hanging from a thread, and a painted glass ball. "Nelson gave me these—gifts from his classroom."

She unwrapped more. A tin man and a lion. "The Wizard of Oz. Did you see the movie? We took the train to Minneapolis to see it. And then it finally came to Frost."

"I was terrified of the witch," Violet said.

"We all were. If Nelson had been any younger, I suspect he would have slipped into my bed in the middle of the night. But he was fifteen, so he pretended well."

Dottie tucked the ornaments back in the box then set it aside and dug further, opening another box, pulling out a stocking, the name NELSON knitted into the top. The next one read MOTHER.

Violet had seen them both when she'd unpacked that box earlier.

Behind it came the tree skirt, made of felt and displaying the nativity scene including the three wise men. Dottie folded it on her lap, ran her hand over it.

"Silly to hang on to all these things. I know he's not coming back."

"It doesn't mean you can't remember him," Violet said. "Just because Nelson's gone doesn't mean your life is over. Or erased." She looked in the box, pulled out a pair of knitted socks. "These are cute."

"He wore those when he was a baby. I'll never forget those big blue eyes. He couldn't crawl yet, so he did this sort of rocking scoot around the house, after me. I'll never forget my father, yelping when he caught Nelson chewing on his toes."

"Where was your mother?"

"She died in childbirth when I was eight, along with my newborn brother. My father never quite recovered. He wanted to fill this house with children." She made a face. "I'm not sure he ever forgave me, either, for not giving him a crowd of grandchildren." She added the stockings to the pile. Then she pulled out a little red bunting. Held it to her nose. "He loved Nelson, though."

"Everyone loved Nelson."

Dottie's eyes glistened. "They did, didn't they? It was like, when Nelson came along, the town of Frost forgave me for my sins."

"It's hardly a sin to follow your heart."

"But what about breaking another's?" She shook her head. "Not a person didn't know that Gordy changed after I left. I always waited for him to marry, but—"

"But he never stopped loving you."

Emotion raked across Dottie's face, despite her casual shrug.

"Just like God never stopped loving you."

Dottie drew in a quick breath then took everything and piled it back in the box. "God stopped loving me the day Nelson died."

Oh, Dottie. Violet kept her voice soft. "Dottie, God's love isn't measured by His blessings. Think about it—what about when there is suffering? Darkness? Storms? Does God love you less?"

Dottie's face hardened.

"I know it seems easier to say God doesn't love you when terrible things happen. But the truth is, God's love isn't measured by the good—or bad—things that happen to us. God loves us, period. He already loved us completely when He sent His Son into our dark, painful, sinful world. We were His enemies, Dottie, and He loved us, even then. I *guarantee* you are not His enemy now. So, the fact is, He still loves you, even though He took away Nelson. And, He's been trying to comfort you—"

"How?"

"By giving you a man who loved your son as much as you did! *Gordy.* God didn't leave you bereft. And, you can never erase the twenty-one years you spent with Nelson." She reached inside the box, pulling out the stocking. She pressed it into Dottie's hand. "You can't erase your son."

Dottie stared at the stocking, back at Violet. "I don't want to erase him. Sometimes, I just can't bear to remember him."

Violet's voice gentled. "But, don't you see? You can, Dottie. You just did. And we're here to share him with you." She folded her hand on Dottie's. "Your Storm House Family."

Dottie ran her finger under her eye. "I knew it was a bad idea to let you into my house."

"I rescued you from the cellar."

Dottie managed a semblance of a smile. "Help me bring these boxes down."

Violet climbed down the stairs and took the boxes from Dottie as she handed them down.

"Just a moment," Dottie said, and disappeared into the recesses of the attic. When she returned, she lowered down a large, glass star.

"I don't suppose you could figure out a way to light this up, could you?" Dottie said, grinning. She climbed down then closed the attic door.

"Dottie—"

"I think you need to stop hiding who you are. Christmas needs you, Sergeant."

"You're not being fair."

"And you're not being honest." Dottie hefted a box. "You can't live your life pretending to be someone you're not." She winked at her. "Even in Storm House."

Violet carried the star down the staircase, following Dottie. She set it on one of the boxes.

The doors to the dining room, where Gordy had abandoned the generator, remained closed.

Upstairs, she heard thumping as the men attempted to escape their icy prison.

Dottie headed to the kitchen, perhaps to make magic with ham.

Violet took one look at Arnie, sprawled on the floor, plowing over a herd of little metal soldiers with a giant green wooden tractor, puttering noises emitting from his pursed lips, and headed through the doors to Santa's workshop.

CHAPTER TEN

Gordy was simply too old to be climbing out of second-story windows and sliding down the rain pipe. He shook his head as Jake finished prying open the window. He'd taken a candle to where the ice piled up in the corners, enough so that finally they were able to wedge it open.

Too old and too large. A slim, fit guy like Jake might be able to fit through there—

"I'm going to need to you to lower me off the edge. I think I can drop from there into the snowbank."

"Really, Jake, I don't know. This is different than when Nelson climbed up to the roof, the main difference being that I was on the ground. Pushing *up*."

Jake glanced over his shoulder at him, grinning. After two days, the man had grown on Gordy. Not quite the Dapper Dan he had pegged him as. Jake had substance behind his charisma. Maybe it was the fact that he wanted to hike out in the blistering wind-chill, drag in the tree, or a portion of it, to create a Christmas world for Arnie, had Gordy second-guessing his own assessment.

In fact, Jake reminded him, more every hour, of Nelson. His ability to find a silver lining, the way he could tease and cajole

Dottie into giving him his way, his thoughtfulness. Indeed, if Nelson had lived, he might have become a man very much like Jake.

Although, with the wind shearing off the top layer of snow, casting it into the abyss beyond like a white whirling dervish, perhaps creeping out on the narrow roof might not be the ideal way to dredge up Christmas cheer. "You're going to get me killed."

"It's snow. It's fluffy."

"It's a long way down."

"Or, we could just stay here until spring." Jake raised an eyebrow. "I'm in if you are."

Frankly, he didn't care if he ever went home. Who, after all, did he have to go home to? His cow?

No, he'd stay until the summer daisies arrived and the lilacs outside Dottie's window came into bloom.

Thank you, Santa.

Her soft voice could turn his chest into a gooey, garbled mess. You're welcome? "Not at all" is what he wanted to say.

Dottie, I loved your boy like he was my own. Of course I gave him Christmas presents.

But, more importantly, she'd known that Gordy had given Nelson the gifts and kept them anyway.

He blinked back the moisture in his eyes—probably from the searing wind that sent the bathroom into a deep freeze.

Why hadn't he ever asked Dottie again to marry him? Their argument in the yard yesterday—was it only yesterday?—rushed back at him.

"You should have married me."

"You should have asked."

"I did, Dottie."

"Was that what that was? Because it seemed more like a tumble in the hay, and a command, issued by a desperate boy."

She'd been right—it was a command by a desperate boy. Too desperate and too young, and not enough of a tender request for her hand in marriage.

Maybe she still would have spurned him, but certainly after she'd returned, lonely, heartbroken, pregnant, alone, he could have asked again.

His pride simply wouldn't allow it.

They'd returned downstairs for their jackets, hats, and boots while Dottie and Violet were hunting through the attic, and now Gordy buttoned up his jacket as Jake squeezed his way through the opening without a problem.

The wind sounded like a locomotive howling, and while the blizzard seemed to have abated, the wind scooped up the snow, turned it into a cyclone. The wind-chill might be forty below, or more. Gordy could make out the barn, however, through the swirling snow, and the cake of accumulation on the roof. He'd have to take a shovel to it and the roof of the house after the storm blew over, or it might cave in.

While Gordy was out in the cold, he should also find and dig out the cellar door, try to get inside and feed the coal furnace, stir heat back into the house.

Jake crouched by the window entrance. "C'mon old man, it's your turn."

"Keep your paws off me—"

But Jake grabbed Gordy's jacket as he wiggled his way out

the window. Gordy closed the window behind him, his chest on fire.

He still couldn't shake the persistent ache in his lower back—probably from last night on the floor. But the cereal this morning had left him feeling nauseous also.

Or, it could be the height. The bathroom window emerged onto the mudroom addition so that the roof extended wider from the house. Still, he imagined that one wrong step might sled him down the side and fling him into space.

"I really do feel old," he said as he inched his way down the side of the roof with Jake.

More than that, this little excursion to the edge of eternity made him consider that he should ask Dottie for her hand again.

Will you marry me?

How difficult could those four words be?

Perhaps as hard as *I love you.*

The wind shook his perch and threatened to whisk his legs out from under him. As if proving his fears, Jake slipped, landed on his backside, and Gordy grabbed at the scruff of his jacket as Jake's legs dangled over the edge.

Jake kicked his way back to the roof. "In my head, this was a better idea."

Gordy stifled a grin as he finally scooted to the edge of the roof. The snow drifted up over the house like a hand, covering the mudroom door and the front porch. Probably it also covered the back of the house.

It occurred to him that they might have checked those windows first before hopping out on the roof.

Still, now that he overlooked it, the drift seemed to nearly reach the second-story roof. He could just reach out his foot and—

His stationary foot slipped, kicked out, and the force of it sent him skidding.

And then he was airborne.

He tried to wind his arms, to maneuver himself upright, but he landed—*boof*!—face up in the snowy drift, staring at the sky as he attempted to catch his breath. It had snuffed out, the wind stealing it with a howl.

"Are you hurt?"

He looked up. Jake peered over the roof at him.

Five feet up. He'd barely fallen five feet, and he felt like he'd been run over by a horse. He sat up. "Get down here."

Jake pushed off and landed next to him, on his feet then falling down beside him. "I feel old too."

"Don't talk to me." Gordy scooted down the bank, landing on his feet, then plowed through the snow to the barn.

While he fed the horse, Jake dug out a couple of shovels. He handed one to Gordy.

Gordy noticed he was employing that strange breathing again—slow, in through the nose, out through the mouth. "Are you going to be okay?"

"It's just the cold. I have to slow my breathing, keep it steady. I'll be fine."

"Do not die on me. I can't carry your carcass back up that snowdrift."

Jake gave him a narrowed-eye look and Gordy smiled. Yes, the kid reminded him of Nelson.

Ice covered the drift against the house, a thick layer of wind-polished snow that required chipping and not a little grunting until Gordy had worked up a thick layer of sweat dribbling down between his shoulder blades. His nose, however, he could barely feel, for the wind. A couple of times he stopped, trying to make out his farm, but the bullet-gray sky still hovered too low. That another storm might be in the making seemed possible.

They finally broke through, and as he cleared around the door, he saw Jake grab his knees, close his eyes.

"Go back to the barn, son," he said, and to his surprise, Jake obeyed. Gordy had wrestled the door open by the time he returned.

"It's the cold. And the work. I'll be fine," Jake said as he waved to Dottie through the mudroom window. They hiked down to the snow-covered tree.

Gordy could use a rest, his back turning to fire after all that shoveling. When had he gotten so old? He watched Jake shake the snow off the tree.

What a stubborn old man he'd been. Stubborn, stupid, and, apparently, old. He should ask Dottie to marry him before he croaked. He gripped his knees.

"You okay?" Jake said, now peering under the tree, as if hunting for something.

"Go up to the barn. You'll find an ax in the utility closet. Let's get this tree inside, let the ladies pretty it up."

Jake hiked back up to the barn. The cold had begun to freeze the sweat inside Gordy's jacket, and he started to shiver.

By the time Jake returned, Gordy's teeth chattered.

"Go inside, Gordy. I can do this."

"Naw—I'll help you." He got up, groaning. Maybe he *should* go inside. But he wasn't quite ready to be mothballed yet. Grabbing the top of the tree, he steadied it for Jake's blows. "Just chop off the top. Leave the rest."

His entire body shuddered as Jake chopped at the cold tree, the blows radiating down his arms, into his brittle bones.

The final whack dislodged the tree from the base and the force of it pushed Gordy back into the snow. He lay there, staring at the pewter sky, closing his eyes. *Yes, Dottie, I should have asked again.*

"You're not going to die on me, are you, old guy?"

Gordy opened his eyes. Then, because he could, he whipped out his leg and tripped Jake. Jake fell in the snow beside him.

Jake lay beside him, gasping. "Okay. Fine. Sorry I called you old. Maybe decrepit would have been better."

Gordy tossed snow at him as he climbed to his feet. He grabbed the end of the tree. "You can just lay there and get some shuteye while I drag this up to the house." He left Jake in the snow as he carried the tree to the house.

Maybe they'd have a merry Christmas after all. Especially since he planned to ask Dottie to marry him the first magical moment he could find.

And this time, he'd do it right.

* * * * *

He was going to die, right here in the snow, with the wind gluing his eyes shut.

And just when he thought he'd laid hold of a piece of the man he'd lost, back in the battlefields of Belgium. A man who helped others.

A man who ladled out real hope again.

Perhaps he was supposed to be here, to help put a smile back on Arnie's face, if just for a day.

If he didn't die first. Jake lay there, watching Gordy drag the tree up to the house, his chest webbing. He needed to get inside. But maybe if he just kept calm, kept breathing, he'd be fine.

He felt as if he might be breathing through a straw, sinking deeper underwater. He blamed the chopping. And the cold. And jumping from the roof. And chopping their way into the house.

And his insistence that he hide his condition from Violet. At home, in this weather, he would do everything, from rubbing his chest with camphorated oil, to preparing a toddy with honey and whiskey.

If he got desperate, he had a machine and a mask that opened his airways.

But of course, he'd left that back in Minneapolis.

He closed his eyes, tried small, more shallow breaths, calm breaths, listening to his rasping. Maybe he should get into the barn, but the hay there might only make it worse.

And he'd smoked the last of his asthma cigarettes.

He always feared that someday he'd start to wheeze in public, that a crowd would form, and then, while everyone watched, he'd suffocate to death on the sidewalk.

But worse, just might be sprawled in the snow, alone.

He'd simply gotten too excited about giving Arnie a Christmas.

No. He'd gotten too excited about the way Violet looked at him, a sparkle in her eyes. Really looked at him. Not as a substitute for Alex, but Jake, the guy who could bring magic to Christmas Eve.

Some magic.

Because being Jake wasn't going to make her forget Alex. Being Jake was lying in the snow, gasping for air.

He didn't want to be Jake.

Jake wasn't enough. Hadn't been enough when he was hauling the wounded back to the field hospitals, hadn't been enough when he was dispensing chocolate in the foxholes, hadn't been enough when he was offering up passages of hope in makeshift chapels, or eulogies at too many battlefield funerals.

He should have picked up a gun instead of a Bible to serve his country.

He pressed his hands on his chest, breathed in through his nose, but the biting wind only made his eyes water, hiccoughed his breath.

He sat up, wheezing.

Gordy had disappeared into the house.

He needed to get inside, to relax.

He needed an inhalant of medicine.

He needed to be whole again.

Please, God, can't You be on my side here?

The wind brushed the tree back where he'd chopped it. Where the tree covered the ground remained a deep well, and he could nearly see the ground. Beyond that, the taillights of the Plymouth emerged. And near the back—

His suitcase. Oh, he nearly cried out with joy. He had another pack of cigarettes inside his suitcase, just in case. Crawling toward it, he picked it up, found his feet.

The wind fought him, but he reached the barn then wrangled

his way inside. The silence accentuated his wheezing as he stumbled to the end of the truck, nearly fell into an empty stall. The smell of hay on a summer day could probably kill him, but today, in the crisp air, no allergens moved to irritate him. He fumbled with the frozen suitcase, finally coaxing the snaps open.

Inside were the letters, a change of clothes, and—hallelujah!—a pack of cigarettes. He pulled them out, his breathing more labored. He couldn't control it now, started to feel the black panic rising deep inside him. Breathe. In through his nose, out…slow down, not so fast.

He pulled out a cigarette, his hands shaking as he tried to light it. But the wind, even in the protected barn, fought the flame.

His eyesight had begun to narrow, a black tunnel.

Breathe. Slow. Easy.

His head spun.

He fell back on the frozen, hard earth while his lungs began to close like a fist. He closed his eyes.

He would have liked to kiss Violet. That thought pulsed inside him as he shuddered, wheezing, forcing himself to keep his breathing slow and shallow. He should have. He should have leaned down and pulled her to himself and made her forget about Alex.

Jake could nearly smell her, the scent of roses and cinnamon. Could nearly feel her hair tickling his face.

Yes, he would have liked to kiss her, to tell her the truth—that he'd been in love with her for years. Would have liked to have been the man she had written to, hoping he'd remember her after the war.

He would have told her that he was proud of her and that she didn't have to hide her past, because he knew it already. And that he loved her.

Yes, he would tell her all that, if he could just breathe one day longer.

He pressed his hands to his chest.

In. Out. Breathe.

Live.

* * * * *

The generator resembled the inner workings of her father's diesel tractor. Violet checked the hoses, the fuel line. In case the injector might be clogged, she disconnected the fuel line then unscrewed the injector. Taking it apart, she took out the BB and the spring, cleaning them with a rag Dottie dug up, then cleared out the hole on one end with a toothpick.

She put the entire assembly back together while listening to the thumping outside, then the clanking as the men chipped away at the door.

Oh, she didn't want Jake to see her with grease saturating her fingers. If Alex hadn't told him she'd changed tires and overhauled engines for four years, she didn't want to cement that image in Jake's head. She rather liked the way he looked at her, without some sort of wariness or even defense.

She'd finally understood the stigma while stationed in Berlin, during the aftermath of the war, when all she did was patch up engines and overhaul carburetors. She'd been walking back to her barracks, and the chatter from a cadre of privates lifted to her ears. *"Maybe she can work on my engine."*

She felt dirty, had even stood in line for a shower, retreating to her bunk despite a USO event. The shows weren't for the women, anyway, the acts intended to please the men. She'd stared at the dusky ceiling, recalling the expressions on her brothers' faces as she'd sat at the dinner table with stained hands, so much like her father's.

When she'd enlisted, she felt proud, but that day in Berlin, she'd wanted to hide. To start over. To be someone else.

Why couldn't she enjoy knitting and cooking and crocheting and gardening, like other women? Why hadn't God made her pretty, and womanly?

Violet screwed the fuel injector back together, hearing steps in the kitchen. Heavy steps. She opened the dining room door. "Mr. Lindholm!"

He was hauling in a beautiful green fir, still dripping with snow. Arnie looked up, and the expression on his face made it all worth it.

"C'mere," she whispered to Gordy, "I need your help."

He propped the tree in the hallway, near the front door, and clomped into the room. Sweat glistened on his face, and he was pale.

"Are you okay?"

"Just one of Santa's elves," he said, and grinned. "And call me Gordy, please."

Oh, she liked him. For years, he'd been the hermit farmer out of town. How wrong the schoolchildren had been to call him Mr. McGregor.

"I need help bleeding the fuel line. Can you rip the pull cord while I bleed it out?"

He nodded and she picked up a rag, holding it at the end of the fuel line. Good thing Gordy had spread out old sheets in the room, although bringing the engine inside had certainly warmed the fuel, turned it less viscous.

Gordy stood over the engine, grabbed the handle, and pulled. Bubbles emerged from the end of the hose as air forced through it. "Again."

"How did you know to bleed the lines?" Gordy asked as he pulled.

"We had to do it every time the tractor ran out of gas." More bubbles emerged.

"Your father taught you?"

She nodded, as fuel finally spurted out of the hose. "That's enough." She reconnected it to the engine. "And, I got pretty good at it in the military."

He stood up, wiping his hands, frowning. "You were in the military?"

"Women's Army Auxiliary Corps. I worked in the motor pool."

She waited for his frown, even the look of disgust.

"Well, I'll be," he said. "Maybe after we get dug out, you can come over and take a look at the Ford. It's got a sticky starter."

She stared at him, nonplussed.

He smiled.

She found one inside to match it. "Can you carry this outside for me? I need to start it."

He hefted it up, marched through the kitchen. Dottie was cutting up ham.

"What are you making?"

Dottie looked up at her. "I haven't a clue." But she winked as Violet trekked through the kitchen on Gordy's tail.

They threw on their coats, their boots and hats, and he carried the generator out to the barn. "Dottie's father wired the barn for electricity after the 1933 World's Fair. He bought this generator there and thought he would be the first to have electricity in Frost. He was."

He bent down, ripped the cord. The engine sputtered, but Violet thought she heard life. "Try it again!"

"There's a plug out here that extends to the house, but it's not going to run the entire house. You'll have to turn off the switch, isolate just the lights in the house."

"Can you do that for me?"

He nodded then pulled the cord again. The generator rumbled and sputtered to life, coughing twice before it died.

Gordy grinned at her as he pulled it yet again. This time the engine caught. "I'll go throw the switch in the house." He disappeared first into the utility room of the barn, emerging with what looked like a tree stand. Then he barreled back out into the cold.

While she waited, she wandered the barn, running her hands down the mane of the horse. In a back stall, an old sleigh, the runners rusty and dug into the dirt, suggested a more romantic era. She unearthed the roadster in yet another stall, covered by a blanket. A faded, red 1929 Ford roadster that, with the right touch and someone to believe in it, might be beautiful.

She was fiddling with the hood cover when movement caught her eye. There, in another stall, a foot—

Jake's foot.

Had he fallen? "Jake?" She found him sprawled on the ground, his eyes closed, holding his chest, his breaths quick, wheezing.

"Are you having a heart attack?" She dropped to her knees beside him. "What's wrong?"

"He's having an asthma attack." Gordy appeared behind her. "Let's get him in the house."

An asthma attack?

Gilmore Jenkins had died of asthma when he was ten years old. She could still remember the funeral, the story of how he'd stopped breathing while working in his daddy's field, turned blue, then white, suffocating while they tried to help him breathe.

Jake had asthma? He'd turned a sort of ashen color in the wan light. He seemed to be gasping now, and as Gordy went around one side of him, to lift him, he opened his eyes.

What looked like horror filled his eyes. His breath—shallow as it was—hiccoughed, then sped up.

"It's going to be okay, Jake. We'll get you in the house."

"Suit…case." He barely whispered the word, but she heard it. His suitcase lay open at his feet, and in his hand he clutched what looked like a cigarette. She took it from him, pocketed it, then closed the suitcase and picked it up.

Gordy wrapped his arm around him and headed toward the house.

The wind seemed even more violent, scraping ice into her eyes as they wrestled their way to the house. They got him inside, peeled off his coat, and Gordy half dragged him into the kitchen.

"Dot—he's having an asthma attack. Get a towel."

She nodded and darted out of the room.

"Violet, in his suitcase—he's got a tin of Elliot's Asthma Powder. Find it. We need to burn it and get him to breath in the smoke."

She opened the suitcase on the table. Clothes, a manila package, shoes, a wrapped package—there, in a tin on the bottom.

"Open it, shake some of the powder into the lid."

Jake sat in the chair, his eyes closed, as if trying to concentrate on breathing. His breaths came shallow and quick.

Dottie returned with the towel. She draped it over his head as Gordy swiped the matches from the stove, grabbed a candle off the table, and lit it. Then he moved it in front of Jake and held the lid over it.

"Breathe, son."

Jake draped the towel over his head, began to breathe in the smoke of the powder.

Violet sank into a chair, her heart clogging her own breath as he inhaled.

"How did you know what to do?" she asked Gordy.

"He told me. That first night. He was trying to find his suitcase."

She wanted to cry for him, watching him struggle to breathe. "How long has he had it?"

"He had it as a child, and it came back when he got sick in the war—pneumonia."

Arnie had come into the kitchen, and Violet put her arm around him, holding him.

"Is he going to be okay?"

"We think so, honey," Dottie said.

She watched Jake as he began to slow his breathing, as it seemed the smoke, which teared her eyes, began to seep into his lungs. Finally, as the powder burned out, he leaned back. Removed the towel and opened his eyes.

Met Gordy's. "Thank you."

"Don't scare us again like that," Gordy said, his voice ragged.

Dottie got up. "I have some tea left."

Gordy reached for Arnie's hand. "Help me put the tree up, little man."

Violet stayed at the table, staring at Jake. She wanted to reach out, hold his hand, but it felt so feeble in the shadow of what had just happened. "I'm sorry about your illness. Alex told me that he'd had asthma too, and how terrible it was not to be able to breathe—"

"Alex didn't have asthma," Jake said quietly.

She stilled.

Jake met her eyes, something dark in them. "Alex never had asthma. Never gave anyone oranges for Christmas, never watched his brother die. Alex stole my life, okay?" His jaw tightened. "He concocted an identity out of my life. One that turned him into a hero in your eyes. Apparently, however, he left out the part where at any moment, he could keel over and die on you on the dance floor." He shook his head. "I don't really blame him for that part, I guess."

Oh, Jake. It was as if she were watching him suffocate all over again, but this time on some wretched lie that he'd worked up inside his head.

Because, as he spoke, his words clicked inside her. No wonder he felt so familiar to her. No wonder she'd had an immediate affinity to him. No wonder she'd wanted to walk into his arms this morning.

He stood up. "The worst part is, you would have really liked Alex. And the Jake he created for you was only the good half of the story. I'm really sorry that neither of them exists."

Then, as he left to join Gordy in the parlor, he dropped the towel into her lap. "And by the way, you have grease on your face."

CHAPTER ELEVEN

"When Alex stole your life, he also left out the fact that you're an idiot."

Jake winced at Violet's words but didn't turn. Not when he knew he had pain etched in his eyes, his face. The last thing he wanted her to see was the shame of her finding him in the barn, gasping his last breath.

Indeed, he wished the life Alex concocted for her had been true. All the strengths, none of the paralyzing weaknesses. He might have conjured up the same lies if he'd been in Alex's shoes.

Violet's hand on his arm turned him. "Did you hear me?"

"Yes. I'm an idiot. Got it." He went to turn away but she wouldn't let him.

"No, you don't. Do you really think I would be angry at you for Alex's tall tales? That you're to blame for what Alex did?"

She was so beautiful it hurt, right down the center of his chest. Those violet-gray eyes, now shimmering, burrowing their way through him, that streak of grease on her face that he longed to wipe away. "I just know that I'm not Alex. I never will be. When I was a child, I was diagnosed as depressed, called weak. But the fact is…I am weak, Violet. You have no idea. So…let's just leave it. I'm sorry I'm not Alex."

"You think I want Alex?"

"Wasn't that why you kept writing to him for the last four years, when all you got back was postcards? I'd say you were holding out for something, yeah."

His words stung, he knew it by the wince on her face. "Thank you for that reminder, Jake. And, you're right. I had hoped that even though Alex knew the real me, he liked me anyway." She reached up and wiped the grease from her face.

"The real you? Like the one who could fix the radio and the generator? The one who worked in the motor pool?"

"You know?" Her voice fell.

A little of the heat went out of his chest then. His voice softened. "Yes, I knew. Why didn't you just tell me?"

"For lots of reasons," she said, her mouth tightening. "For every single time some solider made a crude comment. And the looks the other women in Frost gave me, the rumors I caught about what they thought women were doing overseas." She looked away. "I didn't want you to think those things about me."

"I would never think those things, Violet."

Out of the corner of his eye, he saw Gordy look up from where he was maneuvering the tree into the stand.

Now. Tell her the truth now. The impulse filled his throat, burning as he drew in a breath, his chest bruised and aching from the effects of his asthma attack. *In fact, Violet, I know all about you—*

"I can't believe Alex told you I was in the motor pool," she said.

"Alex was proud of you." *And so am I.* And then, as if his arm had defected and decided to run on its own power, he reached up and rubbed the chaser of oil off her chin. "It's kind of cute, actually."

She stared at him.

Oh, he hated Alex then. "I hate that Alex stole from me all the good things you might have known about me. Now, my life is just a cheap replica of what he embellished."

"But Alex can't steal this."

She surprised him, then. In fact, he might have even stopped her if he'd known, given the fact that little Arnie kept turning around to stare at them.

Or, maybe not, because at least she had the courage to do what he couldn't. She stepped up to him, lifted her face to his, and kissed him.

Kissed him. And, like the idiot that he was—Violet pegged that well—Jake just stood there.

Then, something ignited inside him and he came to life. His hand slid around the back of her neck, his eyes closing as he kissed her back. All that he was dropped away, all the weakness, the shame, the could-have-beens, the was-nots vanished, and he became simply a man kissing the woman he loved.

And oh, how he loved her. Had loved her for years, really— loved her courage and her loyalty and her tenacity, but now, here, in his arms, smelling of gasoline and even the smoke from his asthma powder, he loved her kindness, the way she'd wanted to be for him the woman she thought he wanted.

But he wanted Violet. This one, with a soft but eager touch, the one who burned peaches and couldn't dance. The one who was angry at Alex, not him.

The one who tasted like tea and sugar. She stepped closer into his embrace, wrapping her arms around his waist.

"Ahem."

Gordy's cleared throat stopped Jake from wrapping his arms around her. He leaned back, blew out a breath—he realized he'd been holding it—and smiled.

A blush was working up her face. "I've never done that before."

He ran his fingers along her cheek. "I'm glad to hear that."

She ducked her head. "I'm sorry. It wasn't very ladylike."

He lifted her chin, met her beautiful violet-gray eyes, and kissed her on the forehead.

"So, you weren't the one who rescued Alex from the ice?"

"He rescued me. And nearly died."

"But you were the one who got help."

He lifted a shoulder. She raised an eyebrow. "And the oranges?"

"My Christmas present the year my brother died."

"Influenza, right?"

He nodded.

"Alex taught you chess?"

"Apparently he liked to think that."

Her face softened. "Whose mother died of TB?"

"Alex's. Right before the war. She was our housekeeper."

"The one who made the Russian treats."

He nodded, but her words settled inside him. Russian treats... "I have an idea."

"Please don't say that word. It gives me hives," Gordy said as he began to unravel the lights. The tree nearly brushed the ceiling in the parlor, where Gordy had set it up after moving the radio and the chairs. "Jake's brainy ideas can kill a man."

"Lights!" Arnie said, as Gordy plugged them into the wall socket.

Jake turned to Violet. "Was that the generator I heard running out in the barn?"

She made a face.

Jake ran his thumb down her face, wanting to kiss her again. "Maybe Christmas is on its way, after all."

* * * * *

"Jake, I'm not sure if you're trying to set the house on fire, or just creating a science experiment, but I believe if you continue to boil that can, we may have an explosion on our hands." Dottie stood back, away from the stove where Jake had set the can of sweetened condensed milk, unopened in a pot, bringing the water to boil around it.

"Calm down, Dottie. You'll just have to trust me a little."

"Another Russian recipe?"

He grinned at her as he crushed her stale soda crackers into a bowl.

The vibrant, hopeful Jake of this morning had returned, although he still appeared peaked around the gills. He'd scared her when Gordy dragged him in from the barn, set him at the table looking gray and barely able to take a breath.

So much so that Dottie had even lifted a prayer to heaven, in case the Almighty might be looking down upon them. In fact, if she weren't a Lutheran, but one of those Episcopalians, she might even believe He'd sent one of His angels down to hover among them.

There hummed a sort of Christmas cheer under the layer of chill, warming her from the inside out. A stirring of Christmas past into the Christmas present, Violet dressing the tree with ornaments, and Arnie cranking the Victrola, dragging out her

Christmas records. Gene Autry's "Rudolph the Red-nosed Reindeer" played, and before that, Bing Crosby's "White Christmas."

You know Dasher, and Dancer, and Prancer, and Vixen...

Arnie had reconstructed his train set around the tree, atop the tree skirt, and Gordy had even found the carved crèche up in the attic, setting it up on the sewing table, the sheep in dire jeopardy as the train came over the mountain to plow them over.

She let the memory of Nelson sprawled on the floor as she prepared Christmas Eve dinner tiptoe into her memory like syrup, warm and sweet through her. He'd keep sneaking into the kitchen to stick his chubby finger into a chocolate bowl or lick the whipped cream off the spoon.

Nelson! She swatted at his hand in her memory, chased him out of the kitchen, but lingered there, watching him go over to the tree, take off the ornaments, and play with them on the sofa.

Perhaps no, it didn't hurt to remember him, to allow him in to resurrect the sweet memories, to share them with her Storm House family.

Dottie had even dug out a Hormel foods promotional leaflet and found a canned ham recipe that might actually pass for Christmas dinner. She'd filled her Christmas mold with slices of processed ham then used the rest of her baking powder and flour to make biscuits, which she also filled with pieces of ham. She'd bake it, then make a cream sauce of the hardened chunk of cheese in the fridge and a jar of tomatoes.

At least it would be colorful.

And edible, which she couldn't exactly say for Jake's concoction. "And you're just going to boil the can until it's...tender?"

He laughed. "No. I'm making caramel. The sugar will cook and turn thick. Then I'll pour it over the crackers. It'll melt in your mouth."

"I've never met a man so good at cooking, Jake."

He glanced over his shoulder and she couldn't read his expression. "The hidden talents of a boy who spent his formative years inside."

Oh, Jake. She wanted to press her hand on his shoulder. Or turn him and give him a motherly hug.

She softened her voice. "I remember when Nelson was about five years old, he got the German measles. I had to darken his room so the light wouldn't destroy his eyesight, and he lay there in the darkness, his fever raging, for three days. I was beside myself. I couldn't help my son. He was crying and miserable.

"So, I did the only thing I could. I told him stories. One after another as I fought to keep his fever down. Years later, he told me that he remembered every one of them, although I had no idea what I said. I just remembered praying, and hoping God would help me keep my son alive."

Jake didn't turn, didn't acknowledge her, just kept crumbling the crackers.

"Have you considered that God made you exactly the way He wanted you to be? You're tenderhearted and kind. And maybe being ill as a child helped make you that way."

Jake's jaw tightened. "Yes."

"Jake, I haven't been in church for a few years, I admit it, but once upon a time I was a God-fearing woman. And I remember my Bible. It specifically says that God doesn't expect us to be strong without

Him. That we're supposed to need Him, and there's no disgrace in that. In fact, weakness just might be the mark of a man of God. Don't call yourself weak because of the things you can't do. Call yourself weak when you don't let God take over, do His work in your life."

His shoulders lifted and fell on a deep breath.

"That's the point of Christmas, isn't it? Our weakness, His strength? Him coming to our rescue?"

He picked up the can. Glanced over his shoulder. Met her eyes.

They stood there a moment, her own words resonating back at her. Where had they come from? *Our weakness, His strength. Him coming to our rescue?* Even breaking through the cold barriers of her heart, no matter how much it hurt?

Indeed, God had thawed her heart so much so that she could feel every nuance, every thread of heat emanating through the house. In her spirit.

No, Christmas hadn't given up on her after all.

Jake drew in a long breath. "I'm so sorry about Nelson, Dottie."

His words didn't hurt, didn't pinch. She took them in, tasting their sweetness. "Thank you, Jake. You and he would have gotten along. I just wish I could have gotten one last letter from Nelson. Other women received one from their sons after their deaths—I thought Nelson would have written me one too. Maybe it was lost in battle, but I would have certainly liked to hear his voice, one last time."

Jake leaned down and kissed her on the cheek. "I know what it would have said."

She frowned.

"It would have said, 'Thanks, Mom.'"

She turned away, her eyes stinging.

"Want to see a Russian miracle?"

He opened the can with an opener. The creamy milk had turned brown and thick, into caramel. He poured it over the bowl of crackers and stirred it with a spoon.

The smell, tangy and buttery, filled the kitchen. In it she could taste the sweetness of the coming Christmas Eve. They would share dinner. Tell a Christmas story.

The thought caught her breath. Tell a Christmas story. But yes...she'd tell a Christmas story to Arnie.

Maybe he'd even climb on her lap.

She looked past Jake, out the window. It seemed the wind had begun to die, the storm clearing. She saw sky peeking through the snow covering the window.

No. After everything, God couldn't abate the storm before Christmas Eve.

She wrapped her arms around herself, stifling a shiver as Gordy tromped through the kitchen, little Arnie on his tail.

"We're going outside to stoke up the coal furnace. Time for heat in this house."

Dottie watched them disappear into the mudroom. Funny, until a moment ago, she thought the house felt warm enough.

* * * * *

Gordy just wanted a speck of Jake's Dapper Dan's magic. An ounce, an inkling, just let some of it chip off Jake and onto Gordy.

Then, maybe he'd figure out how to take Dottie in his arms and propose. In the kitchen, or the parlor, under the sparkling lights, with "White Christmas" playing on the Victrola.

Dottie, I love you. He could figure out that much. Beyond that, words escaped him.

Jake made it look too easy.

Jake merely stood there while Violet did the kissing.

It made a guy want to give up. But Gordy wasn't going to let the night go by without asking Dottie. With the storm clearing overhead, he was running out of time.

The wind still wound his scarf around his face, bit at his skin. He'd made Arnie bundle up in an old pair of Nelson's coveralls, still hanging in the back room, not to mention his own wool jacket, hat, and mittens.

"Where's the coal chute, Mr. Lindholm?"

He paced it out from the house and handed Arnie a shovel. "Start digging."

Arnie dove in with gusto, the energy of being cooped inside for two days spilling out in a flurry of snow.

Gordy's back still ached, a low, persistent burn. He couldn't wait until he could sit by the fire, put his feet up, share the evening with Dottie at home.

At home. Only, this wasn't his home. And if he didn't figure out a way to ask her soon, as soon as the storm lifted, he'd be forced to go home.

Back to their separate lives, the magic of Storm House vanished.

Arnie unearthed the handle on the cellar door. "Found it!"

"Good job—now let's cut out the rest of the door."

If they could get inside, they could hand-fill the coal furnace and start the electricity. And next spring Gordy would talk Dottie into cutting a passageway through the kitchen directly to the stoker in case next winter they ended up trapped in another Christmas Eve blizzard.

Not that he'd argue with God for the providence of this one. Gordy hadn't exactly been praying his way through this weekend, but if he had been paying attention, he'd thank the Almighty for His mysterious ways.

For knowing the unspoken longings in his heart.

For Dottie's forgiveness. Oh sure, she hadn't exactly said the words, but the way she smiled at him, warmth in her eyes as she rearranged the lights on the tree, or hung stockings by the fireplace, or even dusted around the crèche he'd retrieved, glancing at him out of the corner of her eye...he could convince himself that she'd forgiven him.

Arnie climbed off the cellar door, and Gordy used the edge of his shovel to pry it open. The smell of coal drifted out of the recesses. He climbed down the steps, Arnie behind him.

"Arnie, grab the clinker out before we fill it up."

Arnie opened the coal furnace, took a poker, and dislodged the donut-shaped clinker. He let it fall on the floor.

"We'll carry it out behind the barn after we get the stove going. C'mere and help me shovel coal into the furnace."

Arnie was a good little worker, digging into the pile, transferring the chunks of coal to the furnace. Gordy shoved the paper he'd brought from the mudroom into the center, lit it with a match, waiting for it to catch onto the coal. Even without electricity, the heat would rise into the house. It would be toasty warm by tonight's Christmas Eve celebration.

Arnie hiked up the clinker on the pole. "I'll go dump this behind the barn."

"You're a good boy, Arnie," Gordy said as they climbed out of the cellar. "I'll bet your daddy is real proud of you." He'd have to return in an hour to load in more coal.

"My daddy is in heaven," Arnie said.

Oh. Gordy's heart gave a little lurch. He'd forgotten. "I'm so sorry to hear that."

Arnie lifted a shoulder, trudging out ahead of him as he closed the cellar door.

Gordy caught up to him. "You must have been pretty young when your daddy went off to war."

"I don't remember him, except for the pictures. Mama misses him, though. She cries sometimes."

"I'm sorry for your mama," Gordy said. "It's hard to lose someone you love." His own words found him, settled inside. *It's hard to lose someone you love.*

Indeed.

Arnie carried the clinker behind the barn, dropped it. Then he stared up at Gordy. "Mama tells me stories, and I say that I remember him, but…" He had big eyes, and they seemed to glisten as he looked up at Gordy. "I want to be a hero like him when I grow up."

Gordy cupped the little boy's chin. "I have no doubt you will be."

Again, Arnie lifted a shoulder. He shuffled past Gordy, toward the house.

Gordy stood there, barely able to make out his porch light in the gloomy day. It seemed to twinkle through the dusk, as if beckoning.

"Arnie, you go on into the house. I'll be in presently."

"Where you going?"

He could get home and back in twenty minutes, probably.

And then he'd really have a proper proposal.

"I'm going to find some magic and give it to Dottie so we can finally be happy."

Arnie grinned up at him like he knew exactly what Gordy meant.

Turning up his collar, Gordy headed down the drive, past the remnant of Nelson's tree, the crushed Plymouth, hiking through the snow as he hit the road. His feet crashed through the drifts, up to his hips in places, and he worked up a sweat, his back on fire by the time he reached the marsh. Here, the snow seemed more pliable, and he tromped his way through, crushing the brittle grasses.

The front porch protected his doorway, but he still had to head out to the barn for a shovel, kicking his way to the door, then wedging it open and sliding through. He checked in on Harriet, fed her, checked her milk bag.

He shouldn't have panicked. Indeed, the milker would probably have to be retired to the slaughterhouse soon. He ran his hand over her back. "Sorry, old girl."

He picked up a shovel, dug his way to his door, then shoved it open.

The chill from the long-dead fire embedded the house. He longed to hear Barnabas's bark, greeting him.

C'mere, old boy. The memory of Nelson walked in behind Gordy, crouching beside the stone hearth, waggling the dog's ears.

Gordy let the memory warm him as he tromped through the

house to his bedroom. He pulled open his top dresser drawer and pulled out a rectangular box, shoving it into the pocket of his flannel shirt. Then, he went to his parents' room.

He hadn't disturbed it since his mother's passing, almost ten years ago. Not that superstition stopped him; he simply hadn't had a reason. Or time.

He found her ring in the top bureau drawer where he'd put it after her burial. A simple band of white gold with two small diamonds, side by side. His father gave it to her on their twentieth wedding anniversary.

Dottie could wear this ring.

He folded it in a sock then shoved the ring into his pants pocket.

In the kitchen, he found a burlap bag and raided his pantry. A tin of cookies, potatoes, another canned ham, some peppermints, and in his icebox he found a crate of oranges. He added five to the bag, relishing the idea of the smiles on the faces of his Storm House family.

Family. He'd begun to think of them all as family. Jake and Violet, his children, Arnie his grandchild.

Dottie, his wife.

The sun had begun to sink into the horizon as he exited his house, pulling the door tight behind him. A shimmering ball of haze, the sunset spilled out cranberry and marmalade along the horizon. The wind found his nose, burned it, whistled in his ears. Already his toes felt thick, his legs numb, but he'd make it across the marsh, back to Dottie's warm house.

The wind chill would trap them inside tonight, but he guessed by tomorrow, everyone could return home.

He tried to imagine Dottie's house quiet, without the ring of Jake's ideas, Violet's humming as she hung Christmas ornaments, Arnie's motoring noises. Dottie, clucking over the mess he might be making.

He wouldn't think about tomorrow.

We're happy tonight,

Walkin' in a winter wonderland.

Despite the trail he'd carved earlier, the way back seemed more difficult, his breath crisp and sharp in his chest. The pain had traveled up his neck, around to his chest, almost a burning. Probably that strange cereal Jake had served them for breakfast.

Gordy's legs turned to anvils as he tromped past the marsh, onto the road. Sweat trickled down his back, his chest. His arm seemed to grow numb, his chest woolen, almost as if his heart had expanded to fill it. He stopped in the road, bracing his hand on the stone wall, just to rest.

But the ache didn't ease, his breaths coming shorter.

He glanced up at the house. Just get inside, get home. He'd simply overexerted himself today.

Get home. Back to Dottie.

Home.

He stood up, took a step, and then the fist around his chest closed and snuffed out his breath. He dropped the bag of food.

Then Gordy pitched face first into the snow.

Home.

CHAPTER TWELVE

There were times when Violet took a square look at herself and didn't understand her own actions. Her own mind.

Some errant, fervent part of herself had grabbed a hold of her common sense and propelled her into Jake's arms.

She'd kissed the man. And, for too long of a moment, he didn't kiss her back. Just stood there, shocked. And right then, she heard it.

A man doesn't like a lady to make the first move. Oh, thank you, Mother.

Thankfully, Jake's shock turned into a response quick enough for her to not disentangle herself and flee the room in shame

She could still taste his touch on her lips—strong and urgent, the husky scent of smoke. Her heart hammered when she remembered the grip of his hand behind her neck, the little noise of surprise—or perhaps desire?—he'd made before Gordy reminded them that he and Arnie watched them from across the room.

Now, Jake had escaped to the kitchen to make some sort of new concoction for Christmas, and Dottie was upstairs rummaging for something, and Violet sat in the parlor, cutting out paper snowflakes with Arnie as if she hadn't just thrown herself at a man she'd only met two days ago.

Although, truth be told, perhaps she'd met him four years ago. Perhaps she'd known him all along.

Alex stole my life. No wonder she felt as if she knew him from the moment he walked in the door. It eased her guilt that much more for falling for another man only hours after finding out about Alex's death.

Wait. She didn't love Jake, did she? Could she love him?

She'd thought she loved Alex, but perhaps she'd only been in love with the hope of love.

In fact, she'd considered nothing of romance when she began to write to him. He'd simply been a soldier, shipping off to war. They'd never exchanged anything but friendly letters. He'd even stopped writing for six months. Silence on his end as she traveled with SHEAF through war-torn Europe, witnessing so many lives destroyed, turned her hollow. She kept writing, however, because it just helped to have someone to connect to, to remind herself that someone knew she was alive and serving her country.

Then one day, a postcard arrived. Not from Paris or London, but Minneapolis. Then Chicago and New York, New Orleans, and finally, a Christmas card.

All sent to her from America. Cheerful greetings with just the words, "thinking of you," and "Alex."

Something about the thoughtfulness of his greetings spoke to her heart.

In a season when she'd felt forgotten, Alex's postcards made her feel remembered.

And, maybe she'd helped him feel…special. *Alex stole my life.* Maybe he needed to be someone different, someone new. Once he returned stateside, to reality, perhaps he didn't know how to tell her the truth. Hence, the cryptic postcards.

His lies might help her forgive Alex, also, for not hopping on a train and finding her.

So why did Jake decide he needed to face her?

"Make sure you hold it tight, right here in the corner, or you'll cut off the center of the snowflake and it will fall apart."

"Did you make the snowflakes in the window at the library?" Arnie asked as he worked the scissors, his tongue caught between his teeth.

"Mrs. Morgan made them," she said.

"She used to scare me," Arnie said, setting down his scissors. He unfolded his snowflake. "But I didn't really know her."

"That's a beautiful snowflake," Violet said as she cut her own. She caught his eye, lowering her voice. "Wanna know a secret?"

He nodded.

"She used to scare me too. But she doesn't scare me so much anymore. I think she was just lonely."

"Because her son died?"

"You know about that?"

He nodded. "His picture is on the wall by the library with the other five men we lost."

Yes. Out of the entire town, they'd only lost five men. A handful of heroes out of all the men in Frost who'd fought. Violet never really considered that before. No wonder Dottie wanted to lock herself in her house. No wonder people called her cursed.

Violet hated the rumors now. Hated that she'd even considered them.

But maybe you couldn't really know a person until you spent time with them. Until you saw them look with love upon another person, until you saw them hold a terrified child on their laps, wrap him in blankets.

Until you saw a man clutch that same child to his bare chest, enduring his cold body to save him. Until you saw his courage as he fought to breathe. Alex might have stolen the facts of Jake's life, but he couldn't steal Jake. Not the man he was. Not his servant's heart, that devastating smile, those eyes that, when he turned them upon her, made her feel like she might actually be beautiful. Even when wiping grease off her face...

He knew. Jake knew about her job.

Had he also known that Alex stole his life? She sat back, unfolding her snowflake to see the design.

He didn't come here thinking he could take Alex's place in her heart, did he?

No...he couldn't have known, could he? Unless Alex told him. But Jake had appeared surprised—even horrified—when she accused him of being the hero and saving Alex from the ice yesterday. No, he couldn't have known about Alex's lies.

Then why the visit?

"Let's pin these to the window, shall we?" Violet said and took Arnie's snowflake to the parlor window. Outside, the sun cooked the horizon, a hot ball against the gunmetal sky. She taped the snowflakes up on the glass, feeling it shake against the wind. The gusts seemed to be fewer between.

"Put this one on the kitchen window," Arnie said. He handed her another finished snowflake.

"This is another pretty snowflake, Arnie." She took it out to the kitchen. Jake was at the sink, washing dishes. He looked at her, his face lighting up. "The lights on the tree really make it festive."

"Did you make that treat?" She motioned to a concoction of caramel on the counter.

He nodded. "Want a bite?" Drying his hands, he nipped off a piece and walked over to her. "Open up."

She grinned then opened her mouth. He dropped it in. Tangy, with a hint of salt, it made her only want more. "What is it?"

"You like it?" He stepped closer to her, running his finger down her face, eliciting a trail of heat.

"Mmm-hmm," she said, touching her hand to his chest. He seemed to be breathing just fine now. She dipped her finger into the well at his neck.

He smiled. "You are so beautiful, did you know that?"

She looked away, but he tugged her chin back.

"You are so beautiful," he said again. Then he kissed her. Sweetly, taking his time. He ran his thumb down the bones of her face before moving his hand again behind her neck. She relaxed into his touch, molding herself to him.

Could she love this man after only two days? He wrapped his other arm around her and she let him deepen his kiss.

This. This is what she'd hoped she'd find with Alex.

Or, perhaps she only dreamed of finding it, period.

She eased away from Jake, smiled up at him. Ran her hand down his now whiskered cheek. It didn't matter why Jake came. Just that he was here.

"Miss Hart, is Mr. Lindholm back yet?" Arnie ran into the

room, nearly banging into her. He was holding the homemade tractor, the wheel off in his hand. "The tractor broke."

Violet took it. "It's not broken, the wheel just came off. Do you have the pin?"

He handed her a long, thin screw. She wiggled the wheel back on the screw, then into the tractor. "I need a screwdriver."

"I might have something," Jake said, and opened his suitcase. Dug through his folded clothes, the brown parcel, until he unearthed a small eyeglass repair kit and handed it to her.

But her gaze had fixed on the package he'd put on the table. An envelope from the US Army, addressed to Jacob Ramsey III. She stared at the date.

October 1945. About the time Alex had begun to send postcards from America. She picked up the package. "What's this?"

It was the way Jake's breath caught, the funny noise he made, the attempt he made to reach out and grab it back that made her pause. That sent the shard of panic through her.

She stared at him. His face twitched, then, his eyes darted away from her. "I meant to give that to you."

The package bulged, the top open. "It's letters." She leafed through them, realization hot, like syrup through her. Her letters.

"What is this?"

"These are—these are the letters you sent to Alex. I thought you might want them back."

Oh. Except…she looked at the package, the date. "I don't understand. Why is this package addressed to you? Over four years ago?"

He picked up the tractor, began to fit the wheel on.

"Jake?"

"He died, Violet." He pulled out the screwdriver, fitted it into the wheel, and tightened it down, not looking at her.

"I know—"

"No, you don't know." He sighed, met her eyes. Swallowed. "He died four and a half years ago, in Germany, in the battle for Berlin. They sent his belongings to me."

Four and a half years…she stared at the letters. "But…no, he sent me postcards. From Minneapolis and Chicago and…" She froze as the truth seeped into her, found her heart. "*You* sent me the postcards."

He handed the tractor back to Arnie. Drew in a long breath. "I never meant…I just…"

"You read my mail."

He nodded. "You were so lonely. And…" He shook his head. "I never meant it to get this far. I just loved hearing about your life and your hopes and dreams—"

"You said Alex stole your life. But you—you stole mine! These letters weren't for you, Jake. They were private and…" She pressed her hand to her mouth, her eyes burning. "You *knew*. You knew that I was a WAAC and worked in the motor pool and…you knew everything. About the cruel things the men said, and how—how I came home. You got my Christmas greetings and my…" Her voice turned dark. "My invitation to the dance."

"Violet—"

"He's not out there." Arnie had taken the tractor, stepped up to the window.

Violet couldn't move. He knew she couldn't dance. He knew about her father dying.

He knew that she hadn't had a date since returning home.

He knew she was lonely. And on her way to spinsterhood.

No wonder he'd jumped a train to see her.

A real hero.

She turned away from him.

"Don't, Jake. Just…stay away from me." She clutched the letters to her chest. "I knew this was too good to be true. The sooner I can escape the lies in this storm house the better."

* * * * *

Jake always believed he could fix nearly anything, but he didn't know how to fix this. He'd wanted to make her feel better, to make her less lonely, but he'd only made Violet feel naked and vulnerable and betrayed.

Exactly the opposite of what he'd intended.

He stared at Violet, her words turning him cold. *Stay away from me.*

Of course. What had he been thinking?

"Do you know where he went?" Arnie said.

Violet looked down at him, frowning. "Who?"

"Mr. Lindholm."

"Gordy isn't here?" Dottie said as she walked into the room. She held in her hand a small, wrapped box. "Where is he?"

"I don't know," Arnie said. "He said he'd be right in, and that was before we made snowflakes."

Dottie glanced at the window then handed the box to Arnie. "Can you put this under the tree?"

She turned to the window. Went to it to stare out. "Where could he be?"

Arnie returned, pressed his nose against the window. "I see him! There on the wall!"

Jake looked up, found him through the darkening window just as Gordy disappeared from view. "Did he just fall?"

Dottie pressed her hand on the window. "Gordy? Gordy!"

The shadows of twilight could just be hiding him, but no, he didn't see Gordy rise.

"I'm going out there," Jake said and headed to the mudroom.

"I'm coming with you." Violet left her package on the table and followed him.

He shut the mudroom door behind her. "Violet—"

"I could have lied to Alex, you know. Every letter, made my life up."

"Violet, I know it was wrong to read your mail, it's just... well, he'd told me about you. He told me how much you meant to him."

"How I was *everything* to him?"

He didn't miss the sarcasm in her voice. He took a breath. "Violet, you're everything to me."

"You don't even know me." She reached for her jacket.

"I do know you. I know you're someone who sacrifices for others, that you believe in love, that someday you'll make an amazing mother. I know that I want to be with you."

"Let's just get Gordy." She pushed past him, out into the biting cold.

The freeze burned his eyes, shredded his breath away as he pulled up his scarf, fought his way down the hill. "Violet!"

"He fell down here somewhere!"

They found him crumpled in the snow beyond the stone wall, in the road, although it seemed a sea of white. Gordy had curled into himself, his breathing shallow, his eyes pained.

"Gordy! What's the matter?"

The air delivered his voice on a puff of white smoke. "I don't know. I can't breathe. My chest, it's—"

"He could be having a heart attack. Let's get him inside." Jake ran his hand under Gordy's back, flung his arm over his shoulder. "Help me!"

Violet took Gordy's other arm. They struggled with him into the house, through the mudroom, onto the kitchen floor.

He moaned, his cheeks whitened with the cold.

"Gordy!" Dottie dropped to her knees beside him.

"He needs a doctor, Dottie," Jake said. "I think he's having a heart attack."

Dottie looked up at him, at Violet. "But the cars are buried. I…"

And thanks to him, they couldn't get them out of the driveway anyway. But— "The sleigh. We could hook up the sleigh to the horse in the barn," Jake said.

"Oh no," Dottie said. "Ollie is not a horse you can hitch to the sleigh. I've never been able to—"

"We'll do it." Jake turned to Violet. "We can do it."

"What, now you can tame animals? What can't you do? Oh, wait, I know. Tell the truth."

He hid his wince. "Dottie. Do you have any aspirin?"

"Yes, yes—"

"Go, get it. Give Gordy one, tell him to chew it up. We'll be back for him."

Jake stood up, caught Violet under the arm. "I need your help."

They had reached the barn before she yanked her hand away from his. She glared at him. "I don't know how to hitch up a horse."

"I do. But I need your help."

She didn't look at him.

In the tack room they found a harness, and Violet helped him smooth it over the horse's body. The horse had wild eyes, bobbing its head as Jake pushed the bit into his mouth.

He bent over, coughing as the horse stirred up dust.

"Take him out of the stall!" he said, coughing. He had to get out of the barn before his bruised lung closed up.

He was near the doorway when he heard the commotion. Violet had the animal by his halter, but he fought for his head.

Jake heard the panic in her voice. "Good...horse. Stop. Please—"

The animal ripped the reins from her hand. She stumbled back as the animal reared. "Jake!"

"Right here—I'm right here." He stepped in, swiped the reins. "Hey there, Ollie, shh." He kept his touch calm, his tone soothing as he settled the horse down. "We need to back him into the stall, hook up the sleigh."

"I don't know how to drive a sleigh."

"I do."

"How did you learn how to drive a sleigh?" She opened the stall.

He should have told her the truth long ago. "I wasn't allowed to do much as a child. I spent a lot of time in the kitchen with the cook. And, with my dad on house calls. He had a horse and sleigh in case of emergencies. I carried his medical bag." He clucked to the horse, moved him back into the stall. "C'mon, Ollie."

The animal snorted, took a step back. "Slide the sleigh guides into the harness."

She angled the guides into the harness.

"Just a little more." Jake ran his hand down the horse's head, calming it, then ran the leads down the back of the harness, tying them off on the carriage. He eased the horse forward. The sleigh, a two-seater, caught, pasted to the earth. Jake kept clucking at the horse as he eased it forward. "C'mon, Ollie."

Ollie nearly tromped over him as the sleigh broke free. He led the animal outside. The night had already descended, dark and starless.

"Hold him while I get Gordy."

But Violet marched past him, into the house. He tied up Ollie then followed her in.

Dottie had Gordy up on a chair, leaning over.

"I'm fine, Jake," he said. "It's just a backache."

"Trust me, you're not fine. We need to get you to a doctor."

"There's a clinic in town, but it's probably not open. You might have to take him right to Doctor Flemming's house," Dottie said.

"I'll show you," Violet said. She had tucked her package under her arm and slid her other under Gordy. "Dottie, can you bring me some blankets?"

Gordy moaned as Jake helped him to his feet. "Violet, you don't have to go. Gordy can show me—"

"Oh no, I'm going with you. And then, after I know Gordy is okay, I'm going home. I'm tired of letting you destroy my Christmas, Jake Ramsey. Go back to Minneapolis." She turned to Dottie. "Thank you for the storm house. Have a merry Christmas."

* * * * *

And just like that, they were gone.

Gordy with them…

But she hadn't said good-bye. And what if he died and…

Dottie refused to think this way. Gordy always came back. Always….

But he'd looked so pale.

Just like her father had, turning weaker and weaker, until he faded out of their lives. She'd walked in one morning and found him gone.

But burying her father didn't compare to burying her son.

And she couldn't bear to bury Gordy.

"Is Mr. Lindholm going to be okay?"

Dottie stood at the window, watching the sleigh take them out of the yard. Jake had a touch, for sure. Ollie scared her, and yet the horse obeyed Jake like he had Nelson.

She pressed her hand on the cold windowpane. "I hope so."

"Maybe we should pray for him," Arnie said, and folded his hand into hers.

She looked down at him, his big brown eyes, that pale face, and his words slipped right through her, landing on her heart.

"Yes. We'll pray for Mr. Lindholm," she said softly. Then, because she didn't know what else to do, she got on her knees, right there in the kitchen. Her heartbeat could deafen her, but she managed to find words. "Please, God, save Gordy."

Because she couldn't bear not seeing him creep over to her house to fill the woodbin, to check the coal stove, to leave pints of cream on her doorstep. She couldn't bear a night where she didn't watch his light turn off after hers.

She wasn't ready to say good-bye when she hadn't yet said hello.

"And help Mr. Lindstrom find his magic. Amen."

She looked at Arnie. "What magic?"

"He said he was looking for magic. He said he needed it, so he could give it to you. So you could be happy."

She stared at Arnie, at those sweet brown eyes. "Arnie, you are the magic." Then, because she was afraid, and because Arnie just kept looking at her, she hugged him.

He smelled of wood smoke embedded in his wool sweater, and an afternoon decorating the pine tree—or rather, stealing ornaments from it.

"Would you like me to tell you a story, Arnie?"

He nodded.

"Let's take our supper and sit under the tree."

She cut them pieces of canned ham, taking another long look out the window. A wan light showed, as if the clouds had parted with the wind, and a winter moon decided to light their path to town. *Please, God, bring them safely to the Flemmings.* The doctor lived in town, not far from the dance hall.

She and Arnie made a picnic in front of the fire and finished their ham casserole. Then, she set the plate of Jake's Russian candy between them.

"Once upon a time, there was a mitten. It was a beautiful mitten, but it was a sad mitten, because it belonged to an old, crabby lady. She had knitted it for her son, see, and he had gone away and left the mitten and the old lady behind."

"Didn't he want the mitten anymore?"

"Oh, I think he wanted it. He just couldn't take the mitten with him where he was going. See, he was going far away to fight in the war."

"Like my daddy?"

"Just like that. So, the mitten stayed with the crabby lady. But she never wore it, just put it in her pocket. And the mitten was very lonely, because it was used to being worn and loved by the boy.

"One day, she dropped the mitten in the snow. She didn't even know she'd dropped it, just kept going on her way. But the forest animals saw it drop. Now, there was a terrible blizzard blowing in, and they were cold. So, first the beaver came, and he decided he wanted to climb in it. Then, an otter came by, and he wanted in it too."

"A beaver and an otter can't fit in a mitten together."

"This was a special, stretchy mitten. And finally, the old wolf came by—"

"Did he eat them?"

"Oh no, see, he was cold too, so he made them move over. The mitten, oh, it stretched and moaned, but it let the wolf in too.

"Finally, a tiny squirrel came by. He was very small, so they let him wiggle in too. But the mitten was very, very full, and ready to break with all the stretching.

"When the old, crabby woman got home, she realized she'd lost her mitten. And, because it had belonged to her son, she went out to find it. She searched everywhere in the woods, under the rocks, in the trees, until she finally found it. But it had been stretched out of size by the beaver and the otter and the wolf. And she was so angry, she wanted to yell at them to leave, that they had destroyed her beloved mitten. But she was cold, from the blizzard. So—"

"So she moved in with the beaver and the otter and the wolf and the squirrel!"

"That's right. They all made room for her in the mitten. And they stayed there, cozy and warm until morning."

"Then what happened? Did the mitten break?"

"No, the mitten was very happy. Because mittens are made to keep things warm."

"But wasn't it all stretched out and lumpy? Like my mittens after they get wet?"

"Oh, indeed it was. But it didn't mind because that only meant that next time it snowed, all the forest animals would have a place to hide."

"What did the old, crabby lady do the next morning? You know, after the storm was over?"

After the storm was over. Dottie stared at the flickering fire, the remnants of Jake's treat in the bowl. The house no longer creaked in the wind, and the coal furnace had warmed the house to bearable.

"I don't know what she did."

"I think she invited the wolf and the beaver and the otter and the squirrel over for Christmas day." He grinned up at her. He'd lost an incisor—she hadn't noticed that before.

"You do, huh?"

He nodded.

"Well, speaking of Christmas, maybe you should go to bed, so that Santa will come."

"Do you think he'll find me?"

"Most definitely." She stood up, and he took her hand. "Can I sleep in the boy's room?"

His question only threw her for a beat. Then, "Absolutely."

She found Arnie a pair of pajamas and helped him under the covers of Nelson's bed, adding another blanket.

"My mommy sings me a song."

Dottie sat down on the side of his bed, combing his hair back from his face. Such a brave boy he'd been to survive the storm. "You love your mommy, don't you?"

"I have the best mom in the world!" He sang it a little, and she caught her lower lip in her teeth.

The best mom in the world.

The song came as if she'd sung it yesterday. She looked Arnie in his eyes, a softness in her chest.

"Jesus loves me, this I know,
For the Bible tells me so.
Little ones to Him belong,
They are weak but He is strong."

Arnie closed his eyes but sang the refrain with her. "Yes, Jesus loves me…"

She heard her own words, let them sink inside her, heat her through until it didn't hurt. "Yes, Jesus loves me."

Maybe God hadn't forgotten her this Christmas. Maybe He hadn't forgotten any of them. Maybe, yes, all she had of Christmas was Jesus. But He was enough.

He was, in fact, everything. "Yes, Jesus loves me. The Bible tells me so."

She leaned over without thinking and pressed a kiss to Arnie's forehead.

"Good night, Mrs. Morgan," he said.

Good night, Nelson. Sleep well.

* * * * *

Cocooned safely in the catacombs of the ice-city of Frigia, Flash Gordon and his compatriots have won the trust of Queen Fria, ruler of the land. When we last tuned into our hero, internationally famous athlete and interplanetary adventurer, he was fighting to find and save his beloved Dale Arden. But, driven by a terrible blizzard into the land of Frigia, and chased by a snow-bear, Flash was taken captive and tortured at Queen Fria's hands.

Queen Fria, however, enticed by Flash's bravery, cut his bonds free and allowed him to roam about the castle. Now, our hero, recovered from his wounds, finds himself in the inner chamber, in the room of gadgets where he can plot his journey to find Dale.

Arnie rolled over under the covers, tucking his knees to his chest. Outside, the sky had cleared, stars winking down at him. *Don't worry, Dale, tomorrow Flash will break free....*

But what about Queen Fria? She would be left alone in her castle, no one left to defend her. Not with Dr. Zarkov and Thun, the Lionman gone on ahead to scout the country.

Her story wheedled inside him. He saw the mitten, misshapen, empty in the snow. It would be buried, forgotten, trampled on.

Destroyed.

He got up, throwing back his covers, and tiptoed out into the hallway. He could hear the crackling of the fire, Mrs. Morgan

humming "Jesus Loves Me" as he watched her rearrange ornaments on the tree.

She wasn't so old, maybe. With her blond hair pulled back, a
scarf around her head, she looked a lot like his mother. Only, tired.
Except, as she returned the lambs and baby Jesus to the manger
and picked up the farm animals and toy soldiers he'd left strewn
around, she didn't even seem that old.

He wanted to go downstairs, ask her for another story. Maybe
she'd let him stay up, wait for Santa Claus.

Pounding at the door, then voices startled him, and he shrank
back from the stairway as she hustled into the kitchen.

And then he heard her—Dale.

No, not Dale. "Mama!" Arnie raced down the stairs, hooking
his hand on the end of the banister and barreling toward the kitchen.
There she stood, dressed in Daddy's beaver coat and hat, her eyelids
frosty, and behind her, the sheriff, blowing on his hands. She caught
him up against her, pressing her cold lips against his neck.

"Arnie, you had me so frightened." She put him down,
crouched, looking him over. She was crying a little, and her eyes
were cracked and red, but he didn't smell whiskey. She pressed her
hand over her mouth then, and her shoulders started to shake.

He put his arms around her. "I'm fine, Mama. I'm safe. See,
I have my storm house."

But she just wrapped her arms around him, held onto him.

"How did you know he was here?" Mrs. Morgan was talking,
her voice sounding suddenly frail.

"Gordon Lindholm came into the clinic with Violet Hart. She
told us where to find him. I brought your horse and sleigh home."

Arnie looked up at the voice. The sheriff, in his oversized coat, his sculpted hat. Arnie shrank back from him, remembering the unfinished lines on the board. "I can unhitch him, stable him in the barn for you, if you'd like, Dottie."

Dottie nodded as Arnie's mother stood. "Thank you, thank you for taking care of my boy."

Arnie looked up at her, and Mrs. Morgan smiled down at him. "He's a very brave boy."

"And foolish! He should have never left the school!" But his mother smiled down at him, and he let the tension in his chest uncoil. "I went there straight from the factory, but you were gone." She looked at Mrs. Morgan. "We stayed there, in the school, all the girls from the mill and me. And another group holed up at the dance hall. Frank Duesy has his snowplow out and is clearing the roads. I followed the sheriff over in the farm truck. Do you need anything?"

Mrs. Morgan wrapped her arms around herself. Shook her head.

His mother took his hand. "Let's go home, Arnie. Tomorrow is Christmas Day. You don't want Santa to find you missing."

But he would find me here. The words nearly broached his lips. Instead, he nodded and scampered upstairs to change.

At long last our hero escapes the land of Frigia, riding the wily Snow Dragon, with its massive teeth. But he waves good-bye to Queen Fria, as she stands in the doorway of her enchanted castle, bidding him farewell on his journey.

Don't be frightened, Queen Fria. The Flash won't forget your great kindness to him and his companions.

CHAPTER THIRTEEN

Sunday, December 25

Jake knew everything about Violet's life.

At least everything she'd written to Alex. Violet tried to catalogue the stories, but they meshed together into a knot of disbelief.

Jake had been lying to her for over four years. Reading her mail, sending her postcards, nurturing the dream that Alex might be waiting on the other end.

Violet just wanted to flee back to her home, forget about Storm House and Jake Ramsey and the fact that he made her feel like a fool.

A pitiful fool. Because every word out of his mouth only confirmed it.

"You were just so lonely, Violet. And it broke my heart. I know it was wrong for me to read your letters. You have to know I didn't set out to betray you. I received Alex's packet and I was curious about this woman who wrote to him. I had to write back, and when you kept writing, I simply couldn't stop."

She didn't strangle him in the hallway of the Frost Medical Clinic only because he had saved Gordy's life. "No doubt about it," said Dr. Flemming as Jake had muscled Gordy into the physician's parlor, then to the medical clinic. Well on his way to a heart attack, Gordy received nitroglycerin, and she and Jake kept watch over him as the blizzard finally wore itself out.

Which meant Jake also had plenty of time to try to plead his case.

"It wasn't about deceiving you. It's about the fact that you were in Europe, alone, and I wanted you to know that someone cared."

"But you wrote to me—you made me believe Alex was alive!"

She'd earned a dark glance from one of the ward nurses for her strident 2 a.m. voice and cut it to low.

"You made me feel—and look—like a fool. Writing all those things to Alex. I even invited him to our Christmas ball."

"You did?"

She'd wanted to slap Jake then, for the look of anticipation on his face. "I invited *Alex*, not you, Jake. I didn't know you existed."

She'd hurt him, then, she knew it, the way his mouth closed, the cool set of his eyes. "Yes, of course. My mother received your letter and she's the one who sent it back."

Return to Sender.

She wanted to send Jake *Return to Sender*. She wound her arms around herself, shivering. "Why didn't you just leave it, Jake? I would have figured it out. You didn't have to come all the way to Frost."

"You would have thought Alex rejected you. I didn't want your heart to be broken."

She'd given a laugh that earned another throat clearing from the nurse. She schooled her voice. "My heart isn't broken. It's *shattered*. Eviscerated. I didn't just lose Alex. I lost the chance to start over, with you. To be a woman without grease on her face."

"But I don't want—"

She'd held up her hand. "I don't want you in my life, Jake. Go home. You delivered your message." And, as if to confirm that indeed, she wasn't at Storm House anymore, that she'd reverted to the soldier she was, she managed to say it all without a hitch in her voice.

Then she'd gotten up and found herself a pew in the chapel and tucked the bundle of letters under her head. She slept there, curled in her coat, letting the creases of the pew pad draw into her face.

She woke in the silence of the hospital, the gray of dawn sifting in through the windows of the chapel. The thunder of her heart propelled her to rise, and she shuffled back to Gordy's hospital room, her breath tight.

Please.

Gordy was still with them, sleeping hard, looking old and drawn in the dusky light.

Jake, however, had listened to her and left.

Have a very merry Christmas.

She flagged down Frank Duesy on his plow just as the sun cast gold over the waves of snow, turning it to gemstone.

"Can I get a ride home?"

He patted the bench seat next to him. "I gotta take another run out your direction anyway."

Violet tucked herself inside the cab, shivering.

Jake hadn't even said good-bye.

It didn't matter. She didn't want him in her life.

Really.

Absolutely.

She could probably sleep until the New Year. "Thanks,

Frank," she said as she stepped out of his cab. The sun had finally appeared, turning the sky a pale blue, cloudless. She stood for a moment, remembering the blue sky over the Trianon Palace Hotel in Versailles, after S.H.E.A.F had moved them there from London. A clear sky, without smoke or the debris of battle to mar it. A sky of hope.

"You sure you don't want me to run you to Johnny's place?"

"No. I'm sure my mother is worried." She shut the door, waving to him. He saluted to her then continued down the highway out of town, snow rolling off the side of his shovel like waves.

She had to hike through the drifts to the front door. The porch had protected it, but as she opened the front door—she expected at the least heat, if not the smells of Christmas day—a gasp of cold met her. The house shuddered as she shut the door behind her, caught in a silent chill.

"Mother?"

Her voice echoed against the walls of the house, and she listened, nothing but her heartbeat in her ears.

Mother? I'm home. She heard her voice echo back to her as if it might be two years ago, the moment she'd arrived home from her service in Europe. She'd wore her dress uniform, carried her army-issue duffel bag over her shoulder.

She hadn't really expected anyone at the train station. Just a feeble hope put her mother, her brothers there.

She'd braced herself for the fact that her father would be absent.

Violet had stood in the foyer, letting the duffel fall from her shoulder to hit the wood floor. The daisy clock in the kitchen ticked out her heartbeat. Her home smelled the same—lemony cleanser, the fragrance of pot roast, the redolence of family life. She spotted new sofas, the cushions wrapped in plastic, and a fancy new television set in the family room where the Wurlitzer once sat. She walked into the kitchen and discovered it empty. No casserole in the oven, no fresh-baked molasses cookies in the jar.

Water plinked into the sink from the rag hanging over the faucet.

She watched it gather on the edge, drop into the porcelain, bleed down into the drain.

"Violet?"

The voice turned her, and she found a smile as her mother swept into the room. Frances hadn't aged a day, it seemed, although as she drew closer, Violet could count more lines around her smile. "When did you get home?" She pulled her daughter close, and Violet closed her eyes, breathing in her mother's smell, talc and rosewater.

"Just now."

Frances held her at arm's length. "I'm so sorry. I have it on my calendar for next week." She pressed her hands against Violet's face, her dark eyes softening. "You're home. Finally."

Violet wove her fingers into her mother's. "I'm sorry I couldn't come home for Daddy's funeral."

Frances's eyes filled. "It happened so fast—Johnny didn't make it home either. But I gave him your father's watch, and that seemed to help. Johnny is so much like him, you know."

Violet watched as her mother put her purse on the table, pulled off her gloves.

No, she didn't know. Johnny wasn't at all like Daddy save his dark hair, the mischief in his eyes. He didn't have a mechanical bone in his body. She, however, was identical to her father.

Her voice shook. "Daddy promised me that watch, Mother."

Frances opened the icebox, pulled out a casserole. "It's a good thing Thomas and June are coming over for dinner. I made extra."

"Mother, the watch. Why did you give it to Johnny?"

Frances glanced at her. "It's a man's watch, Violet. It doesn't keep time, anyway."

It has its own mind, Vi, just like you.

"Go change out of those clothes and put on something pretty." Frances picked up a match to light the oven, smiled at her. "We're going to have a celebration."

A celebration because June was expecting.

And, oh yeah, that Violet had made it home from war.

Probably, it only felt that way.

"Mother?" Violet now called again as she dumped the package of letters onto the kitchen table and shucked off her coat. The electricity had probably stopped the coal stoker in their house too. She stopped at the foot of the stairs and called again.

Had her mother not made it home from the dance hall? Then again, Violet *had* taken the Plymouth.

The Plymouth. She'd have to ask Frank to pry the car out of the tree. Maybe after he'd gotten the roads cleared. She could park it in the garage, try to repair the radiator, the damage to the headlights.

It would probably never run the same again, however.

Mother had probably headed home with June and Thomas. Violet should probably get her boots on, find her snowshoes, and hike back into town, but first she needed to get the stove running, find something to eat, and…

And read those letters. She wanted to see what kind of things she wrote, decide just how embarrassed she should be.

How transparent had she been to Alex, really? She'd told him about her life here in Frost, but had she told him how the news of her father's passing had turned her inside out? That she couldn't dance but longed to?

Had she told him about the watch? And the fact that sometimes, when she lay in her bed, she wondered why she wasn't like other women?

Oh, shoot. Of course she did. She closed her eyes, shaking her head against the brutal truth. Jake knew her life. He knew her secrets. He knew her dreams.

Yeah, now she felt naked.

Pulling on her jacket, she headed downstairs to the cellar, thankful for the stairway her father put in. The coalman poured the coal in through another opening in the house, but it allowed them to access the furnace through the kitchen.

She checked the clinker then added paper and fuel to the center and lit it.

The paper flamed, then the coal began to burn. She shut the door. The heat would rise through the grate in the parlor. Maybe she'd take a pillow and blanket and park herself on top of it, try to press some warmth back into her brittle bones.

Returning to the kitchen, she found cheese and mincemeat and made herself a sandwich. Then, pouring a glass of milk, she retrieved the letters.

A bath would come next, but not until she had some real heat in the house.

She poured the contents of the envelope on the table then started to fish through it. Her early letters were thinner, probably less of herself in them as she talked about life at Fort Meade, or in London. Her last letters, however, contained the challenges of seeing so many people without family, without homes, without hope. She'd hated the brutality of war, wondered if there might be anything good waiting for her.

She read her last letter, sent from Berlin, a month before she shipped home. She'd been transferred to working in the chow line at one of the refugee camps, alongside the Red Cross workers. Meal after meager meal she handed to sallow, starving mothers, their children even more saggy beside them.

She simply longed to return home, to be safe, and away from the suffering. And yes, she'd hated herself for her weakness.

Getting up, she left her lunch and went upstairs to her room. She'd kept Alex's letters too, in a drawer in her desk. She fished them out then brought them back to the kitchen table and began to sort through them. Only a fool would not have noticed the change in handwriting, but then again, a gal not looking closely might not have noticed.

Thinking of you, Jake had written on his first card, sent from Minneapolis.

Stay safe, he'd written on another, featuring photos from the 1933 Chicago World's Fair.

From New York City, he'd chosen a card of the Metropolitan Opera House. *This reminded me of Versailles,* he'd written.

Had he ever been there? She had written to him about it.... Oh, he was too clever.

More postcards—of flowers in Washington, DC and then more of Minneapolis, one from London.

What did he do that he traveled so much?

I did a lot of things. Not all of them am I proud of. And none of them were very exciting.

He did do a lot of things—he cooked, and knew how to save a child from hypothermia, and could spot a heart attack, and soothe a horse, and...

I knew you were lonely, and I wanted to help.

What kind of man did that? Reached out to a person he didn't know? Was he some sort of shrink? *I didn't imagine that we'd meet. I just thought I'd let you know that someone cared until that some-day when you'd meet someone else and stop writing. I didn't mean for it to go this far. I never thought you'd fall in love with Alex.*

Fall in love with Alex?

Alex made her feel as if someone were listening, but Jake had found her in a storm. Jake had made her feel like she was worth fighting a storm for.

At least Storm-House-Jake did.

She put her head down on the table. But the storm was over.

And Jake was gone.

Stomping sounded on the front porch. She lifted her head as Johnny plowed into the house, his cheeks rosy. "Sis! You're okay!"

He unwound the snowy muffler from his face. "I'm sorry it took so long to get here. We wanted to wait until the storm passed, and then last night, well, we were all tucked in, see...but we figured you were okay." He slapped his gloves together, snow chunking off them. "The house feels cold. Did you forget to feed the furnace?"

She stared at him. "What are you talking about? I just got home too. I thought…you didn't know I wasn't here?"

Johnny's eyes widened. "No. We figured you headed home in the storm. Mother said you went to change clothes."

"I went to get the star from Dottie's house."

"Dottie?"

"Dorothy Morgan? She lives in that old Victorian?"

"Right. Of course…but—you were there? You weren't here?"

Did anyone care where she'd holed up in the storm? She stood up. "Is Mother okay?"

"She's cooking up a frenzy at Thomas's place. We've all been there since Thursday. They're fixing Christmas dinner right now. Mama told me to run out and ask you what's taking you so long." He gave her a look. "You look tired."

She pinched the bridge of her nose, trying to make sense of his words. "You mean you weren't even worried about me? You didn't wonder if I was okay out here?"

"Sorry. Should I have been worried? You're a take-care-of-yourself gal, Violet. I didn't know we were supposed to be worried."

A-take-care-of-yourself gal. Yep, that was her. Practically a man.

"Forget it. I…I'm tired. I think I'll stay here. Don't worry about me."

"For Christmas?" Johnny's eyes widened. "You want to be alone on Christmas?"

And right then, it hit her.

She *had* turned into Dottie. A woman who pushed all the

people who loved her out of her life. Maybe out of pride, maybe out of shame, but still, she'd be alone on Christmas.

But Dottie didn't want to be alone any more than Violet did. And it might take someone storming into her life, into her storm house to rescue her.

Not unlike Jake did for her.

"Mamma said to hurry—"

Violet rounded on him. "Johnny, just hold your horses. We'll get there when we get there. I gotta change, and then you're going to run me back over to Dottie's house. She's not spending one more Christmas alone."

She turned back to the letters, began to collect them. One of them caught her eye. She picked it up and read the script.

Her heart stopped right there, a ball of heat in her chest.

It couldn't be. She read the script again.

The storm had blown in a Christmas miracle.

* * * * *

"You're still here?" Gordy opened his eyes. "I feel as if I've been trampled by an ox." His chest burned, his arms soggy, his eyes weighted. And, across the room in a chair slouched Jake, looking as if he had been standing right behind him during the trampling.

Jake didn't rouse at his word, as if he hadn't heard him. Jake bore two days of whisker growth, a rumpled white shirt over a pair of jeans that looked like they'd belonged to Nelson, and enough sag in his face to know something despairing happened since Gordy had taken off for his house in the cold.

Like the fact that the last clear thing Gordy remembered was landing face down in a snowdrift. Or, the fact that he'd had a faint, dark memory of Jake and Violet shouting. And, the most glaring—Gordy was no longer at Dottie's house.

Something sharp and antiseptic pinched his nose, and footfalls on linoleum outside his open door clipped past him down the hallway. With the squeal of the bed beneath him, Gordy put the pieces together.

As if to confirm, a nurse walked by, her dark hair pinned up under her cap, wearing a dark blue sweater over her uniform.

"Nurse? How long have I been here?"

She stopped. It seemed she looked familiar, but he didn't know every face in town. She approached his bedside. "Oh, Mr. Lindholm, you just came in last night. You'll be fine." She patted his leg, but her voice had awakened Jake, who shook himself and sat up, yawning. He drew his hand down his face then scrubbed both hands over it.

"You look about how I feel," Gordy said.

Jake looked at him. Gave a half-grin. "You're a tough old geezer. Had to haul your carcass through the snow. What were you doing tramping around in the blizzard?"

Gordy looked away. Shook his head. "Doesn't matter now."

His golden opportunity, the storm house magic had passed. He wasn't sure how he might land on Dottie's doorstep again— not without a reason, and…

He didn't know what to say, anyway. So he had a ring. He and Dottie would return to watching each other's lights across the marsh, nothing but cold words on their lips as they avoided each other. Nothing would have changed.

Storm House was over. And with it, the capturing of the past, the reaching for the future.

"Really," Jake said. "Because when the nurses undressed you, they found this in your pocket." He held up the sock. "I made sure it wasn't lost because it sure looks like a pretty ring."

The ring. He met Jake's eyes, but he was shaking his head, wearing a smirk. "Gord-o, you went out in the storm because you want to propose to your lady."

"And nearly died doing it. What does that tell you?"

"That you're a romantic."

"And you need a good kick in the head."

Jake spilled the ring into his hand. "She'll say yes, if you ask her."

"I don't think so, Jake. Probably my old ticker knew that, was sending me a shot across the bow. Dottie and I...we're like oil and water."

"Naw. You and Dottie are just set in your ways. But you two saved Arnie. And you raised Nelson together. I was talking to some of the nurses around here. You didn't tell me he earned a bronze star."

"He received it after he died, but I never doubted he was a hero."

Jake slid up his chair. "He wasn't the only one who won a medal, was he, Gordy?"

"What did you do, go through my pockets?"

"I told you, the nurses gave me your belongings. A victory medal, from World War I? I didn't know you served."

"Just for a year."

"And you were going to give the medal to Arnie, weren't you?"

"The kid needed something for Christmas."

Jake drew in a breath, nodded. "We met his mother and the

sheriff at the hospital last night. I told her he was at Dottie's. They headed over there to pick him up. I'm sure he's back at home by now."

"Arnie's mother came to get him? That means Dottie's alone on Christmas Day?" Oh, Gordy might as well just crack his chest open, let Jake take a good look inside for the tone of his voice.

Jake worried the ring around his index finger. "Tell her you love her, Gordy. Marry the woman."

Gordy looked away. "I don't understand it, Jake. Why put us in that house together? Why shake things up? Things were fine as they were."

"What are you talking about?"

"Storm House. Being trapped in there only made me soft. It made me realize what I didn't have. I was fine before I—"

"Before God brought you in from the cold? Before you remembered what it was like to have people in your life who might go out and find you in a snowdrift?"

"I didn't need anyone looking for me."

"Yes, you do. You do need people looking out for you. You're so afraid that Dottie will turn away from you that you won't even knock on her front door."

"I blew it with her years ago."

"Yeah, you did. But apparently God's giving you a second chance."

"By sending the storm?"

Jake smiled. "And, by sending me."

"What are you talking about?"

Jake set the ring on the table. Then, he reached behind him

and pulled out his wallet. "If you want to marry Dottie, Gordy, I can help with that."

He was pulling something from his wallet, wearing an expression Nelson wore the day he arrived on Gordy's doorstep, his enlistment card in hand.

Indeed. Jake flashed him an ID. His military ID.

Gordy stared at him. "You're a priest?"

"A chaplain with the US Army. I'm currently on leave, but I believe I still have the power to marry you."

"But—but what about Violet? You *lied* to her. What kind of chaplain does that?"

Jake's smile fell. "A stupid, sinful one. One who wishes he could regret it." Jake raked his hand through his hair. "I know I shouldn't have read her letters, Gordy. Alex's package came to me, and I was trying to figure out how to write his eulogy, so I read his mail, just to see who might be writing to him. She moved me, Gordy. And…" He closed his eyes, running his fingers across them before he stared at Gordy. "But I'm not sorry, and that's the problem. I wish I could be." His eyes were cracked, tired.

As was his voice. "You were in war. You know how it is. Three days of rain and mindless shelling while you hide in your slit trench. I'd listen to the 88s and then the P-47s dive-bombing us, and I was the one who had to keep everyone calm. I'm pulling the wounded out of the trenches, I'm comforting the dying, then I'm handing out chocolate in foxholes. And every day, I'm watching men lose their arms, their legs, their lives, and I have no idea the condition of their souls. It's worse watching a man bleed out—not knowing if he's right with God, ready to meet his maker. It's a wretched thing to watch someone who is broken of body, but worse to watch a man broken in spirit, but unable to reach out for God's grace."

"That's what broke you, wasn't it?" Gordy said it softly, because he knew it would hurt.

Jake met his eyes. Nodded. "Helpless. It was too much for me. I couldn't bear not being able to save lives, and the darkness found me." He leaned back, ran his hands on his pants.

"I remember once, after a battle, looking up and thinking, if I could turn off the war, shut my ears to it all, the sunset could transport me away. Copper sunset silhouetting the birch trees against the indigo sky. A pale fingertip moon above as if God had given it a stamp of approval. All that beauty against so much loss. The paradox could take my breath away."

He looked at Gordy then. "Not unlike grace. Powerful. Unexpected. God's salvation against the blackness of our souls."

"Christmas," Gordy said softly.

"Storm House," Jake said. He clasped his hands together, tucked them between his knees, drew in a breath. "Once you get a taste of grace, it's so overwhelming it can bring you to tears. Especially when you're caught in the darkest night. Or the cruelest storm. That's what Violet's letters were to me. A storm house."

A storm house. Yes, Gordy understood that. Perhaps Dottie, the light across the marsh, had been his storm house for years.

Jake looked at his hands. "I couldn't help but write to her. And I couldn't stop. But the lying ate at my soul."

"Which is why you came to Frost."

"The truth is, I was hoping that, somehow, she'd know that it wasn't Alex but me writing to her. And that there was someone behind the postcards who truly cared. I told myself that maybe, for her, my postcards were grace too."

Gordy drew in a long breath. "I heard her tell you to leave."

Jake pressed his hands together. Nodded. "I probably should get home. I have soldiers I need to check in on at the VA hospital, broken men who are spending this holiday alone."

"Like Violet."

He looked up, and Gordy raised an eyebrow.

"And Dottie," Jake said slowly.

Gordy reached out, picked up the ring. "So, Rev, what are we going to do?"

Jake shook his head. "Violet doesn't want me."

Gordy smiled. "Good grief, son, don't you know anything about women? Go tell the nurses that I want to check out of this hotel."

* * * * *

Dottie should have known it would come to an end. Of course it would, because every time she believed in something, when she starting thinking that she and God might be even, He reminded her of her sins.

Her mistakes.

Her losses.

She sat on the sofa, her legs curled to herself, tucked under a quilt. She'd sat there most of the night, watching the flames flicker out and die in the hearth, listening to the blizzard blow itself out, staring at the lights of the Christmas tree.

Watching the lone package underneath. Why hadn't she given it to Arnie before he left? A stupid gift, really. What had she been thinking, caught up in the drama of the storm house, thinking the child would want a gift from her?

He'd practically flown into his mother's arms, couldn't wait to leave her home.

And Violet and Jake certainly hadn't returned. Not that she expected them, really. They had their own families, their own lives.

Lives in which she wasn't included.

Dottie's stomach rumbled. She still had the ham casserole she could heat up, really celebrate the day of Christ's birth.

She lowered her head to her knees. *Please let Gordy be okay.*

Okay, fine. She had to talk to God. Because frankly, she had no one else.

Or…

Mama, look what Santa brought me! Nelson came in through the mudroom, holding a package wrapped in burlap, his bright blue eyes gleaming. Dottie's heart stopped then swelled in her throat as she watched Nelson unwrap the burlap. A boxed train set sat inside, and he pulled it out, piece by piece, barely able to contain his joy.

Thanks, Gordy.

Years followed, with toy soldiers, an airplane kit, a BB gun, and finally the .22. Hunting trips, driving lessons, even that time Gordy taught him to box.

Gordy had raised Nelson too.

The truth caught her.

Gordy *had* been Nelson's father.

How many nights had she sat by Nelson's bed, praying that he would grow up to be a good man.

Gordy had taught him how.

Gordy had taught him to be a hero. Taught him how to fight, yes, but taught him also how to be a man of honor.

Maybe God is giving you another chance to make things right between you and Gordy.

Dottie's fingers went to her lips. He'd kissed her.

Kissed her. Just like he had in the barn so long ago.

Marry me, Dottie. You know you belong with me.

Yes. Yes, Gordy.

The word pulsed inside her, longing to push out. It didn't matter that he hadn't asked again. Didn't matter that he never used the three words, I love you. He'd shown her every day since then.

She had been a stubborn, prideful old woman, and she might have rattled around this too-big house—a house meant for family—for the rest of her days.

If it weren't for God and the blizzard and three strangers.

She saw Arnie, then, under the tree, playing with the train set. Saw Violet dancing in handsome Jake's arms. Saw Gordy with Arnie in his embrace, the boy sprawled against his chest.

Her Storm House family.

Come, Lord Jesus, be our guest. Her prayer resonated through her.

Perhaps Jesus *had* arrived this Christmas. Maybe He'd arrived in the storm, in the form of three strangers who needed a home. Maybe He'd arrived in the form of a little boy, cold and hungry.

Come, Lord Jesus, be my guest. In her life, her heart. In Storm House.

And let these gifts... Gifts like Gordy and Violet. Like Jake... and Arnie.

To us be blessed.

Blessed—remembered, loved.

Wasn't that the point of Christmas?

I don't celebrate Christmas anymore. Her conversation with Violet drifted back to her. *There's nothing left in it for me.*

What had Violet said? *Except, of course, Jesus.*

Jesus.

All these years, she'd thought God had taken away her reason to celebrate Christmas. But Christmas gave her son back to her. Christmas delivered her the one thing the world, and the war, wanted to steal.

Hope.

Hope invited her in from the storm.

Hope could keep her warm, keep out the chill of death.

Hope protected the memories she'd locked away.

And hope, despite the pain of it as it crept back into her life, showed her how to live, and to celebrate again. She pushed the quilt off, stood up. She had Hope in the form of the star sitting on the dining room table.

Heading upstairs, she combed her hair, brushed her teeth with the water she'd thawed, then washed her face. Okay, she'd apply some lipstick.

Then, Dottie rooted through her closet until she found a sweater—red. And a matching scarf to hold back her hair.

She looked tired, but it was an improvement.

She stood outside Nelson's door for a moment before taking a breath and entering.

In her memory, Arnie lay in the bed, humming "Jesus Loves Me."

Little ones to Him belong. They are weak but He is strong.

She rooted through the closet until she found Nelson's limp duffel bag she'd stashed away after the army sent it home with his belongings.

Then she returned downstairs, found an old creamery box from the entryway, and set it inside the duffel. In that, she loaded in the star.

She added Arnie's gift too. Just in case providence cast Arnie into her path.

The sky had released the power of the storm, leaving behind a beautiful blue-skied day. Dottie bundled up, wearing not only Nelson's coveralls and parka, but his wool rabbit hat and a pair of double-lined mittens.

Then she ventured outside.

The wind had died, but a nip in the air burned her eyes. She trudged over to the barn. The generator seemed to be puttering, coughing, nearly out of gas, and she found her father's wooden skis and poles before she turned it off.

The barn went dark, but she pulled the skis outside and strapped them onto her boots. Good thing her father had been as eccentric as people said he was.

She stopped by the tree on the way down the hill, inspecting it, and the Plymouth crushed beneath. Yes, the tree hadn't needed much to come down, the way the wood seemed brittle and rotted. Probably she would find another pine, plant it in the spring.

She let a smile find her, the winter wonderland charming her as she headed toward town. The Pikes' dog ran out to the road and followed her. Maybe she'd let herself get a dog too, like Digger,

Nelson's old beagle. *Please, Mom,* he'd said that year Digger arrived on her doorstep.

She'd had Gordy to thank for that too.

But really, she couldn't blame him. How could she say no to Nelson?

The memories warmed her as she skied into town, the duffel bag over her shoulder. Snowmen and caught fireflies and nights camping out in the backyard. She'd taught him to ice skate on the pond, and taken him driving in her father's truck when he turned eight. No wonder Gordy had to take him in hand—she was probably to blame for the day he drove the old roadster into the marsh.

Sweat piled down Dottie's back by the time she reached the dance hall. The giant tree in the circle hung thick with snow. She took off the skis and parked them next to the building. Then she shook off the tree, stepping back before the snowfall blanketed her.

The utility room in the rec hall had a ladder, and she pushed the door open. The chairs and tables still set up for the dance evidenced an abandoned evening. She found the ladder and dragged it out.

Setting it against the tree, she dug the feet into the ground, retrieved the light, and started to climb.

Oh, God, please don't let me fall.

The top was stiff with cold, but she managed to whittle the cone onto the top. The long cord ran fifteen feet to the bottom. She climbed down and plugged it into the receptacle with the other lights.

Hopefully the electricity would return soon and turn the Bethlehem star from a pretty plastic and gold ornament to a shiny beacon of hope.

She stood with her arms wrapped around herself, staring up at the light.

Then she returned to the rec hall, strapped on her skis, and headed to the hospital.

CHAPTER FOURTEEN

My heart isn't broken. It's shattered.

Violet's voice thundered in Jake's head as he squeezed inside Father O'Donnell's sedan. He'd seen the priest in the hospital and bothered a fellow chaplain for a ride. For Gordy's sake.

Gordy sat in the front seat like a schoolboy, despite his feigned casual conversation with the priest.

At least one of them would get the woman he loved.

Eviscerated.

Jake couldn't scrape her voice from his brain. *I didn't just lose Alex. I lost the chance to start over, with you.*

No. No she didn't, and that was the whole point. Jake knew her better than anyone perhaps.

Or...wanted to.

But, *eviscerated.*

He'd never seemed to have the right words, the right actions to save lives. He should have known that he would just make things worse.

Gordy's voice still rang in his head. *But—but what about Violet? You lied to her. What kind of chaplain does that?*

Indeed. A wretched chaplain. A chaplain who couldn't tell the truth, let alone save souls on the battlefield.

A chaplain who hadn't even been able to help himself.

I'm sorry, Lord. I know I let You down. He'd been praying that prayer for the better part of four years, even as he made his way back to the States, as he counseled veterans to hang onto their faith, their hope.

He felt like a hypocrite.

He'd just wanted to make a difference, to offer hope and faith in a time of darkness.

The town had begun to dig out from the storm. Despite it being Christmas Day, Jake saw a few men emerge from the Catholic church, digging out the front walk, probably for Mass, as well as unearth the nativity scene in the front yard. A plow had churned away much of the piles of snow on the road, but only a narrow path cut through town. The snow frosted the park into a merry wonderland, rolling hills of icing, green pine trees heavy with dollops of snow.

They drove over the stone bridge. The river had frozen solid, in mid-gurgle, frothy ice like fingers crawling upon whitened stones.

"So all four of you bunkered in at Dottie's place?" Father O'Brien was saying.

"Little Arnie Shiller too. He was pretty stiff when we found him."

"He should probably see a doctor," Jake said from the back seat.

"Jake saved his life," Gordy said.

The priest glanced at him over his shoulder. "Where did you serve, Chaplain?"

Jake tried not to wince at the label. But he couldn't hide from the truth forever. "Traveled with the 4th Armored Division as they retook France."

"So you were in action."

"I didn't carry a weapon. But yeah, I was right there, in the trenches. Mostly for morale and hauling out the wounded, but of course, we had services when we could. One day I counted over a thousand caskets. I can't tell you how tired I got of being wet and cold." He looked away. "I was wounded in the Battle of the Bulge and sent stateside. I lost a lung, had trench-foot and pneumonia—"

"He nearly died," Gordy said, glancing back at Jake.

Something about the smile on his face made Jake's throat fill.

"I thought about volunteering," O'Donnell said. "But there were plenty of wounded men—and women—who needed me here in Frost."

Jake stared out the window, at droplets of melting snow tearing down the glass. "That's also when I began to show symptoms of my childhood asthma returning. It didn't really surface until I returned to the battlefield. They finally reassigned me to work in the VA hospitals, counseling vets. Sometimes I get through to them."

"And sometimes you don't," Father O'Brien said softly.

"I had a man commit suicide a couple of weeks ago. I went to visit his family last week in Davenport."

Eviscerated. He heard it again.

"If I was a good chaplain, I would have seen it coming. I would have known what to say. Especially since I lived through it. But I have no words to erase the pain of war. And hope seems sometimes so...fragile in the face of it."

"Hope, however fragile, is the one thing that keeps us from getting lost," Father O'Brien said. "And we, as men of God, can't stop the pain. We can only apply the comfort of God to it."

Except, he hadn't exactly comforted Violet, had he?

Jake stared out the window as Dottie's house appeared through the spindly trees, a regal green Victorian frosted with snow. He hadn't seen it in the daylight, really. It resembled something out of a Grimms' fairy tale with the turret, the balconies, the gingerbread trim.

Father O'Brien let them off at the end of the drive. "I'll be coming back this way later. If you want a ride back into town, let me know."

The sun hung high in the sky, brilliant and shiny, the sky a perfect blue. Jake stopped for a moment as they trudged up the hill. It reminded him of that day in Meuse, a day off of the shelling, and the French refugees and the prisoners, when he'd held services and served communion under a camouflage canopy, hidden from the enemy's eyes.

Gordy opened the door to the mudroom and tramped inside.

It felt intrusive, suddenly, to just walk in. Storm House didn't belong to them. Or maybe it once did, but perhaps it wasn't their storm house any longer.

"Gordy—I think we should knock."

Gordy considered him then drew in a breath and knocked. "Dottie! Merry Christmas!"

No one answered. Gordy peered in the window. "The house is dark."

He opened the door before Jake could stop him. "Dot?"

No Dottie at the sink, washing dishes. No Dottie clucking over their boots, with snow dissolving on the kitchen floor.

"Where is she?" Gordy asked, like Jake might know.

"I don't know."

"But…where would she go? It's Christmas Day. She doesn't have anyone." Gordy's breath caught then, and he cringed. "I didn't mean it like that."

"Of course not. She has you."

Gordy turned, and for the first time since Jake met him, the man appeared confused. Nonplussed. "Do you think she went to my house?"

"No, Gordo. I think she went to the hospital."

"But I'm not there."

"Do you need to sit down?"

Gordy considered him, shook his head. "No, this isn't going to work. She's not at the hospital. She probably went to Violet's house for Christmas. They seemed to get along well."

Gordy tramped into the next room. Slumped down on the sofa. "I'm just kidding myself here. She doesn't need me. She doesn't want me. I'm just a foolish old man."

Jake stood at the doorway. "I don't understand you, Gordy. You've loved this woman for nearly thirty years and you're giving up? Why?"

"Because I've lived across the pond from her for my entire life, that's why. Never once after she returned home did she even invite me inside. I'm not the man she really wanted. She didn't run away with me, she ran away with TJ Morgan."

"Do you seriously think Dottie wants some gangster? He lied to her, he stole her heart, and he left her with a son to raise. *Please.*"

"I'm just a farmer. I'm not eloquent. I'm not dapper. I usually smell like the barn."

"Then take a shower."

"Dottie deserves someone who can love her the way she deserves to be loved. She needs someone more...someone more than me."

"What is it with men who always believe they have to be someone else in order for a woman to love them?" Violet stood in the doorway, holding a bag. She put it on the table. "I don't understand any of you."

Violet. Jake just stared at her, his heart cutting off his breathing.

She'd cleaned up, her dark hair in rolls around her face, her skin porcelain and white, her lips...

He looked away before his desire could betray him.

Eviscerated.

Except, she didn't appear eviscerated as she tugged off her gloves and set them on the table. "Where's Dottie?"

"We don't know. We just arrived. We thought she might be with you."

"She's not with me." She stood there, her hands on her hips, her mouth in a perfect bud of consternation. "But she should be. So, gentlemen, I'm going to unload these groceries, and then we're going to go find her."

They were?

She turned and carried the bag to the counter. Gordy was staring at him. Raised an eyebrow.

"What do you want me to do?"

Gordy shook his head. "Practice what you preach. Finally."

Jake glared at him, but he drew in a breath. "Violet, can I talk to you?"

She was adding cream and a ham to the icebox. She looked up at him. "No. I need to talk to you." Then, while his heart stopped inside him, she closed the door and stepped up to him. He stilled as she touched her hand to his cheek. "Thank you, Jake."

Thank you?

She must have read the question in his eyes. "The fact is, you cared about me, and I see that now. I know you weren't trying to deceive me as much as make sure I wasn't alone."

He caught her hand. "You weren't alone, Violet. I thought of you every day. In my mind, I saw you in your uniform, changing a tire, greasy and getting no respect from the men you worked with and I—I wanted to be there. I wanted to round on those jerks in Berlin and tell them just what you'd given up. How you were there to serve your country, just like they were. I wanted to be there in the kitchen when you came home to an empty house, welcoming you, and hold your hand when you hiked out to your father's graveside. I wanted to track down Johnny and wring his neck for taking your watch, and I wanted to tell every man in Frost that only a beautiful woman—inside and out—could have the courage to do what you did."

She blinked, looked away. "I didn't know that."

"I couldn't tell you without telling you that Alex had died, and I knew you were already grieving your father. But that's no excuse. At the least, I should have been honest with you three days ago. But you looked at me like I might be a real hero. Someone like Alex, and I wanted to be that." He stepped away from her. "I did serve in the war, Violet, but I was not in the infantry. I was a chaplain. I'm still a chaplain. I didn't fire a weapon, I just did a lot of ducking."

She frowned at him. "Are you kidding me? I met the chaplains. They went in right beside the troops. They were shelled in the trenches, strafed by German P-47s. And they did it to offer hope and light to the soldiers. The chaplains fight with the Word of God at their side. It doesn't make them less heroic, but more."

His chest tightened. He turned away.

"That wound on your chest. You got that fighting for your country." She stepped up to him. "You're a hero in my book."

Her words only burned inside him, however. "No, Vi, I'm not. I had a nervous breakdown in the field. I..." He closed his eyes, seeing it all again. "I survived my wounds and asked to go back, but although my body was healed, my soul wasn't. I'll never forget, we were rolling into Dieuze and I came upon this hole in the ground. There was a young woman in there with her baby. The woman was a skeleton, dirty, her body so thin I thought it might crumble. She'd been living in this hole—there was a makeshift fire, and a blanket, an old piece of wood pulled over the top. She held up her baby to me—she wanted to give it to me. But it was gray, and already dead. I stood there, overwhelmed by the horror of it all. The men who lost their legs and arms, their souls shattered. The ones who called out to me, repenting even as they died. The others who went down cursing. I tried to offer hope and words of faith...but as I looked at this woman, it seemed so empty. I was helpless." He opened his eyes, wiped his hand across his wet cheek. "I just woke up one day and couldn't move from my bunk. They had to send in medics." He stared at his hand. "They sent me on a medical separation to Minneapolis. It took me four months to recover." He shook his head. "I'm a disgrace to the chaplaincy."

"Oh Jake, that's such a lie." She pressed her hand on his cheek, warm, soft. "Everyone feared losing themselves in the war. There were days when I was so afraid, I could barely get out of my bunk, we were behind enemy lines in one of the most fortified compounds in Europe. But I saw refugees every day—a twelve-year-old girl with her arm blown off, toddlers dressed in rags and starving. Mothers leaving their babies on the side of the road, dead. I wanted to lose my mind too. It didn't make me weak. It made me human. And it made you understand the defeats of others."

Her voice softened. "Do you seriously think that Arnie would have lived without your calm thinking? Or that Gordy would be alive and agonizing over how to propose if you hadn't made him believe he could? Or that I would be back here, with food, trying to figure out how to cook if you hadn't believed in me? You might not have served us communion, but you served grace and hope and life and healing. You're a chaplain at heart, the hands and feet of Jesus."

The hands and feet of Jesus. He drew in her words, longed for them to touch him. "You said I eviscerated you."

Oh, could he sound any more pitiful?

"You did. But you also put me back together." She looked away from him, a blush pressing her cheeks. "You read my letters."

He swallowed. "I know, and I wish I could say I'm sorry for reading your mail. I am sorry for hurting you. But you have no idea what they meant to me. I received the package of Alex's belongings, with your letters while I was in Minneapolis, recovering." He met her eyes then. "Your voice healed me."

"And your postcards gave me strength." She caught his hand.

"You know me, Jake. The real me, not Storm House me. You know my fears and mistakes…and I guess that's the point. You know me…and you're still here."

Thank you, Gordy, for needing a ride to Dottie's. Jake squeezed her hand. "I'm still here."

"And Alex is not."

Jake didn't understand her words. "He's not?"

"He's not. And I'm not sure he ever would have been. We were just friends, even if I hoped for more." She shook her head. "But I was never Alex's girl. Not when I was really in love with you."

Oh. *Oh.*

"I forgive you, Jake," she said.

He couldn't help himself. "Violet." He leaned down, cupped his hand behind her neck, and kissed her. She tasted of coffee and smelled fresh, as if she'd showered, and made him feel like he'd spent a week in a foxhole. But she molded herself into his arms as if she didn't care, so he kissed her like she belonged there.

Had always belonged there.

Violet. He knew he didn't deserve this.

But that's what grace was about.

"Oh, for cryin' in the sink." Jake looked up, and Gordy stood at the door, shaking his head. "Some guys have all the luck."

Violet smirked, turned away.

Gordy brushed past them, into the mudroom.

"Where are you going?"

"To find Dottie. It's time she and I had a little conversation of our own."

"Don't forget the ring!"

Violet looked at Jake. "He's got a ring?"

"Yeah, and you're right—he's going to propose if he doesn't keel over first. Listen, old guy, you can't go traipsing out there. The doc said to take it easy."

"What, you going to tote me to town again with the horse and sleigh?"

"If I have to."

Gordy stared at him. "My truck won't start."

Jake smiled. "Good thing for you, we have a mechanic in the house."

She drew in a breath. Glanced at Jake.

"I'm talking about you there, Sergeant. I don't know the first thing about vehicles."

She smiled. "I need to find Dottie too. I have to give her this." She pulled a letter from her pocket. "You're not going to believe what I found." She smiled up at Jake with those beautiful eyes. "God brought us a Christmas miracle after all."

She handed the letter to Jake as she pulled on her coat.

Jake stared at it. The envelope was addressed to *Dottie Morgan, Frost, Minnesota.* "Where did you get this?"

Violet pulled out her mittens, her eyes shining. "I found it in the packet of mail you gave me. I think it must have been on Alex when he died. He was probably waiting to send it stateside."

"Why would he have it?"

"I told you. I introduced them at Fort Meade. They were in the same company. They must have become friends."

"What is it?" Gordy asked, pulling on his fur hat.

Violet took the letter and handed it to Gordy. "It's Nelson's last letter home."

* * * * *

"Gone? What do you mean he's gone?"

"I'm sorry, Mrs. Morgan. Mr. Lindholm's not with us anymore."

Dottie stared at the young, pretty nurse and wanted to reach across the desk and slap her. No.

No...

She walked away, gulping in her breath as she reached for a bench, lowered herself onto it.

No. This wasn't right. She pressed her hand to her chest. No, God couldn't do this to her. Not again. She closed her eyes.

In her memory, she saw the car drive up her driveway. Saw the Lutheran pastor and the uniformed soldiers exit. She'd stood at the kitchen window and wanted to refuse them.

No.

The two representatives from the military and her long-time pastor sat in her kitchen on a sunny spring day, the violets blooming outside her window, a lazy wind playing with the eyelet curtains, and destroyed her world.

No.

Gordy couldn't be gone.

She curled her hands in her lap. Because if he was...

Because if he was, then she would stand at his grave and tell him the truth. That she still loved him. That she'd shared the best part of herself with him—Nelson. That they'd been a family, of sorts.

It hadn't been enough. But it had been more than she deserved.

She pressed the heels of her hands to her eyes. But, no, she couldn't say good-bye—not—

"Mrs. Morgan, are you okay?"

She looked up. Christine Flemming stood over her, looking prim in her nurse's uniform, her blond hair pulled back. Dottie remembered when the nurse checked out all the Nancy Drew mysteries in the library.

"I... No, I'm not. I—I came to see Gordon Lindholm."

"He's not here anymore."

"I..." She closed her eyes. "Thank you, Christine."

But Christine stepped closer. "You don't understand. Mr. Lindholm left the hospital over two hours ago. He's fine."

He's fine? "But last night—"

"He had an angina attack. My father brought him in and treated him. He spent the night and we discharged him today. We told him to go home and rest."

Oh, the old coot! Dottie got up. "Yes. Well. Fine. Thank you, Christine."

"Merry Christmas, Mrs. Morgan."

Merry Christmas, indeed. Oh, what a fool she'd become. Here she'd conjured up a happy ending for them that he clearly didn't share.

Gordon had checked out and returned home. Without a word to the cranky woman across the marsh, pining away the night hours, worried sick for his health.

She should go dunk her head in the creek, slap some sense back into herself.

Dottie strode by the nurses' desk. Stopped. "One should be aware of the syntax of their words before they use them," she snapped at the nurse. "Merry Christmas."

She stormed out of the building, her breath hot against the crisp air. Now she had to ski home, with nothing waiting but her disgusting canned ham casserole.

Merry Christmas, indeed.

Dottie gritted her jaw against the rush of heat into her eyes. Well, perhaps the whole thing had been a sort of dream. A story stirred up by an old, desperate woman.

All she had left was her soggy, misshapen mitten.

She snapped on her skis, heading down Main Street. The sidewalks weren't yet plowed, and she skated on top of the snow, working up a sweat.

She'd go home, take down that wretched tree, toss it out into the backyard. Maybe take an ax and chop up the remainder that blocked her driveway. She'd call Frank and get him to tow Violet's car from her yard.

By tonight, she'd have her house cleaned up, everything back to normal.

Storm House, indeed.

The remnant blizzard wind chapped her cheeks as she passed the town hall, with the display of Christmas books in the library window, its dark mournful eyes following her. She skied past the grocery store parking lot then the pharmacy, with Santa in the window, and the bank's display of a Christmas wonderland. Miller's Café was dark today—no lonely souls eating alone in the tan vinyl booths. She passed the jewelry store, averting her eyes, and stopped to rest at the corner of First and St. Olafson.

A glittering of light caught her eye. Probably the sun, now dropping in the afternoon sky, turning the pallor of the horizon to purple and red. She looked up, staring at the tree at the end of the street.

Was she imagining it, or had someone lit her star?

Perhaps the electricity had been restored?

She frowned, stood, skied closer.

But no, the rest of the tree lights remained dark.

And then she heard it. The rumble of a generator thrumming against the crisp air. She skied out past Main Street, toward the park, and that's when she saw them.

Gordy, Jake, and Violet. They stood, staring up at the tree, their hands in their pockets, stamping their feet.

Her storm family.

No. But she couldn't stop the rush of warmth. It seeped through her, into her pores, her once brittle bones, turning her spirit inside out.

Her storm family had turned on her light.

Violet saw her first. "Dottie! We were just on our way to the hospital. Well, actually, we were on our way before, and then we saw the star and I thought maybe the generator could help light it." She lifted her shoulder. "It'll be pretty when the sun goes down."

"It's pretty now," Dottie said. Her gaze fell on the way Jake held Violet's mittened hand. And how Violet glowed.

She glanced up at Jake, at his crooked grin, the twinkle in his blue eyes, and smiled. Well done, Jake.

Gordy stood behind them, his hands shoved in his wool jacket, looking at her with an expression she couldn't place. His truck, still covered in snow, was parked next to the community center. "Hello, Dottie. We were looking for you."

"Glad to see you're alive," she said, not quite meaning her tone the way it emerged. "Did you shave?"

"They did it at the hospital," he said. And ran his hand over his smooth chin, as if inspecting it.

He looked nice without his beard, younger perhaps, but she wasn't going to say that. In fact, seeing him out here, in public, outside the confines of Storm House, she tasted their old, charred relationship. Like she should rightly ski right past him.

And that's how he wanted it, wasn't it? Because he *hadn't* gone to her house—hadn't gone looking...

Wait— "You were looking for me? Why?"

Jake looked at Violet, and Dottie couldn't discern the texture of his smile. Nor hers as she said, "I never told you that I saw Nelson at Fort Meade when I was stationed there. He came through, on his way to London. I introduced him to Alex. They were in the same company."

"Nelson knew your friend?"

"More than that," Jake said. "Alex and I crossed paths a few times while we were in Europe. He told me about a friend of his who'd died saving his life. He was a sniper, and he'd held off a squadron of German soldiers as Alex and his squad escaped. They awarded him the bronze star for it. Posthumously."

Dottie nodded. "Your friend was one of the soldiers my son helped save?"

Violet nodded and pulled out an envelope. "I found this in the packet of mail that Alex sent to Jake. I think maybe Nelson must have asked him to carry it, in case anything ever happened to him. Or maybe Alex just took it off him. Whatever happened,

Alex never got that far. I don't know how long he carried it before he was cut down too, but it was in his belongings. It must have gotten shuffled into my packet of letters. I found it this morning."

Dottie had stopped breathing. Stopped thinking.

"It's from Nelson. It's his letter home," Jake said softly.

Dottie's hand shook as she took the letter. The envelope bore the stains of war—sweat, or dirt, rumpled and smudged.

But on the front was her name, in Nelson's fine script.

"His letter. Nelson's letter." She closed her eyes, pressed it to herself, drew it in.

Nelson's letter.

She looked at Violet. "Thank you."

Violet covered her mouth with her hand, nodding.

Then Dottie turned to Jake, her eyes wet. "You did this, Jake. You did this wonderful thing." She stepped up and put her arms around his neck. "Thank you for bringing my boy home."

Jake held her, his arms strong like Nelson's, and for a moment, she felt unbroken, whole. Loved.

"You always had Nelson. God just used us to help you remember it," Jake said softly as she released him.

She pressed her hands to his cheeks. "God used *you*, Jake, for all of us. You're a good soldier, and a good man."

He swallowed, and Dottie saw him blink hard, look away.

Violet took her hand. "Dottie, Christmas hasn't forgotten you."

She didn't know why, but she couldn't help but look at Gordy. He swallowed, his eyes wet. Smiled at her.

A smile of forgiveness. Of intimacy.

She smiled back.

She wouldn't read it now. She would savor it, sitting beside her tree, the crackle of the fire at her feet, the sounds of family—

Dottie turned to Jake, to Violet. "You will come for Christmas dinner, won't you? I know I only have canned ham—"

"I brought dinner, Dottie. I cleaned out my mother's fridge. She's making dinner for the family at Thomas's house," Violet said.

"We're not having dinner." Gordy finally spoke from behind Jake, his voice dark. "We're not going anywhere until I say something."

"Oh, Gordy, I'm cold. And hungry. Can't it wait?" Dottie said.

"Not one more day, no." He pushed past Jake, took off his glove, and touched her hand.

She stared at his grip as he knelt before her.

"What on earth are you doing?" But she'd started to feel her heartbeat in her chest, pounding. Really?

"What does it look like? Now, just wait a second while I figure this out."

She stared down at him, at the way he fumbled in his pocket, the way his breath sped up, the way he seemed to be gathering himself and—

"Yes, Gordy. Yes, I will."

He looked up at her. "I haven't asked yet."

"Well, for Pete's sake, ask me already."

"Fine. Marry me, Dottie."

"Oh, Gordy, that's not a proposal!"

He got up, his eyes dark. But he took her face in his warm hands. "Dottie Morgan, I love you. And I have since I was nine years old, chasing you around in your barn. I loved your son, and I have been true to you every day of my life. Please, please, will you marry me?"

She had little in her but a nod. Now, that was a proposal. "About time." Then, with all of Frost watching, she stepped up to him, gripped his lapels, and pulled him down for a kiss.

The years flushed away. She felt in his touch the sweet familiarity of Gordy, of a man who had shown up and loved her from the edge of her property, waiting for the day a storm would blow him into her house and stir her cold heart to flame.

Gordy, sweet Gordy. He kissed her like they were sixteen, or perhaps twenty, with their future spooling out before them.

He lifted his head. Grinned at her. "I have a ring."

She laughed. "Well, then, I guess I'll invite you over for dinner." She looked at Violet, wrinkled her nose. "But only if Jake's cooking."

* * * * *

It should have always been like this. Dottie pulling out the seat beside him, Jake and Violet at their places around the table. Gordy drew in the smell of dinner—ham and mashed potatoes, biscuits and canned peaches. The fire crackled in the hearth, the smell of the pine tree redolent in the parlor.

"So, when's the big day?" Violet said, sitting down beside Jake.

Gordy caught Dottie's eye. "Sooner, please?"

"Oh, Gordy...I..."

"I'll help plan it," Violet said. "We can do it next Saturday night, a New Year's wedding. We can have it at the dance hall."

"I'm getting married in a church, thank you." Dottie looked

up at Gordy and he could get lost forever in her smile. How had he waited twenty-six years to ask her again? "I missed that the first time around. I'd like to have it last this time."

"Of course." Violet reached out for Jake's hand. "But the reception could be at the dance hall. It's already decorated."

"And who would come?"

Violet stared at her. "The entire town of Frost?"

Dottie shook her head. "No one wants to—"

"They'll be there," Gordy said. He took Dottie's hand. "Let's do it."

"Gordy—"

A knock came at the mudroom door a second before the door flew open. "They *are* here, Mama!" Arnie tromped into the kitchen. His cheeks bright red, his breath short.

"What on earth?" Dottie rose to her feet.

"Hey there, soldier," Jake said.

"I'm so sorry, Mrs. Morgan," his mother said. "But we were on way home from Mass and Arnold had to stop in. He said he had a gift for you. I don't know what it is."

Arnie pulled out a package, wrapped in a hankie. "It's for you."

Dottie took it, opened it. Gordy tried to hide his expression, but really, a pair of worn mittens?

"Because yours got lost in the snow," Arnie said.

He didn't understand women at all because Dottie knelt beside him and pulled the boy into her arms, her breath shuddering. Dottie didn't even wear mittens, did she?

"I have something for you too." Dottie stood up. "Please, Kathryn, come in. Join us."

"Oh, no, we couldn't."

"Yes, you could. This is, after all, your storm house family. You're welcome here, Kathryn."

Kathryn hesitated.

"Please, Mama?"

She pressed her hand to her mouth. Nodded, her face flush with emotion.

Dottie tugged Arnie's hat from his head. "But you're dripping all over my floor. So take off those boots and get your present from under the tree."

Arnie scooted into the mudroom and left his boots there, emerging also without his jacket. Even Kathryn had unbuttoned hers, although she left it on.

"I think she means it," Jake said and got up to help her off with her coat. Violet stood to gather more plates from the cupboard.

Arnie sped into the parlor and returned with a wrapped package. He scooted up to the table, his eyes shining. "I knew Santa would find me here."

"Indeed," Dottie said softly.

Arnie ripped off the wrapping and found a box. Lifting it open, his mouth widened into an O. "This is real swell." He pulled out a model bi-plane, painted red, a number on the side.

Gordy recognized it as one of Nelson's. A box-top plane.

Arnie zoomed it through the air, with the appropriate noise.

"Be careful with that now," Kathryn said.

Gordy looked at Jake, who knew way too much about him for Gordy's good. He almost felt Jake's finger in his spine. He might be glad when the man left town. Fine. "I have something for you too, Arnie." Gordy felt eyes on him as he found his jacket. "I didn't wrap it."

He handed the rectangular box to Arnie. "This is because you're a real fighter, Arnie. And someday you're going to be a hero, just like your daddy."

Gordy didn't look at Kathryn.

Arnie opened the gift. "Wow. Is it real?"

"It's real." Gordy knelt before the boy, took the victory medal out of the box. "I got it because we won the Great War. But it belongs to you now." He pinned it on Arnie's sweater. "Because you're a soldier too."

"A real live medal." Arnie looked up at his mother. "I'm a hero!"

Kathryn smiled. "Yes, indeed you are."

Dottie wiped her cheek.

Arnie pulled up a chair beside Gordy, so Dottie moved to the end and set a plate for Kathryn at the other end.

They stared at the food for a long moment. Then Jake held out his hands. "Let's pray."

Gordy took Dottie's hand, then Arnie's. He held his mother's, and she reached out for Jake, who entwined his fingers through Violet's. She smiled up at Dottie and folded her hand into hers.

"Together now."

Gordy heard the prayer inside, even as he spoke it.

"Come, Lord Jesus…be our guest, and let this food to us be blessed."

He was releasing Arnie's hand when he heard Dottie's voice, sweet and full of warmth.

"And may there be a goodly share, on every table everywhere."
Amen.

* * * * *

Dear Mother,

You know that I would have wanted to return home
to you. Right now I can imagine you sitting at the
kitchen table, and I know I have broken your heart.
I know how difficult it was to let me go, to wish me
farewell on the train station steps that day. You smiled
and told me that I looked handsome in my uniform.
You pressed a bag lunch into my hands for the ride, my
favorite, minced ham.

I remember that Mr. Lindholm stood just down the
row, watching me also. I shook his hand good-bye and
I asked him to take care of you.

He promised me he would, but I didn't need it. He's
always taken care of you, even better than I ever could.
He took care of us both, Mother.

He taught me, too, how to be a son, or a brother. I
am a better soldier because of Mr. Lindholm.

I never thought war would be a constant drizzle of
noise and wetness and fatigue. Remember that Saturday I played football in the mud and the rain and came
home with a fever? You were there to doctor me back
to health. I think of that, as if you were here, and it
gives me strength.

I know that I am okay, now. I've never believed

that heaven was a celestial place, but rather filled with prairie grasses and the hush of the wind through the cottonwoods. It smells of the cattails and milkweed in the marsh and the fragrance of fresh-cut grass. It's filled with fireflies and birds greeting the morning, and I am sure that someday I will see Digger loping toward me, his shoe-sole ears flopping.

I'd like to think that I will be able to see you, to watch you make pie, cutting off a piece of the crust for me to make my own, sprinkled with cinnamon and sugar. That in the fall, you will hunt for a pumpkin and decorate the house with pussy willows and cat-tails, that you will spin stories for the children at the library, and most of all, light the Christmas star on the tree in town. I think I can already see it from here.

If I could ask you one thing, it would be this. Tell Mr. Lindholm thank you for the train set. And for teaching me to hunt. And for not ratting me out when I stole his medal and wore it to school. (He caught me playing with it in his barn, but you never knew it.) Invite him in and let him sit at my place at the table.

I loved him too, Mama.

I know you'll miss me. I will miss you too. I already do.

Thank you for letting me serve my country. Thank you for being my mother. You were the best a boy could have had.

Your son,

Nelson

The fire crackled in the hearth as Dottie folded the letter back up. She pressed it against her chest, inhaled. The fingers that had held her heart so tight loosened with the reading, and she took a full breath without agony for what seemed like the first time in years.

"I miss him so much it takes my breath away," Gordy said. He sat beside her, his arm around her, silent through the reading of the letter. "But he is right. You were an amazing mother to your son."

Dottie covered his hands with hers. "*Our* son, Gordy. Our son."

* * * * *

Arnie lay on his bed, his hand pressed to the medal, now pinned to his pajamas. He stared out the window, at the dark sky, the stars like snowflakes.

Mama was banging around in the kitchen outside his door, perhaps putting away the leftovers Mrs. Morgan sent home with him.

Don't worry, Dale Arden, we're safe now. But I promise to visit Queen Fria, and Thun and Dr. Zoraff.

And beautiful Aura, with the long dark hair.

Outside, the stars seemed to wink at him, as if approving. His father might be out there among them, perhaps seeing his medal. Perhaps smiling.

Arnie traced the cold outline of it, pressed his finger into the point of the star. Over his bed, the airplane dangled on a piece of fishing line. Mr. Lindholm had offered to take him fishing in the spring.

Arnie rolled over and groped in the darkness for the flashlight hidden under his bed.

Then he pulled a Little Big Book from under his pillow and tucked the blanket over his head.

Outside the wind shuddered his windowpane. He wound his cold toes together and flipped open the page to where Flash Gordon was escaping the torture chambers of King Vultan....

And so our intrepid adventurer, armed with his newest weapons, has found at last his beloved Dale Arden. Warm and full, he sets out for another interplanetary adventure, ready to conquer his foes with his compatriots, Thun of the Lion Men, Dr. Zarkov, Fria the Ice Queen, and beautiful Aura by his side.

EPILOGUE

"Just press on the gas when I tell you to."

Violet blew on her fingers then held the rag to the fuel line. "Okay, Jake!"

He pressed on the gas, and the fuel popped and bubbled out, until it finally settled into a steady flow. "Okay, that's good. Turn it off."

Jake turned off the power to the roadster then hopped out, blowing on his hands. "Are you sure you want to take this thing out tonight? It's going to be cold."

"We'll bundle up. And it's only to the dance hall. Only, after hearing about your story of crashing your jeep into a tank, I'm not sure you should drive."

"Do I mention the tree outside? Hmm." Jake grinned at her then held up his greasy hands. "I still can't believe you got this thing to run."

"It just needed a rebuilt carburetor."

"And the brake lines replaced. And fresh fuel."

"Dottie said that Nelson drove it into the pond. I can't believe he couldn't figure out how to get it running again."

"Not everyone is as brilliant as you," Jake said, coming close, catching her chin with his hand. He kissed her, sweetly, full of mischief, and when he pulled away, he wore grease on his nose. She nipped it off.

"I think it'll make a nice wedding gift, don't you?"

"I hope Dottie is wearing something warm."

"I think she's wearing something practical."

He looped his arms around her. "But please tell me you're not."

She grinned at him, pushing him away. "You'll have to wait." But no. She had a dress, a new dress that fit her curves and dispelled any lingering librarian images.

Funny what a good-looking man on her arm could do for her reputation in town. And in the space of a week, no less.

And not just any man. A chaplain. A decorated chaplain, one with a purple heart and a bronze star.

That was a story she was glad Alex hadn't known. It belonged to Jake.

She closed the hood of the car. "Let's start her up, take her for a spin."

To her surprise, Jake took the passenger seat. But he braced himself as they drove down the hill, out past the stone walls. The Plymouth would take a bit more repairing than the old roadster, with the front grill smashed, the radiator destroyed. But she'd pulled it into her father's garage, had already started working on it in the evenings.

Last night, her mother had even brought her out coffee. She stood in the glow of the light from the house, watching her.

"You really do have your father's talent," she said quietly, then returned to the house.

Violet would take that as a compliment.

They motored down Third, over to Saint Olaf Street as the sun began to sink into the far gray horizon. The star radiated from the top of the tree, and would soon light up Main Street like a postcard.

"I need to get ready," Violet said. "Do you mind taking the car back?"

"Oh, I think I can manage," Jake said. "I'll pick you up in an hour."

He let her off at her house, the drifts now piled high along her walkway. Johnny and Roger had worked all week digging out the house while her mother camped out at Thomas's. Violet spent every day at Dottie's, preparing for the wedding.

One week? But what, really, did they have to wait for?

She scrubbed off the grease, put her dark hair up into rolls, and wiggled into a white and red swing dress, a pair of dancing shoes.

She pinned on her hat for the ride, a little pillbox, and was waiting by the door when Jake showed up.

His trip back to Minneapolis to retrieve his dress browns had paid off. He appeared resplendent as he offered her his arm, helped her out to the roadster. He covered her legs with a blanket.

Dottie was waiting in the church vestibule when they arrived, twilight falling through the church windows, painting the sanctuary. Through the glass doors, Violet spied Gordy, looking too dapper for his own good in a suit. No other guests sat in the pews, the moment private between them and their witnesses. Dottie wore her hair up, curled back, and Violet nearly fell over when she saw the pale yellow dress, as cheerful as a spring morning. Covered in lace, it came with a short veil and pillbox headpiece and long white gloves.

"Why, Dottie."

"Just hush now." But she looped her arm through Violet's. "You're supposed to just hold me up here."

So, she did. Delivering Dottie to her new husband, at the altar, where Dottie's pastor married them and Jake and Violet signed their approval.

Violet and Jake drove Gordy's truck to the reception.

Her mother had turned out the best in Frost for the party, the women baking up their goodies, trundling them out to the dance hall. Twinkly lights, still affixed from the night of the cancelled dance, sparkled throughout the room.

The Hungry Five had set up again, apparently hungry to play.

Violet stationed herself by the door, waiting for Dottie and Gordy to arrive.

"Miss Hart!"

She turned and spied Arnie strutting up to her, looking dangerously grown up in his suit and bow tie. He grinned at her.

"You lost another tooth."

"And look at my medal!" He pointed to the victory medal Gordy had given him.

And then they arrived. Gordy and Dottie, swinging into the reception as if they might be teenagers, grinning, glowing. A brand-new life together for the new decade.

"You're next, you know," June said into her ear as they toasted the couple with punch. Violet glanced at Jake. Maybe. Or maybe they'd simply correspond until...

"She is most definitely next," Jake said, his eyes shining.

Oh. Well.

The band played "Baby, It's Cold Outside," and Jake teased her with the lyrics until he coaxed her onto the dance floor.

Gordy had his arms around Dottie, something too wonderful on his face to bear.

They caught up to Arnie, dancing with his mother. He grinned up at them. His medal glinted on his chest.

Violet stepped on Jake's toe. "I'm sorry!"

Jake grabbed her before she could spin away. "Don't give up on me, Violet. I won't let you down."

"Oh, Jake. You've never let me down." She smiled at him. He bent down, whispered the steps in her ears. "You are exactly the man I hoped for."

As they neared midnight, the dancing ceased and they gathered around the punch table for Dottie and Gordy's cake cutting. The couple fed each other, laughing as the townsfolk of Frost counted down to the New Year.

"C'mere," Jake said, taking her hand. He pulled her away from the town, the counting, the celebration, and outside, into the crisp, quiet cold. They stood in the darkness, the tree sparkling against the night, the star shining into the darkness.

"Happy New Year, Violet Hart," Jake said, then tucked his arms around her. He kissed her, and in his touch, she tasted their tomorrows as snow began to drift like fairy dust from the sky.

AUTHOR'S NOTE

The idea of a book that took place in a Storm House simmered in my mind for the better part of two years. I came upon the concept while walking with an older friend in our small town. She pointed out an old house on the corner, one that looked like it might have grown there, with the weeds around the porch, the overgrown maple in the front yard, and said, "That was my Storm House."

She then went on to explain that, back in the day when she attended school in our town, she lived an hour away, out in the woods. For her, and other children who lived out of town, they were assigned a Storm House—a place to escape to in the storm. Apparently, families signed up to act as Storm House hosts, and at the beginning of the school year, the school educated children on where to go. I've also heard storyteller Garrison Keillor talk about Storm Houses in one of his monologues, and when I mentioned the concept to my parents, who hailed from South Dakota, they knew exactly what I meant. I have a hunch this concept might be something particular to the snowy regions of the world.

The notion intrigued me. My friend said she made up stories, as a child, of escaping to her storm house in time of need, of the family she might find there, of being fed hot cocoa and cook-ies. It made her feel safe, even if she never needed it.

I wanted to write a story about this Storm House, about how four "strangers" might find healing and comfort, but also how being trapped might churn up old secrets and hurts. What if two of the characters were estranged, but had once loved each other? And what if, inside Storm House, a miracle happened?

It did for me, as I wrote, because suddenly the spiritual theme began to take place. When I wrote this line, "I don't cel-ebrate Christmas anymore.... There's nothing left in it for me," and answered with, "Except, of course, Jesus," I simply stared at that, letting it sink in. Jesus is the only reason we can celebrate anything. The only reason for Hope. Without Him, life blind-sides us, traps us, steals our joy. We become Dottie.

Jesus is our Storm House. Our safe place. Inside His arms, we find family, comfort, and hope, and the courage to face our secrets and discover forgiveness. He gives us that place of peace inside the storm.

Is your world "cold outside"? Maybe you need a Storm House. A place of safety, comfort, a place to feel Hope again. I invite you to find Jesus. He is enough. He is, in fact, the answer to everything.

As I struggled through the writing of this book, God took me into His Storm House protection and provided me with fel-low travelers who stopped to encourage and assist with this story.

MY DEEPEST THANKS GO TO:

Curt and MaryAnn Lund for letting me quiz them about life in the 1940s. I'm sorry I asked you if you had electricity. Really, I realize you're not that old. Now, please, could you carry out the clinker?

Rachel Hauck, for being there for every chapter and helping me dream up Arnie.

Ellen Tarver, aka my secret weapon who knows how to help me get the story just right, and can make blini with the best of them.

Nancy Toback, and her amazing polishing abilities! Thank you for the details!

Susan Downs, my amazing editor, for her brilliant ideas (thanks for the title!) and for believing in me. Your encouragement means the world to me.

Andrew, Sarah, David, Peter, and Noah. Your hilarious version of *Baby, It's Cold Outside* will forever be my favorite. You are the people I'd want with me in my Storm House.

Blini Recipe (from Susie's Russian Recipe Book)

2 eggs

1 teaspoon salt

2 tablespoons sugar

2 cups kefir (or whole milk)

1 teaspoon baking soda plus enough vinegar
    to make 1 tablespoon total

2 cups flour

Mix eggs, salt, and sugar together well. Add milk, baking soda, vinegar mixture, and flour to make a thick batter. Mix well until smooth. Add 1 cup water to thin mixture; mix well again (should be the consistency of thick cream).

Heat a small fry pan. (Russian hint: Put a small amount of oil in a cup. Spear a small piece of potato on the end of a fork and dip it in the oil. Use the potato to grease the pan lightly.)

Using ⅛ cup batter, pour into the pan. Pick up the pan and slowly turn it to distribute the pancake evenly and thinly along the bottom of the pan. Cool until edges curl slightly (about 30 seconds), then turn for another 20–30 seconds.

Serve immediately, filling with jam, fresh fruit, or butter and sugar. The Russians then fold each blini in half, and then in half again to resemble a triangle. They often will pour sour cream over the top of it, but we prefer a dab of powdered sugar. Or, if you have leftovers, fill with browned ground beef and onions, seasoned with garlic, roll up, and refry in a small amount of oil until crispy brown. Delicious for both breakfast and supper! (Or when you are trapped inside your house with nothing to cook!)